# KING OF KINGS

## MJ PORTER

Boldwood

First published in Great Britain in 2023 by Boldwood Books Ltd.

Copyright © MJ Porter, 2023

Cover Design by Head Design Ltd

Cover Photography: Shutterstock

The moral right of MJ Porter to be identified as the author of this work has been asserted in accordance with the Copyright, Designs and Patents Act 1988.

All rights reserved. No part of this book may be reproduced in any form or by any electronic or mechanical means, including information storage and retrieval systems, without written permission from the author, except for the use of brief quotations in a book review.

This book is a work of fiction and, except in the case of historical fact, any resemblance to actual persons, living or dead, is purely coincidental.

Every effort has been made to obtain the necessary permissions with reference to copyright material, both illustrative and quoted. We apologise for any omissions in this respect and will be pleased to make the appropriate acknowledgements in any future edition.

A CIP catalogue record for this book is available from the British Library.

Paperback ISBN 978-1-83751-180-8

Large Print ISBN 978-1-83751-176-1

Hardback ISBN 978-1-83751-175-4

Ebook ISBN 978-1-83751-173-0

Kindle ISBN 978-1-83751-174-7

Audio CD ISBN 978-1-83751-181-5

MP3 CD ISBN 978-1-83751-178-5

Digital audio download ISBN 978-1-83751-172-3

Boldwood Books Ltd
23 Bowerdean Street
London SW6 3TN
www.boldwoodbooks.com

*For a man I never met who inspired my love of history, my great-grandfather, George Fullerton (1897–1924).*

'Here King Edward died at Farndon in Mercia, and very soon, sixteen days after, his son Ælfweard died at Oxford; and their bodies lie at Winchester. And Athelstan was chosen as king by the Mercians, and consecrated at Kingston; and he gave his sister across the sea to the son of the Old Saxons.'

— ANGLO-SAXON CHRONICLE, D TEXT, FOR 925

'Here fiery rays appeared in the northern part of the sky. And Sihtric perished and King Athelstan succeeded to the kingdom of Northumbria; and he governed all the kings who were in this island: first Hywel, king of the West Welsh [read South Welsh], and Constantine, king of Scots, and Owain, king of Gwent [read Strathcylde], and Ealdred, Ealdwulf's offspring, from Bamburgh, And they confirmed peace with pledges and with oaths in a place which is named Rivers' Meeting on 12 July; and they forbade all devil-worship and then parted in concord.'

— ANGLO-SAXON CHRONICLE, D TEXT, FOR 926(CORRECT TO 927)

# CAST OF CHARACTERS
(ALL HISTORICAL UNLESS UNDERLINED AND THEN FICTIONAL CHARACTERS)

# The Family of Alfred the Great

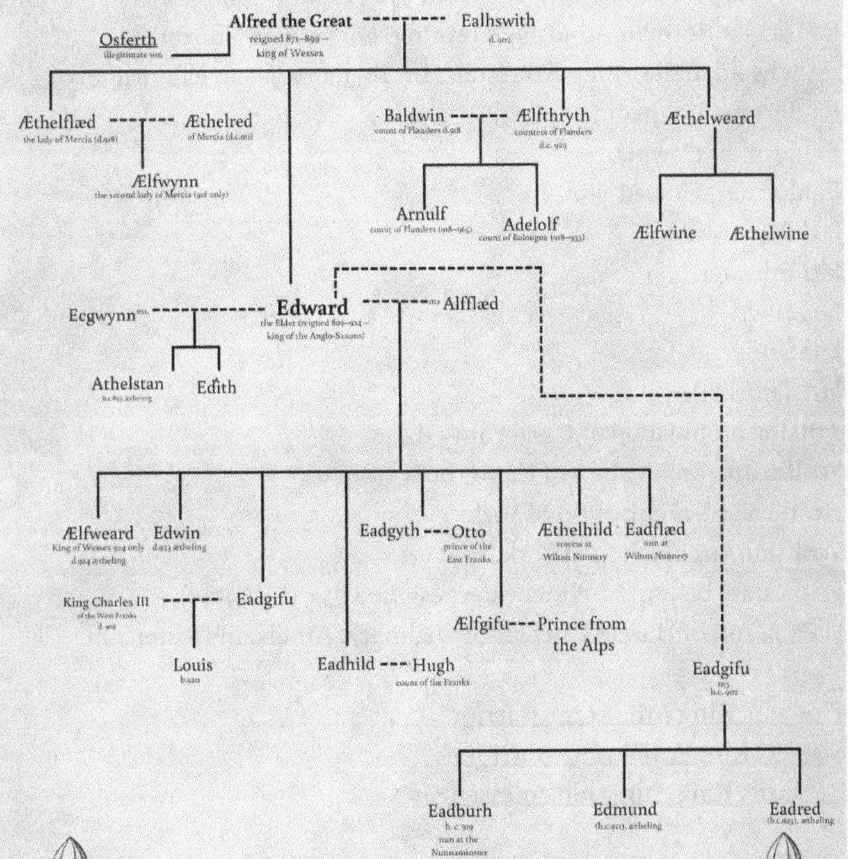

**Alfred the Great** — — — — Ealhswith
reigned 871–899 — d. 902
king of Wessex

Osferth (illegitimate son)

- Æthelflæd — — — Æthelred
  the lady of Mercia (d.918)   of Mercia (d.c.911)
  - Ælfwynn
    the second lady of Mercia (918 only)

- Baldwin — — — Ælfthryth
  count of Flanders d. 918   countess of Flanders d.c. 929
  - Arnulf
    count of Flanders (918–965)
  - Adelof
    count of Boulogne (918–933)

- Æthelweard
  - Ælfwine
  - Æthelwine

Ecgwynn(m1) — — — **Edward** — — — (m3) Alfflæd
              the Elder (reigned 899–924 —
              king of the Anglo-Saxons)

- Athelstan (b.c.893, ætheling)
- Edith

- Ælfweard
  King of Wessex 924 only
  d. 924 ætheling
- Edwin
  d. 933 ætheling
  - King Charles III — — — Eadgifu
    of the West Franks
    d. 929
    - Louis
      b. 920
- Eadgyth — — — Otto
  prince of the East Franks
  - Eadhild — — — Hugh
    count of the Franks
  - Ælfgifu — — — Prince from the Alps
- Æthelhild
  vowess at Wilton Nunnery
- Eadflæd
  nun at Wilton Nunnery
- Eadgifu (m3) b.c. 902
  - Eadburh
    b. c. 919
    nun at the Nunnaminster
  - Edmund
    (b.c.921), ætheling
  - Eadred
    (b.c.923), ætheling

## The English Ealdormen

Ealdorman Wulfgar
Ealdorman Æthelfrith of Mercia (d.c.915), an ealdorman and father of Ælfstan, Athelstan, Eadric and Æthelwald
Ealdorman Athelstan of the East Angles (from 932), an ealdorman, married to Ælfwynn, the lady of Mercia's daughter
Ealdorman Ælfstan of Mercia (from 930), Ealdorman Athelstan's brother
Eadric, Ealdorman Athelstan's brother, not yet an ealdorman
Æthelwald, Ealdorman Athelstan's brother, not yet an ealdorman
Ealdorman Guthrum
Ealdorman Oswulf
Ealdorman Uhtred
Jarl Regenwald
Jarl Inhwaer
Jarl Hadd
Jarl Scule
Jarl Thurfrith
Athelm, archbishop of Canterbury d.926
Wulfheard, archbishop of Canterbury from 926
Hrothweard, archbishop of York
Wulfstan, archbishop of York from 931
Frithestan, bishop of Winchester resigned 932, died 933
Hakon, son of Harald Fairhair of Denmark, Athelstan's foster son

Flodwin, King Athelstan's warrior
Sigelac, King Athelstan's warrior
Beohtric, King Athelstan's messenger

**The Scots**

The succession strictly alternated between two lines of succession
Constantin, son of Aed, king of the Scots (reigned 900 onwards)
Ildulb, son
Amlaib, grandson
Aed, son
Cellach, son
Alpin, son

Mael Coluim, Constantin's designated successor, the son of his predecessor, Domnall
Denewulf, Constantin's messenger

**Strathclyde**

Donald, previous king of Strathclyde (once allied with Constantin)

Owain, king of Strathclyde

**The Welsh kings**

Hywel, king of the West Welsh, (Deheubarth) known as Hywel Dda
Owain ap Hywel, Rhodri ap Hywel and Edwin ap Hywel, Hywel's sons

Idwal, king of Gwynedd
Elisedd, Idwal's brother

Owain, king of Gwent
Morgan ap Owain, king of Gwent after Owain (his son)

Tewdwr ap Griffi ab Elise, king of Brycheiniog

Gwriad, king of Glywysing

## The independent kingdom of Bamburgh

Ealdred, king of Bamburgh (died 934)
<u>Ealdwulf, his son</u>
<u>Hild, his wife</u>

## The Dublin Norse and their allies

All claimed to be descended from Ivarr, the Viking raider who led the Great Heathen Army of the 860s

Ragnall, died c.921, a grandson of Ivarr, claimed Jorvik (York), once allied with Constantin and Donald II of Strathclyde

Sihtric, king of York, died c.926, married Athelstan's only natural sister, Edith

Gothfrith, king of Dublin, grandson of Ivarr
Olaf Gothfrithson, son of Gothfrith

## The notable families of West Frankia

Charles III m. Eadgifu, daughter of Edward and Ælfflæd
Louis, their son

Hugh the Great, married Eadhild, daughter of Edward and Ælfflæd

Heribert of Vermandois, Charles III captor and jailer

## The king of East Frankia

Henry the Fowler
Otto married Eadgyth, daughter of Edward and Ælfflæd

**Note on names**

The unwary traveller to this period of time will be faced with a profusion of names for the men and women in this story. Names may be given in Welsh, Gallic, Old Norse, Old English or with modern spellings. As such, you may find Olaf/Anlaf/Amlaib and be surprised to discover these are all the same person. You may find the name Eadward used, although the most common form is Edward. Equally, Æthelstan is the correct form of Athelstan. You will find names used interchangeably if you consult different sources, and secondary sources. The choice taken will depend, quite often, on the main sources the writer uses and on their own personal preference. I have attempted to use the names that are most recognisable for the individuals involved. Welsh and Norse convention usually names someone as the son of their father, e.g. Olaf Gothfrithson is Gothfrith's son; Owain ap Hywel is the son of Hywel. Names are often reused throughout the generations in all societies and, in England, families often name all of their children with names that begin with similar letters, e.g. Athelstan, Athelwald, etc.

All quotes from the Anglo-Saxon Chronicle are taken from *The Anglo-Saxon Chronicles* M. Swanton ed. and trans.

# GLOSSARY

*Ætheling* – meaning 'throne-worthy', the title given to a son of a king, whether or not they were considered the heir to the kingdom. As such, when Edward the Elder became king, his brother, Æthelweard, and his young sons, Athelstan and Ælfweard, were all classified as æthelings in the available charter evidence. Æthelweard's brother was the son of King Alfred, and Alfred's sons were therefore also his sons.

*Ealdorman* – an ealdorman ruled an ealdordom on behalf of the king. These were often areas roughly parallel with the ancient Saxon kingdoms of Mercia, Northumbria, the kingdom of the East Angles, Kent and Wessex, or may be subdivided further. These positions were rarely hereditary. Indeed, ealdormen would often have landed wealth elsewhere in the kingdom. It's believed that some landed property might have been assigned to the ealdormen to assist them in ruling their areas of control. There were strong ruling families and, occasionally, the position did pass from father to son, or brother to brother. This was not common practice.

*Jarl* – the Norse version of an ealdorman. This would lead, in the eleventh century, to the ealdordoms becoming known as earldoms (jarldoms) under the Danish king, Cnut.

*Witan* – an assembly of the noblemen, women, members of the religious orders including archbishops, bishops, abbots and abbesses, king's thegns and thegns, and also ministers/advisors to the king. They had a say in voting for the next king, and supported the king in governing the kingdom.

# PROLOGUE
## SEPTEMBER AD925, KINGSTON UPON THAMES, THE KINGDOM OF THE ENGLISH

*Athelstan, king of the English*

The church at Kingston upon Thames is full, the smell of incense heavy in the air. Expectant faces look my way, some friendly and open, others more hooded and some overtly hostile, and that's just amongst the members of my family.

These are my people, and I rule them as king. This ceremony will officially mark me as anointed and raised above all by the Almighty God. And for the first time in the history of the Saxon people, I'll be crowned as king of the English people, with an actual crown. No warrior helm will grace my head, marking me as a warrior and only then a king, for all that I am a warrior and proud to be one.

No, my holy men have decreed that it's time for a change. No longer will men be known as the king of the Anglo-Saxons or the king of Wessex. From now on, kings will be the king of the English. A new coronation service has been written by my holy men, and a new crown has been moulded and fitted to my head. It's made of the lightest gold and embellished with the finest jewels. It's beautiful to behold.

It will fit me perfectly and will denote me as no other king of the House of Wessex has yet been marked. Not my illustrious grandfather, Alfred, who brought his religious conviction to bear in crushing the Viking raider menace and holding Wessex complete against the attack. Nor my father, Edward, who continued my grandfather's work and added Mercia and much of the lands conquered by the Norse interlopers to his kingdom.

My father's work in Mercia unsettles me still. The fate of my cousin is an uncomfortable reminder that my father was ambitious, despite the connections of family and kin. His actions will always make me wary of the damage those who share blood can cause one another. Some say he ruled Mercia as overking of my aunt and her husband, Lord Æthelred. But without my aunt, on Wessex's northern border, Wessex would have succumbed to the attacks of the Norse from Jorvik and the Danelaw, and perhaps even from the Welsh of their many kingdoms. I know that. I fought in those battles when I was old enough. I became a man during those attacks. My aunt, Æthelflæd, not my father, made me who I am today.

My father, King Edward. A man I respected and loved, and yet who decreed that despite the expectations of my grandfather, King Alfred, I would not be sole king of the Anglo-Saxons after him. No, Edward divided his recently formed kingdom, giving Wessex and Kent to my stepbrother, Ælfweard, a youth younger than I, though barely. Ælfweard had never been tested in the ways of war, but was proficient in the skills of diplomacy needed to survive at the riven Wessex court. I was to hold only Mercia.

I didn't curse my father for his choice in sundering the united realm of Mercia, Wessex and Kent, even though I did question the righteousness of such a gesture. In splitting the only recently formed kingdom of the Anglo-Saxons, Edward made a mockery of all he did to my poor cousin, Lady Ælfwynn. He stole her birthright, claimed it as his due, and then, at his death, thrust its governance upon me, for he knew Ælfweard would never be able to hold Mercia. Ælfweard, a man who never lifted a blade to defend the kingdom of Mercia from the blades of the bloody Norse. Ælfweard, a man who would sooner raise his wine glass to his lips than a seax into the belly of his enemy.

My father, with such an act, proved that he should never have taken Mercia from my cousin. It was hers to rule. Not that I had long to question my holy men or decry my father's good sense. Ælfweard shortly joined my father in his heavenly splendour, even before his coronation could take place. So that it was I who acceded to the kingship of Wessex and Kent as well as Mercia, almost as if my Lord God denounced the division of our mighty realm as much as I did. My aunt was a woman of deep religious beliefs, and my father was a man of politics and war. It seems my aunt won much favour with our Lord God, after all.

Not that the Wessex witan was keen to accept me, preferring instead my other stepbrother, Edwin, full brother to Ælfweard, and just as much a drunken sot. His mother's family laboured to bring Edwin to the kingship forgetting that Edwin had never lifted a blade in anger either. How foolish he was to think himself worthy of becoming king. It took little more than a daring raid on Wessex shores by some wayward Norse warriors for my kingship to become so much more acceptable.

I also have the support of my cousin, Lady Ælfwynn. She's the daughter of the lady of Mercia, Lady Æthelflæd, and the woman who should have ruled Mercia after her mother's death, if my father had not secreted her away after only six months of ruling to live out her life in one of Wessex's many nunneries. I'm only grateful that now Ælfwynn wishes me to rule with her full support. I've freed her from captivity. I've united her with her lover, and now she'll support my rulership of Mercia. Together, we'll ensure Mercia doesn't falter because of its unification with Wessex. Mercia will not simply be a buffer zone between the Danish Five Boroughs, known as the Danelaw, and Wessex. Lady Ælfwynn watches me now, a faint curve to her delicate lips, a larger bulge at her waist, should she stand. My cousin will have the life my uncle would have denied her and I've gladly returned to her.

While I've fought for battle and glory, using my sword, shield and seax to drive the Norse from the land of Mercia, I've not fought in the arena of the Wessex witan. What an unpleasant experience, and yet, I emerged as the king, and Edwin did not. He didn't have the support of his stepmother, and without Lady Eadgifu's assistance, our father's third wife, Edwin was never going to be proclaimed as king of Wessex and Kent, her beloved homeland.

This means that only a year after my father's untimely death, the kingdoms of Mercia, those parts of the East Anglian kingdom that my father lately reclaimed, Wessex and Kent, are reunited again under one ruler. The Saxons, or rather, the English, have just one king. And this is my moment of divine glory, when, before the men and women of the Mercian and Wessex witan, I'll be proclaimed as king over all.

A prayer is intoned by the archbishop of Canterbury, Athelm, appealing to God to endow me with the qualities of the Old Testament kings: Abraham, Moses, Joshua, David and Solomon. As such, I must be faithful, meek, and full of fortitude and humility while also possessing wisdom. I hope I'll live up to these lofty expectations.

I'm anointed with the holy oil and then given a thick gold ring with a flashing ruby to prove that I accept my role as protector of the one true faith. A finely balanced sword is placed in my hands, the work of a master blacksmith, with which I'm to defend widows and orphans and through which I can restore things left desolated by my foes, and my foes are the Norse.

Further, I'm given a golden sceptre, fashioned from gold as mellow as the sunset, with which to protect the Holy Church, and a silver rod to help me understand how to soothe the righteous and terrify the reprobate, help any who stray from the Church's teachings and welcome back any who have fallen outside the laws of the Church.

With each item added to my person, I feel the weight of kingship settle on me more fully. I may have been the king of Mercia for over a year now, the king of Wessex and Kent for slightly less time, but this is the confirmation of all I've done before and all I'll be in the future.

It's a responsibility I'm gratified to take, but a responsibility all the same. From this day forward, every decision I make, no matter how trivial, will impact someone I now rule over.

The prayers continue around me, but I'm looking at those I now rule, specifically my second stepmother Eadgifu, a little younger than I, although she produced three children for my father before his death.

She's resplendent in the front row of the church. She's serene in her place as king-mother; for all that she's not my mother. I have her support and the support of her young sons and daughter, and this, too, was vital when the men of the Wessex witan arraigned themselves against me, pushing for Edwin to become king. Her children are here, young Eadburh, all serious with her hands held reverently before her, Edmund and even small Eadred, little more than a tottering child. I smirk at his bright face and beaming smile as he sucks on a wooden toy, dripping drool down his fine tunic.

Lady Eadgifu will rule my household for me, and in payment, and in part to fulfil my wishes, I'll remain celibate, choosing never to marry and, in doing so, not disrupt the ruling line which must pass to my young stepbrothers, Eadgifu's sons, after my death. And if I live to old age, then their sons can rule in my stead.

I catch Lady Eadgifu's gleaming eyes with a solemn nod of my head, and she inclines her head in acknowledgement that the new king has marked her with special favour. She's a woman who knows the worth of her good looks and uses them. She dresses carefully, the colours sombre but pleasing to look at. Her children mirror the shades she chooses in their clothes, and together, all five of us are embellished with the wyvern of Wessex, for all I also wear the double-headed eagle of Mercia picked into my tunic with gold thread.

Lady Eadgifu must be pleased with the way events have played out. I think she misses my father, her husband, but she must have known when they married that, in all likelihood, he would die before her. But with our agreement, she's lost nothing. She's still the queen of the Anglo-Saxons, as she was consecrated, at my father's command; still the mother of the king and likely to be the mother of kings for many long years yet to come. She's known as the lady of Wessex, for all that's not her actual title. She's a woman of Kent, but as so often has happened in the past, Wessex overshadows all else.

And I? I'm the king, as my archbishop, Athelm of Canterbury, proclaims to rousing cheers from all within the heavily decorated church at Kingston upon Thames, a place just inside the boundaries of Wessex but not far from Mercia. It's festooned with bright flowers and all the wealth this church owns. Gold and silver glitter from every recess, reflecting the glow of the hundreds of candles.

I'm more than my father, Edward, was and I'm more than my grandfather, Alfred, was. I'm the king of a people, not a petty kingdom, or two petty kingdoms, with Kent and the kingdom of the East Angles attached.

It's done. I'm the anointed king of the English, the first to own such a title. I'll protect my united kingdom, and with God's wishes, I'll extend its boundaries yet further, clawing back the land from the Five Boroughs and bringing the kingdom of the Northumbrians, and even the independent realm of Bamburgh, under my command.

As the cheers reverberate throughout the confined space of the church, I hold my joy in place. It would not be kingly to sit and grin. Instead, a regal expression touches my face, a small tug of my cheeks to show my understated joy at becoming king of this proud people. Whatever we achieve in the future, my name will always be the first to be known as the king of the English; the king of the English people; the survivor of his father's dynastic politics; and the boy his grandfather, King Alfred, once designated as the future king of his realm. I only wish Alfred and Edward could see me now and know that my legacy is far from done. There's more to be done for the Saxon peoples, united now as the English, so much more. And I will start by turning my gaze toward the Norse kingdom of Jorvik, or rather that of York and Dublin, held by the grandsons of Ivarr, he who first led the Great Heathen Army to these shores, and left in his wake a trail of destruction that resonates to this day.

# PART I
# THE PATH TO PEACE

# 1

## OCTOBER 925, WINCHESTER, THE KINGDOM OF THE ENGLISH

### *Eadgifu, the lady of Wessex*

King Athelstan is calm as he faces the men and women of the witan. He wears the clothes of a king, and he looks comfortable with his supporters before him. I admire him. There are many here who are still uneasy at his kingship, and yet he presses on, regardless. And his intentions far exceed anything his father, my late husband, might have thought to bring about.

I was unsure about Athelstan. I hardly knew him, raised as he was in Mercia, not Wessex. A stranger to Wessex, for all he was the son of the king of Wessex. But now I watch and, I confess, a small smile plays on my lips. The more I witness Athelstan and his ambitions, the more I appreciate that my decision to support him in his bid for the kingship was correct.

These men can't complain about Athelstan's plans, and I know he has the full support of his sister, even as he makes the proposal. His sister, Edith, will marry the Norse self-proclaimed king, Sihtric of Jorvik – or York, as my people call it. It's an astounding piece of diplomacy, and not just because it so closely mirrors his father's intentions with my namesake, Eadgifu of the West Franks, married to Charles III, king of the West Franks, Edward's oldest daughter born to his second wife. That the union has proven to be anything but without incident for Eadgifu is irrelevant. While she might currently shelter in Wessex while her husband has been deposed of his kingship, to be held in captivity by one of his ealdormen, a son has been born to Eadgifu and her husband. At some point in the future, it's to be hoped that young Louis will reclaim his kingship of the West Franks. And that Queen Eadgifu of the West Franks will leave the Wessex court and make my life so much easier.

That said, Louis is a delightful child, similar in age to my sons. They're friends and enemies, as children of such age must be. It's a pity the same can't be said for Louis' mother, who's bitter and shrew-faced. It was much more enjoyable at court when she was over the Narrow Sea in West Frankia.

'The alliance will unite the Norse kingdom of York with that of the English,' Athelstan confirms, his voice commanding. I wait to see who'll argue with him. Should they think to do so, I can imagine his counterarguments. He need only mention the treaty his grandfather promulgated with Guthrum, leader of the Viking raiders, over fifty years ago, that brought about the division of this island with the Norse Viking raiders, but in doing so, saved Wessex and much of western Mercia for the Saxons.

With this piece of diplomacy, Athelstan brings to a conclusion his years of warring beside his aunt, Lady Æthelflæd of Mercia, pushing back the boundaries of Mercia, taking back the Norse settlements of the Five Boroughs: Nottingham, Leicester, Derby, Stamford and Lincoln, claimed for so many years by the enemy of the English Saxons.

'But my lord king.' The first voice to speak as Athelstan finishes laying out his plans before the witan is Ealdorman Wulfgar. I'm far from surprised. Ealdorman Wulfgar thinks much of himself, and his unease about events since my husband's death is well-known. He supported Ælfweard, the son of Edward and his second wife Ælfflæd, to be the next king of Wessex. But Ælfweard died only sixteen days after his father.

There was hardly time to even argue over whether his kingship would be supported by the witan or not.

Wulfgar is also an ally of the exiled Queen Eadgifu of the West Franks, and her remaining full brother, Edwin. Not that I believe Ealdorman Wulfgar was as effusive in his support of Edwin as the next king of Wessex after Ælfweard's death. The ealdorman might not be convinced of Athelstan, but for Edwin, familiarity certainly bred contempt. My husband's third oldest son is a real fool. But still.

'Yes, Ealdorman Wulfgar.' Athelstan's words are filled with respect. Athelstan doesn't belittle his supporters. It makes a pleasant change to the way I watched my husband treat his ealdormen.

'This man, Sihtric, is our kingdom's greatest enemy. He and those who ruled before him have done little but persist in warring against us. You would be sending your sister to live amongst heathens.' With such words, Ealdorman Wulfgar thinks to play to the wishes of the archbishop and bishops. And it might sometimes work to his advantage, but if King Alfred is remembered for his deep piety, then Athelstan is not far behind. In time, I believe, he might well become more well-known for his works of religious conviction than even his grandfather.

'Lord Sihtric will convert to our one true faith,' Athelstan assures the ealdorman, still gracious, stressing the use of the word 'lord'. 'My sister is firm in her beliefs. She'll ensure he's a fervent convert, and through her work, she'll guarantee that our faith reaches more of the Norse in York.'

'But, my lord, what of Lord Sihtric's sons?' And still Ealdorman Wulfgar persists. I wonder whether this unease is because he doesn't know Athelstan's full sister, just as he doesn't truly know Athelstan. But Athelstan is close to his sister. I can imagine that this move has not been made as though he was the imperious king and her his to command. I can well imagine that Edith might even have made the suggestion herself. She, like her brother, has been raised in Mercia. She, like Athelstan, has been living for much of her life in what has, at times, been little more than a war zone between the Mercians, Welsh and the men and women of the Five Boroughs.

'It's unfortunate that Lord Sihtric is so blessed with children from previous...' And here Athelstan pauses, perhaps considering his father's marital history – one man with three wives and children numbering into double figures because of that. Or perhaps Athelstan contemplates how best to describe the fashion amongst the Norse of not remaining joined to the same man or woman throughout their entire lives. Again, not so dissimilar from my husband. '...unions,' Athelstan pronounces. He's always ready with diplomacy. 'But Lord Sihtric has assured me, should the marriage prove fruitful, it's those sons, born to my sister, who'll rule in York after his death.'

A murmur of unease ripples through the members of the witan at that. No ruler of York has lasted a lifetime. Many of them survive for a few years. If they survive their rulership of York, then they can claim the kingship of Dublin, the Norse kingdom separated by land and water, most often ruled by two kings, one senior, and one junior, all claiming descent from Ivarr, one of the men who brought the Great Heathen Army to our shores. But there are few enough men who manage to do both, and all must be warriors.

'Then you're envisioning a time far in the future,' Ealdorman Wulfgar presses. Perhaps, now, he's beginning to understand Athelstan's ambitions.

'I am, yes. Such unions, as that of the exiled Queen of West Frankia, my sister, Lady Eadgifu, are for the future. Far in the future, in most regards.' I daren't look to Edwin, or even the exiled Queen Eadgifu as Athelstan speaks. And yet, his words are filled with respect. His stepbrother and sisters from his father's second marriage might well resent him, but Athelstan doesn't share such thoughts about them. Despite everything.

'And so, she'll live the rest of her life amongst the heathens, and then one day, her son will rule York,' the ealdorman surmises.

'It's to be hoped, yes,' Athelstan concedes. 'The archbishop of York will, of course, support her. And it's not as though our faith is unknown to those living in York.' This is perhaps the problematic part. Athelstan's grandfather, Alfred, married his aunt, Lady Æthelflæd, to the lord of Mercia, Æthelred, but in all their years together, they only had one daughter, Ælfwynn. While Lady Æthelflæd wanted her daughter to rule after her, my husband had other ideas and stole her away from Mercia, locking her inside one of Wessex's strictest nunneries, where none could find her. Ælfwynn is now wed to a son of a powerful Mercian ealdormanic family, and has given Athelstan her blessing for him to rule Mercia in her stead.

But what if the same happens with this union with Lord Sihtric of York? What if the only child produced is a woman? If Ælfwynn couldn't rule Mercia, which is wildly less violent than York, then how could a woman rule there? But these are arguments for the future. It's to be hoped that a son is born and that he lives to succeed his father in good time. The rulers of York do not follow the same succession rules as Wessex and Mercia. For them, the ruling family is much wider: fathers, sons, brothers, uncles and cousins. All of them have a claim, similar to the land of the Scots, even further north. And yet there's the possibility that a child, half-Saxon, will one day rule in York, and that might mean that one day, in the distant future, my sons will rule over a united realm of my birth kingdom of Kent, Wessex, Mercia, the kingdom of the East Angles, the Five Boroughs, and York as well.

Of not just the English but also the Norse.

'Then I wish her well with that,' the ealdorman murmurs, and it seems that no others will argue against the plan either. That's because they already knew. But Athelstan, king of the English, is keen to do everything according to protocol. He hasn't yet faltered in his ambitions.

# 2

## 927, YORK

*Athelstan, king of the English*

'Sister.' She inclines her head, even while her gaze is elsewhere. She's hardly changed at all in our time apart. Not that she's been married for the entirety of our eighteen months apart, or in York, for all that time. No, her husband, Lord Sihtric, played me for a fool, assuring me of his honourable intentions, undergoing baptism, taking my sister as his wife at Tamworth, only to change his mind, cast her aside, and apostatise.

Still, I'm to have the last laugh there, for Sihtric is dead, and his chosen heir, Gothfrith, is far from York, still in Dublin, if the rumours are to be believed. But I'm not, and neither is my sister.

Edith smiles at me, hands clasped demurely before her. Her marriage hasn't been what she wanted, but now she's free. She was a queen in name for a short period of time. It suited her. But now, she's a widow, and that's entirely different.

'Brother.' I'm pleased she names me as such. 'When this is done, I wish to withdraw into a nunnery.' I nod in understanding. I knew this.

'I'll be honoured to name you as my sister and to know you're happy doing God's work,' I intone, but a smirk on her full lips has me reconsidering whether her intentions are quite so religious after all.

'I merely wish to never have to endure such a marriage again. I don't want to be a mother. Look what happened to our own. No, I'll stay behind the protective walls of a nunnery, and from there, I'll keep abreast of all that happens in this land while being content to be aloof from it.'

I would argue with her, but I follow her reasoning. 'Then you have my thanks for all that you've done. Your name will always be remembered in connection with the assimilation of York into the English kingdom.'

For a moment, she's silent, weighing my words. Then she nods, and her blonde hair, so similar in colour to mine, shimmers with the sunlight. 'And now, I'll have the archbishop proclaim you as the rightful king of York. He'll be pleased to have a Saxon, not a Norse warrior, as king.'

Still mounted, with my warriors ensuring the path into York is secure, we progress inside.

It feels strange to be here. The name of Jorvik has been used to replace York by the Norse, but this place is still, at heart, a Saxon enclave, and now, with the imposition of my rule, it should remain as such.

I've no plans to remove the Norse women, men and children who live here. I've no intention of stopping them from trading and making a living. My desire is singular: to prevent the Norse from ruling it as part of their combined kingdom of York and Dublin. Yes, these kings can rule in Dublin. It's not my plan to claim Dublin. They're welcome to it. My eyes are sighted, rather, on the East and West Frankish kings. That's the only sea I mean to one day crest when my nephew is proclaimed as king of the West Franks. To bring that about, I'll do all that's necessary. But, and I never forget this, if I can achieve my ends using peaceful means, then I'll do so. I've fought against the Norse for all of my life. Peace will be a welcome change.

'Tell me,' my sister says to me when we're seated in the archbishop's hall, having taken the submission of the leading men and women, the archbishop conducting a mass to celebrate my triumph, 'how are our stepmother and her sons?'

'Lady Eadgifu, the lady of Wessex, as it's necessary to term her now to avoid confusion with our stepsister, is well. She isn't often at court but is happy to raise her children away from the glare of the witan and their complaints and slights. She comes when I have need of her particular skills, and she is skilful. Our father should have allowed her much more sway. She would have been far more useful to him than just the means by which he claimed control of Kent.'

'Brother, you sound as though you approve of her?' Edith doesn't hide her surprise as she drinks, sparingly, from a goblet of watered-down wine.

'I think I admire her, yes. Our father would have done well not to bother with his second wife, the Lady Ælfflæd, but the lady of Wessex is a clever woman. She knows her worth.'

'Does she now? And what, she has more worth than I do?' There's a bite to Edith's voice, and I turn to her, surprised by the flash of fury in her bright eyes.

'I'm sorry, sister dearest. The man gave his word. Lord Sihtric assured me you would be honoured as his wife.'

'Well, he lied, as all of these Norse seem to do. I'm simply pleased he's dead. I'm also delighted our union wasn't fruitful. But,' there's a wistfulness to her voice that I can't ignore, 'I would have liked the reputation of our aunt. I should have liked to ride into battle and command warriors to obey my orders.'

'And you would have been a fine commander,' I assure her. 'But, for you, bloodshed wasn't necessary.'

'No, it wasn't,' she confirms with a twitch of her lips.

'Tell me, how is our cousin?' I ask instead, keen to turn her thoughts aside, and I confess reminding her of the fate of Lady Ælfwynn, my aunt's daughter, is a way of making her appreciate how lucky she has been. Her marriage might have been a failure, but at least she wasn't locked away from all she loved, against her will, by her uncle.

'She's well. Very well. She enjoys being a mother.' A softness touches my sister's lips, and for a moment, I consider offering her a union with another man. 'Don't think I ever wish to endure the same. Not for love and not for country. No, brother. York is yours, and the only blood that was shed was my own. And that's all I'll share in this life to advance your claims.'

'Of course, sister,' I confirm. I want her to know I'll abide by her wishes.

'Like the lady of Wessex, one marriage is enough for me in this life, even if it was only a short one. Now tell me, brother, do you mean to march on Bamburgh, the kingdom of the Scots, or on Strathclyde?' Edith has a sharp mind, but then we spent many years together. She knows what my aunt dreamed, and she knows that I share the same wishes.

'No, sister. I have other plans for the northern kingdoms. Hopefully, they'll also be accomplished without bloodshed.'

# 3

## JULY 927, YORK

*Athelstan, king of the English*

'My lord king.' The voice is stringent with worry, and I turn to face Cousin Athelstan. We share a name, and he's wed to my cousin, Ælfwynn. It causes confusion. But not for us. I'll name him as a cousin to prevent confusion. Others might have less savoury names for him.

'What is it?' I query. He's not yet an ealdorman, although I have intentions to name him as one as soon as time allows. With York secured, I must look to the kingdom of the East Angles. It was entirely overrun by the Norse, but now it's keen to accept my dominion after my father conquered much of it. And Athelstan, alongside my cousin Ælfwynn, would be perfect for ensuring the men and women of the kingdom are loyal to me, their king.

'Reports of an enemy war host, from the west.'

This is news to me, and I turn to focus on him, ignoring the sharp gasp my sister emits and the way she grips my sleeve tightly. She's known war for much of her life. No matter how unwelcome this news is, she'll not panic as others might in this situation. But the news is unlooked for.

'Tell me,' I demand.

'From the east. They say it's Lord Gothfrith of Dublin.'

'Damn,' I explode and then wish I hadn't. For a moment, and only one moment, my heart thuds at this unlooked-for problem, but I was never going to hold York without others wanting to challenge me.

'Have the men prepared and ready to counter the attack,' I instruct Cousin Athelstan. I know he'll carry out my commands promptly. In fact, he's probably already sent men scurrying to inform those on duty that they're about to experience more than just another day of drearily watching the gates to ensure no enemy seeks entry into York.

'How many?' This is always the most important question.

'Difficult to say, perhaps as many as a thousand, but really, fewer than five hundred, if the scouts are to be believed.'

'Then we'll prevail. Our numbers far exceed theirs, even if there are a thousand of them.'

'My lord king,' and Cousin Athelstan moves aside, others following on his heels as he barks commands. I look to my squire, but he knows my mind and has already run to fetch my byrnie, helm and warrior's weapons.

'You'll remain here and hold York for me,' I instruct my sister. For a moment, I think she might waver, but her resolve returns, and she inclines her head, finding the strength I know she owns. Perhaps, after all, she will be able to emulate our aunt.

'The people of York are beloved to me,' she confirms. I wonder how much good work she did in York during her time here. I consider how many she fed throughout the cold winter. 'They'll not hurry to welcome this Gothfrith, for they don't know him. I don't believe he's ever stepped foot inside York.'

I nod, pleased by her strength of will. I didn't invite her to York to witness a battle but rather for her to see what her marriage had gifted to the English kingdom. I wanted her to know that her pain and suffering were not in vain. That her humiliation for the abrupt ending of her marriage was not her fault.

'I'll go to the church,' she confirms. 'I'll have the archbishop summon the populace to join with me in prayer.' I lean over and place a warm kiss on her forehead. Beneath my lips, I can feel the frantic beating of her heart, but she fixes a smile on her face. 'Stay well, brother dearest and my lord king. You have held the kingdom for too short a time to lose it once more.' Her words are strong, speaking of all she's endured, and I stand and stride away.

Edith has watched me ride to war many times in the past. She knows, as I do, that I'll return. All the same, at the doorway, I pause and glance back at my sister. She's shadowed by the candlelight and the flames of the hearth fire, and not for the first time, I consider if she resembles my mother. I have no memories of Lady Ecgwynn and none would ever speak to me of her after her death. When my father took a new wife, Lady Ælfflæd banned all from speaking of her, as though she could forget the king had loved his first wife, whereas his second was merely a match of political expediency.

I wish I could remember my mother. Even Aunt Æthelflæd, normally so eager to speak of my childhood to me, had no memory of her. Æthelflæd had been long married to my uncle Æthelred of Mercia before my father married. The two never met. I know it was a source of some ill will between my father and my aunt. That ill will only hardened when my father took the advice of his new wife and had his two children sent to be raised in Mercia, where she could no longer be reminded of their existence. And more importantly, so my father, Edward, could be made to forget his oldest children and, in the same breath, his first wife as well.

Outside, the sound of rough voices drowns out even the thunder of horses' hooves over the roadways. York is a place of little plan, and yet, the roads that dissect it do allow easy access to the gates and over the bridge spanning the river.

Cousin Athelstan, true to his word, has summoned my commanders and ealdormen and now informs them all of the coming advance. All that remains is for me to determine how we can counter this threat.

'My lord king.' Ealdorman Guthrum bows his head at my arrival, and each head then bobs in turn. My men are fiercely loyal to me. Guthrum, just as Cousin Athelstan, has known me for a long time. Guthrum is from the Norse Five Boroughs, and Cousin Athelstan's father, Æthelfrith, was an ealdorman of Mercia. I've ridden into battle many times with both men. We've fought, not quite side by side, but almost so, as we've slowly beaten back the Norse and their desire to hold the Five Boroughs and the eastern side of Mercia. We know what it is to fight the Norse, even if Gothfrith is unknown to us.

'They must have used the overland route,' Ealdorman Guthrum informs everyone. 'It smacks of arrogance.' Fury thrums in his voice. His ancestors might have been Norse, but Guthrum has long considered himself to be Mercian.

'Perhaps it does,' I confirm, perplexed, for I should have known about this long before now. Unless. Well, if they've killed people loyal to me, I'll ensure they pay for such crimes.

'Shall we hide behind these walls or fight them outside York?' This I direct to my ealdormen, and battle commanders, and also Cousin Athelstan and his brother, Ealdorman Ælfstan, who replaced his father as one of Mercia's ealdormen.

'Outside York.' Cousin Athelstan is quick to reply, his brother nodding along with him. Ealdorman Guthrum grunts his agreement, but I expect some dissension.

'Is that wise, my lord king?' Of course, it's Ealdorman Wulfgar who thinks to question me. I allow the moment to elongate, for Wulfgar to consider what he said, perhaps to reconsider it as well. He doesn't. 'Indeed, my lord king, your father and aunt, and your grandfather before them built a series of burhs for people to shelter behind so that they could defeat the Norse.'

'They were for men and women, children, those too young to fight, and those too old, and to ensure the good people of England didn't die because they had nowhere that offered protection. We're all warriors here, are we not? We don't need walls to shelter behind. We'll meet this threat and defeat it.'

'My lord king.' His bow is obsequious but lacks sincerity.

'Cousin Athelstan, Ealdorman Ælfstan, you'll hold the land to the right. Ealdorman Guthrum, you'll have the land to the left. Ealdorman Wulfgar, you and I will take the brunt of the attack.' Wulfgar looks fit to spit as I make the pronouncement. It'll be good to show this Wessex ealdorman how war is conducted against the Norse. My father was too often likely to leave his ealdormen in Wessex when he fought in Mercia. But there's no longer any need for me to do that. My stepmother has a firm command over Wessex while I'm absent. Not even my stepbrother and sister can cause difficulties while Lady Eadgifu, and my relatives, Lord Æthelwine and Ælfwine, sons of my grandfather's youngest son, and Lord Osferth, the son of my grandfather, are there to support her. I'm confident that even in my absence, Edwin and his sisters can cause me no harm.

'My lord king,' and my squire arrives, leading my horse, a tall animal, nostrils flaring, the ring of iron on iron, alerting him to the fact that we must ride to war again.

'Come on,' I murmur to him. 'Let's show these Norse how true-born kings conduct themselves in battle.'

# 4

## JULY 927, OUTSIDE YORK

*Cousin Athelstan of the English, King Athelstan's ally*

Not for the first time, I marvel that near enough two thousand men can be so silent. There's the odd chink of a weapon being moved, but above all it's the snap of Athelstan's battle standards, pulled sharp in the wind, that fills the air.

Opposite us, within sight, I eye the advancing warriors who've been brought here by King Gothfrith of Dublin. I wonder whether he knew of Athelstan's actions in York. Did his warriors come to make war, or are they surprised to see England's king ready to face them? Perhaps, as so often in the past, when the kingship of York fell vacant, Dublin's king merely expected to claim it, as his due. Maybe none of his warriors expected to do more than quell the populace.

Ahead of me, the archbishop accompanies Ealdorman Guthrum as they move to the middle of the two forces. Athelstan will offer a peaceful resolution, and if that fails, he'll offer nothing but blades. I can't see that a descendant of the Norse bastard Ivarr will accept anything but war. I thrill to know that.

Finally, three of the Norse men are forced to confront the English delegation. From here, it's impossible to know about what they speak. I can't see the faces of the archbishop, the ealdorman or the man holding Athelstan's battle standard, but I can see the Norse faces. They're unhappy. Well, that might be an understatement. They look ready to spit seaxes. I wonder if one of them is Gothfrith? I met Sihtric at Tamworth, when he wed the king's sister, but Gothfrith is an unknown. They say he's also a grandson of Ivarr, the Viking raider who led the enemy sixty years ago when they overran the kingdom of the East Angles. I think he's more likely to be a great-grandson, but what do I know? I've not spent my life keeping track of Ivarr's too-numerous spawn.

'What do they speak about?' my brother, Ælfstan, leans over to ask me. He's older than me by five years, but people say we look alike, not all that different to Athelstan the king, in all honesty. We share the same blue eyes, the same blond hair, but Athelstan is the king, and we're merely his loyal followers. I smirk. I'm a little more than that. I almost still can't believe that I'm wed to Ælfwynn, Athelstan's cousin, and the Lady of Mercia's daughter. But I am, and we already share a son. I'm sure that more will come.

'The weather,' I exhale, eyeing my brother as though unable to believe he would ask such a question. My brother fixes me with his startling eyes, and I chuckle. 'Of war and peace, I would imagine.' Only then there's no more time to talk. Instead, a rumble of unease echoes through the collection of men. I consider what I've missed as my eyes rake in the area before us. Whatever it was, the ealdorman and the archbishop have finished their conversation and now make all haste to return to the line of the king's men.

'It'll be war, then?' My brother shrugs, his arms flexing behind his shield, even as I reach for my seax.

'Aye, it always is with these daft bastards,' I confirm, looking to ensure the men I'll fight with are ready and prepared.

'Advance.' The cry comes only just as the ealdorman and archbishop return to the English side of the battlefield. I begin to go forwards, in the front of the line of shields, ready to kill one of the enemies. I have no love for the Norse. I've fought them before. They're no better than the

Mercians, or rather, the English, at the game of war. And their warriors can wound, and be wounded, just as easily as those men who surround me. We'll be victorious. We'll defeat the Norse and hopefully kill Gothfrith as part of the offensive. Admittedly, if Gothfrith perishes, there'll be another to take his place, but at least it'll be one less of Ivarr's pestilent offspring to kill.

'Hold.' I know it's not King Athelstan's voice that rises above the battlefield, but all the same, we obey the commands. I risk lowering my shield to see what the enemy is doing. They're advancing against us as well, but their line is ragged and filled with gaps. These men aren't used to fighting together as a cohesive force. They lack the strict battle formations of the English. Not that it will make them less deadly, but it's to be hoped that we can overpower them.

Another cry ripples through the air, and with a quick glance to ensure we move as one, the shield wall resumes its forward momentum, and I'm soon rewarded by a ricochet of wood crashing on wood. The enemy is there, just to the side of me, and I prepare to attack.

A smile touches my lips, and then I'm holding my shield firm, even as I reach over the held shield, slashing my seax against the wood of the linden board that greets mine. My wife has fought the Norse enemy, and now I'll do the same. I'll make this kingdom safe for my son, Æthelwold.

My blade reappears, free of blood. This time, I jab and then slash, working it behind the shield of my enemy. I can hear his heavy breathing. I almost stamp on his feet as the shield wall bucks and sways like a branch in a storm. I duck aside from a blade that thinks to slice open my neck, and then I reach higher, jabbing downwards, and this time, I feel the pressure beneath my blade give, and the sharp bite of blood mists the air. A shriek of outrage follows the wound, and I hack once, twice, three times, and the cries still, and the force against my shield abruptly disappears.

A tight smirk on my lips, for I know the man is dead, but another soon takes his place. And now there are spears as well to try and skewer our enemy with.

The slaughter has only just begun.

# 5

## 927, OUTSIDE YORK

*Athelstan, king of the English*

The Norse have never known when they're beaten. Today is no exception.

I'm surrounded by my warriors, most of them the remnants of my aunt's Mercian force. We've fought together many times before. We'll fight again. Or maybe we won't.

Despite the desires of those who wish I didn't engage in the coming battle, I know it's important to take my place amongst my warriors. I may well have undergone my consecration with a crown, not a helm, but I would never have been in the position to do so had I not first been a warrior and a lethal one at that.

My father fought his enemy, but it was my aunt and uncle who taught me the rudiments of how to command and be lauded as a warrior king. Uncle Æthelred was a fine warrior, his life taken from him too soon. Aunt Æthelflæd was a wise strategist. I was honoured to fight for her and in her name. Now, I must ensure others feel the same about me.

I watched the archbishop and ealdorman attempt to bring about a peaceful resolution. My terms were simple. The Norse could leave this place, now, without loss of life. I would not give them York. I would not even discuss that demand. If they didn't leave, it would be war. I doubt they gave it much thought. It's not the way of the Norse to consider anything but bloody slaughter.

My seax is bloodied in my hand, the hold on my shield firm. This isn't my first shield wall. I remember that occasion far too well, standing shoulder to shoulder with my Mercian warriors as we battled at Tettenhall. My father's men were there that day, but I fought as a Mercian. I was proud to take my first kill, even though I vomited all over myself afterwards, the stink of the dead and dying overwhelming me.

My uncle came to me and praised me for the men I had killed. My father didn't.

Now, I remember all that I've learned over the many years in between. I must stab and thrust with my seax. I must jab and defend with my shield. I must protect my brothers in arms, and I must kill as many of my enemies as it's possible to kill.

I turn to the warriors who protect me. Flodwin and Sigelac are my age. We've fought since we were old enough to hold a blunted blade. They fought with me at Tettenhall. I trust them with my life, and in return, they trust me with theirs.

'Hold.' The cry echoes from my mouth. I can feel that the tension in the shield wall has been compromised. We need a moment or two for everyone to regather themselves. I'm breathing hard. Sigelac, little more than his beady eyes showing beneath his helm, turns and offers me a wink.

'My lord king, they're hungry to die,' he crows. I grin in return. Sigelac is joyful on the slaughter field.

'Their Gods will be busy this night,' Flodwin intones, his own voice lacking any of Sigelac's joy. Flodwin fights like the very devil himself, but it brings him no pleasure. Unlike Sigelac.

'Advance,' I cry, content we're ready to continue the battle. I hear the cries of wounded men and the shrieks of those surprised to feel the first bite of a blade. I press my shoulder to my shield, and we take a step forward and then another. Only on the third do I feel reciprocal pressure. A war axe looms large at me, and I duck aside to avoid it, my seax held in my right hand, not my left.

Flodwin knocks the blade aside, growling menacingly in his throat.

I stab with my seax through the gap between my shield and that of Sigelac's. A shriek assures me that my enemy is wounded. And yet, a seax still snakes between the two shields in return. Sigelac notices the action first and stabs down with his seax in his left hand. We're opposites in strength and all the stronger as a group for that. The foul breath of my opponent fills the air, but I can already sense my enemy is weakening. I doubt they ventured to York expecting there to be a bloody fight to the death.

I stab once more and also jab forward with my shield, aware that there's someone now facing me who's taller than I am. He'll try and use his greater reach to strike against me. He won't be the first to employ such a technique, and it'll be far from my first bloody wound.

And so, I stab and jab again, unsettling him, making him rethink his footing. And I do it once, twice, three times in rapid succession. I wish I had metalled boots, and then I could stamp on his foot as well, but I don't. My equipment is heavy enough as it is without encumbering me with something so heavy.

'Kill him,' Sigelac huffs, and I realise he has the arm of his foe held tightly over both of their shields, exposing the man's underarm. I reverse the grip on my seax and stab upwards into where I know his lifeblood will quickly leak away. I meet the horrified eyes of Sigelac's opponent, missing a front tooth and with a drooping black moustache covering much of his cheeks, where his helm doesn't do so.

I grimace into his face and quickly retrieve my blade, the rain of his blood drumming over the agricultural land that should only be home to plants but, for today, is being put to a different use.

I hear the thud and refocus on my tall foe. He's finally regained his footing, distracted as I've been by Sigelac's opponent. Once more, a blade winds over my head, but Sigelac is more than aware of what's been happening. He reaches upwards, a man as tall as my opponent, if not taller, and I hear an unholy shriek of pain, and suddenly Sigelac is chuckling, holding the man's arm for all it's no longer attached to his body.

It won't be long, I'm sure of it, until the shield wall of our opponents shatters. Either that, or we'll entirely overwhelm it, and no one will leave here alive.

I think of my battle standard, held behind me, and whether Gothfrith employs the same. I should like to personally take his life. Then I can truly claim York through military might and not through my sister's marriage.

'Where is he?' I ask Sigelac, as he has a better view of the battle site.

'His banner is to the rear,' he informs me, derision ripe in his voice.

'Then he doesn't fight for his men,' Flodwin glowers. Flodwin believes all men should fight for their men or with their men. Certainly, no lord should ever expect a man to die without being prepared to make the same sacrifice.

'It seems not,' I confirm, concentrating once more on my foeman. He might be lacking an arm, and blood might be dripping down his byrnie, but he fights on, desperate now, and using his weight against my shield. He's finally realised he faces the king of the English. Should he die here, killing me in the process, then he'll have made a name for himself. But it seems his allies don't think the same.

I don't realise it's happening, but suddenly, the enemy shield wall has gone. Flodwin and Sigelac have no enemy to face and only just keep their feet as the other shields are removed, but my opponent remains. I don't lower my shield but instead spread my stance, prepared to face him.

'Don't assist me,' I urge Flodwin and Sigelac, but in that, I include all of those in my fighting force. This man might not be Gothfrith of Dublin, and neither is he more than a few moments from death, but I'll finish this.

My opponent thrusts his shield at me, and I duck away from the force of the blow. It would have hit me firmly on the nose, temporarily blinding me. I keep my shield just in front of my chest, seax ready in my hand. This fight is entirely one-sided, but that isn't in my favour. My opponent, eyes reddened with rage, pain and fury, swings his shield as though it weighs little more than an acorn, the blows wide, all of them coming for me. I scamper backwards, mindful that I don't wish to fall. Neither do I wish to falter when I can feel the eyes of my warriors on me.

I'll kill this man.

With his next wild strike, I rush him, my feet fleeing over the ground, and his shield is no good to him now, for I'm between it and his body. I meet his eyes, stabbing below his byrnie, the heat of his blood hot in my face. I continue to stab. He has no hand to punch me with, but he does release his shield and beats against my back. The blows are fierce, driving the air from my body, but still, I stab and slash, forcing my blade through the thickness of his byrnie. And slowly, so slowly, for some time, I fear the battle will never be at an end, his blows fade to little more than the gentle drum of rain on my back, and he falls to the ground, eyes rolling in his head.

I gasp in much-needed air and turn to meet the eyes of my warriors. Sigelac watches me with a smirk on his face. Flodwin is less effusive.

'He's getting away,' are his only words of praise, and I know immediately who he means.

'Chase him.' I urge those of my men with enough forethought to have already found themselves mounts to chase down the retreating enemy. 'Bring him to me, alive,' I caution them, and the thunder of hooves over the dead and dying almost drown out the shrieks of men trampled by my horsemen.

# 6

## JULY 927, BAMBURGH

*King Ealdred of the independent kingdom of Bamburgh*

'Tell me,' I demand from the messenger before me. He has an arrogant tilt to his head, but then, he's one of Constantin of the Scots' messengers. As such, I expect this kind of behaviour.

'The Norse have lost control of the kingdom of York.'

'And?' I counter, but I suspect I know the answer.

'Athelstan of the English has claimed the kingdom for himself, through the union of his sister to Lord Sihtric, citing the marriage as a means of legitimising his actions.'

'But what of Sihtric's heir, Gothfrith?'

'In Dublin at the time, and then, when he deigned to appear, chased from York by the English king's warriors. We don't know where he is at the moment,' the man confirms. Why Constantin should know before me is a mystery I'll solve when this conversation is at an end. I have eyes in York, but clearly none loyal enough to inform me of what's happening there. For now, I'm unsure how I feel about the news that my southern neighbour, Athelstan, is now a fellow Saxon. Should I be pleased? Frustrated? Even worried? I just don't know. I suspect, though, that King Constantin of the Scots has an opinion on the matter. My southern neighbours, Norse for many long years now, have always been an unruly bunch.

'Then he has only himself to blame,' I muse, without sympathy. While Sihtric's death was a shock, his alliance with the English king had been the greater shock. Gothfrith should have moved long ago to remove Sihtric from York. The Norse of York simply don't ally with the English. The Norse of York believe only in extending their reach into the formerly Mercian kingdom, now incorporated into Athelstan's England.

'King Constantin orders you to be alert to King Athelstan's next move.'

'Why?' Now he does have my interest. 'Does Constantin suspect that Athelstan will move further north? Cast his eyes towards Bamburgh, the kingdom of the Scots or even Strathclyde?'

The messenger, with a beaker of ale in hand, nods along with all of my suggestions.

'He would not be capable.' I muse, hoping my words are correct but fearing they might not be. The Viking raiders, now known as the Norse, long ago ran amuck throughout the ancient kingdom of Northumbria. My family held firm to the rocky outcropping of Bamburgh, high upon its peak, with the sea almost surrounding it, and making it easy to defend from all who might think to take it. Nothing else of the once mighty Northumbrian kingdom survives. Not a single member of its royal family yet lives. But I've endured against the Norse, as my father did before me. I don't intend to allow a fellow Saxon to take Bamburgh from me.

'King Constantin believes King Athelstan capable of anything he puts his mind to. After all, he forged a marriage alliance to bring the York kingdom into the sphere of his family, and now he controls it. He suspects King Athelstan plans on other advances as well.'

I shake my head, dismayed by the news. I'm well aware of what Constantin will demand next. We're allies but uneasy with one another. Still, there's nothing like a combined perceived threat to unite us.

'He urges you to be on your guard and keep a careful watch on the south.'

'I imagine he does,' I confirm moodily, only for my eyes to be caught by a movement behind the messenger. I wait, impatient, as my seneschal comes towards me, eyes gleaming. 'What is it?' I demand to know.

The man, who's served me for many years, and who well knows the messenger has come from King Constantin, bows quickly and then grimaces.

'An embassy from the English king begs for admittance to speak with you,' he informs me, his tone reassuringly bland.

'Well, my friend, it seems the next phase of the English king's plan has already begun,' I murmur to the messenger. Only then do I turn to my seneschal.

'How many of them are there?'

'A small force, no more than fifty, flying a banner of the English king.'

'And they wish to gain entry?'

'They do, my lord. One of the ealdormen, I believe, leads the embassy.'

I sigh heavily, almost wishing that I'd had no warning of what to expect and, certainly, that Constantin's messenger wasn't here to witness all of this.

'Allow them entry,' I concede. I look to my wife, noting that her eyes never leave my face. She's sitting with her women, some of them working on embroidery, although her hands are lax in her lap. Perhaps, I consider, I would welcome a new wife, one who might be more fruitful than the barren husk to whom I'm wed. But not, I reconsider, if it means giving up my kingdom to the English king. After all, rumour has it that King Athelstan has many sisters in need of a husband.

I'll listen to what this ealdorman has to say, but I can't see I'll be welcoming of whatever suggestion he brings. Unless. Well, unless there's a good reason for me to do so.

I feel the gaze of Constantin's messenger later as the English ealdorman makes his bow before me. He's a man who knows the importance of ceremony. He might have ridden to get here, no doubt through the terrible winds of the most recent days, but he looks immaculate. His tunic is liberally covered with the religious symbols of our God so that I might think him a priest, not an ealdorman.

'My lord.' The man's voice is unctuous. 'My name is Ealdorman Wulfgar. I'm sent by Athelstan, king of the English, to broker a peace accord between your kingdom and his own. As you know, my lord King Athelstan is now king of York, both through marriage and conquest.' The man speaks well, his words clearly well practised. My wife, seated beside me now, watches the man with curiosity, the most interest I've seen from her in the last five years.

'And what will I gain in exchange for such an accord?' I question, aware that Constantin's messenger watches on.

'Peace, my lord king. You'll gain peace,' the ealdorman offers menacingly, and a shudder passes down my spine at the words. 'Ah, but I'm neglectful. The king of the English has bid me bring you a gift.'

The man turns, and another steps forwards, carrying a reliquary festooned with more gold and silver than I have in my vault.

'What is it?' I stand, perplexed. The ealdorman smirks and then opens the reliquary, and I shudder once more. Encased, against the reddest silk I've ever seen, is a hand, a skeletal hand, but one all the same. I bow and try and find a smile for my face.

The warning could really not be any clearer.

'Peace it will be then,' I confirm, despite my wife's sharp hiss of disbelief and the grunt of an oath from Constantin's messenger. King Athelstan has returned to me an ancient and prized relic: the arm of King Oswald, sainted king of Northumbria. A man killed in battle against the Mercians. Whatever the religious importance of the item, I know its true meaning well enough. I don't wish to die in battle. I'll accept this peace, no matter what King Constantin of the Scots, my ally, might advise.

# 7

## JUNE 927, THE KINGDOM OF THE SCOTS

*Constantin, king of the Scots*

'He did what?' I rage.

'He was presented with some relic or some such and immediately capitulated,' my messenger informs me while I growl angrily, looking out at those within my hall. The men and women surrounding Mael Coluim absorb my attention. I should do more to make my unhappy feelings known on the matter of their split loyalties. Mael Coluim wishes for my death, but not as much as I hunger for his. Mael Coluim is my acknowledged heir. He's not my son. But that's the way of kingship amongst the Scots. To try and change it would cause more trouble than acknowledging Mael as my heir.

'What was this relic?' I muse. I know King Athelstan is a religious man. I don't decry him for that. But Ealdred? I would never have expected it from him.

My messenger, Denewulf, a man of the Scots people, for all he's as comfortable in the kingdom of Bamburgh, shakes his head once more. Perhaps then, there are some things he doesn't understand.

'And my lord king,' the man continues. I furrow my forehead and think of dismissing him, but he's insistent.

'What is it?' My words are too sharp, and I should settle myself rather than reveal my full fury.

'I also bring news that the English ealdorman wishes to speak to you as well.'

'To me?' I grip the arms of my wooden seat, seeking the reassurance of its solidity beneath me as my world lurches alarmingly. I'm the king of the Scots, overlord of the kingdom of Strathclyde. What does the upstart English king think he has to say that would interest me?

'Yes, my lord king, to you. I swore I'd bring you my word when the embassy was denied entry into your kingdom. Here, my lord king,' and the man offers a tightly rolled parchment. I shake my head, denying what it is and what it will contain.

'You should not have given your word,' I grumble, furious with my messenger. Already, I'm thinking of the worst possible thing I could do to him. Perhaps I'll send him to the furthest reaches of my kingdom, to Cait, to live amongst the seafaring folk of that kingdom, to work on the fishing boats as they try and avoid the Norse and their ships from the Orkneys. A smirk almost touches my lips.

'It was that, my lord king, or there would have been a battle, and I assure you that the English king's warriors are more than a match for your own.' The man speaks boldly, his words eliciting a roar of fury in my head as I stand and simultaneously snatch the offered parchment and slap him hard across the face. The blow is unexpected, and he staggers to his knees, fury in his normal placid demeanour. I'd do worse to him, but now I feel the eyes of all on me, Mael Coluim above all others.

Blood drips from the man's nose, pooling onto the floor, as he spits aside a bloody gobful. I breathe heavily. I should rather ride to war against the upstart English king than have this, this scrap of parchment brought to me by a man I've always trusted.

'He thinks to make a peace with me as well,' I growl, and my messenger, sitting back on his knees, grins, the action filled with derision and a complete lack of respect.

'He means to make you his bitch, along with King Ealdred, King

Owain and King Hywel,' the man gasps, his chest heaving with amusement. I move towards him as though to strike him once more, only for my son, Ildulb, to appear at my side.

'Father.' His back to those in my hall, he speaks into my ear, his word a sharp bark but muttered at little more than a whisper. 'Now is not the time to show any weakness or dismay. Remember, you're the king of all the Scots. Athelstan is merely the king of Wessex.' I appreciate my son's calming words. He's not my heir, but he should be, if only we didn't practise the art of choosing a king from alternate ruling lines. I succeeded Mael Coluim's father, and one day, he'll succeed me. My son will have to wait for Mael Coluim's death before he can rule. In the meantime, I share more with my son than I do my heir.

'He's a bastard,' I seethe, and my son nods but then steps aside.

I bend to the messenger and offer him my arm while my son, still with his back to everyone, opens the parchment.

'My apologies for my lack of restraint,' I offer loud enough that all can hear, and I mean it. My messenger bows his head low, even as he accepts my assistance. I raise my voice. 'It's a poor king who takes such umbrage from his messengers, men who are merely doing their best for their kingdom. Bring the good man ale and fine beef, ensure he has all he needs and can rest before I send him on a return journey.' I eye Denewulf keenly, and a tight smile plays on his lips at my words.

'I think,' he whispers, 'such an action would perhaps be repaired should the king gift something of great value to the man aggrieved.'

I growl angrily, thinking I could too easily slap him once more for such cheek, only I don't. He means to test me.

I smile, turning him so that all can see the face of the man with his bloodied nose and blood-splattered tunic.

'I gift to this man, in recompense for my actions, the finest horse from my stables. Ildulb,' my son turns and discreetly hands the parchment back to me behind his back, 'will escort you when you've been feasted, and then he'll ensure the stablehands don't try and hoodwink you into making a poor choice.'

My son inclines his head to me, his eyes flashing with his own fury. It seems that while he cautions me to be mindful of the effect the English king has on me, he's no better.

Mael Coluim stands, no doubt, aware that all is not as it should be. His eyes narrow, and he takes a step forward, but I don't beckon him to my side. Instead, I return to my chair, the messenger gone from before me, and as I open and close my tightly clenched hand in an effort to drive the ache from it, I read the words sent to me by one of King Athelstan's scribes. There's no need for someone to read it to me. It's written in Latin, the language of our God, and I read the words myself easily. But their intent is clear for me to see. King Athelstan, king of the English, means to have peace on this island.

I find a smirk on my face, wave the parchment before me so that all of those curious eyes know I'm going to speak about it, and lift my voice high.

'It seems, my good people, that we're to have a peace accord with the English king. And without any warfare. We must drink to that.' And I beckon for my servants to serve wine to all assembled. Hastily, the liquid is splashed into cups, beakers and even bowls for those who don't have a drinking vessel.

'To peace with the English king,' I proclaim. I must find good humour in this startling new arrangement and face the English king's embassy. I only hope that nothing more than peace is required.

# 8

## 927, THE KINGDOM OF STRATHCLYDE

*Owain, king of Strathclyde*

I eye the men before me. Two of them arriving within the same morning, one from the king of the Scots, the other from the king of the English. I can't see that any of this is good news for me.

I forced the messenger from Constantin to wait out of spite and little more. Now, it seems I did the right thing.

I consider what whispers I've heard from Norse Dublin and Saxon Bamburgh, and I hold a little grimace in place. It seems that they're quite likely true, and yet, I confess, I know that they already are. Not only do I have these two messengers, but Gothfrith of Dublin, the defeated, is also my guest. I keep him close, aware that at some point King Constantin of the Scots, my overlord, alas, will demand that I return the stray lord to him. I should like to witness that meeting, but know that I won't.

'Come.' I beckon the messenger from the king of the Scots forward. I can't remember his name, but I recognise him, all the same.

'Speak,' I announce, noticing that his nose has been bent out of shape since I last saw him. I wonder who saw to that, but then, I have spies within Constantin's royal court, just as he has some amongst mine. I smirk to see the physical evidence of King Constantin's fury.

'My lord king, Owain of Strathclyde, from his lord king of Dal Riata, Fortriu, Cait and Athol, Constantin of the Scots.' I just stop myself from rolling my eyes at the insistence on such a title. I know what Constantin is. He's the king of the many Scots people. Once, they may have been known as Dalriatians, the people of Fortriu, Caitians, or Atholians, but now they're merely the people of the Scots, just as Athelstan calls himself king of the English. I consider whether the two men who take up so much of my concern realise how alike they are. I doubt it. Men never know themselves as well as others do.

'Get on with it,' I snarl.

The messenger, a flash of mutiny in his eyes, begins to speak.

'My lord king, King Constantin sends word that you're to join the English king's treaty. You're to dispense with Gothfrith, of the Dublin Norse. Send him back to Dublin, and ensure none ever know he was here, with you.' I startle at this and narrow my eyes.

'The king truly means to abide by the terms of the English king?' I'm astounded.

'Indeed, my lord king, he does, and as such, and before my English counterpart can tell you as much, you're to prepare to meet at Eamont, in northern England, in a handful of days. All has been agreed with the king's embassy, and you're to do as your overlord commands.'

I feel my eyebrows arch at that. I almost splutter with indignation but hold myself firm against the temptation.

'King Constantin has agreed on this without first asking me?'

'King Constantin has no need to ask for your permission,' the messenger retorts. His tone infuriates. It seems that whatever passed between him and King Constantin, it's all resolved, and now he speaks with the arrogance of a man high in the Scots king's regard. I might just have to break his nose as well.

'And the terms,' I hiss with a tight breath.

'Perfectly acceptable,' the messenger confirms. His voice is thick with the tongue of the border regions between the kingdom of the Scots and the kingdom of Bamburgh. Every now and then, he uses a word I know to be Norse, and another that is Scots, and another, Saxon. He's a mix of all there can be in these troubled hinterlands. Not for the first time, I consider what he did to earn the prized position of Constantin's messenger between his kingdom and that of mine and Bamburgh.

'Should I not speak to the English messenger?' I jibe. 'Speak for the people of Strathclyde?'

'No, my lord king.' He uses my title, but his delivery lacks all respect. 'You hold this kingdom at the bequest of King Constantin. You have no authority to do anything that would set you against your overlord.' That word once more, how it grates.

'All the same, I'll at least speak with the man. He's come a long way.'

'Perhaps, my lord king.' And the messenger bows from my presence as I beckon for the English messenger to be sent my way.

'My lord king, warm wishes from King Athelstan, most holy king of the English.' The man bows low, almost touching the floor, and although I was determined to be unctuous to him, I quickly change my mind. This man knows how to show respect.

'What's your name?' I query.

'I'm Beohtric, my lord king.'

'Speak, I'm eager to hear from my neighbour.'

'The English king is keen to forge an alliance with all of his neighbours. An agreement has been made with King Constantin of the Scots, with King Ealdred of the kingdom of Bamburgh, and the English king hopes you'll also join the peace accord.'

A peace accord, is it? I consider the idea of that.

'I'm led to believe that King Constantin of the Scots has already spoken on my behalf.'

A flicker of uncertainty covers the man's face, and I look to Constantin's messenger. Has he made a fool of me?

'My lord king, Athelstan, king of the English, understands that you're king of Strathclyde. Is that not correct?'

'Yes, yes, that's correct,' I answer, perhaps too hastily.

'Then King Athelstan would welcome your agreement to the accord as well.'

I nod along, turning to Denewulf. I've finally remembered his name.

He watches, his lips downturned. I think I might just play along with this.

'Then, I'd like to discuss terms,' I conclude, and a beaming smile touches the face of Beohtric.

'I'll have the king's embassy, led by Ealdorman Wulfgar, visit you,' he confirms, bowing once more, and striding from my presence. I smile as well, considering what I might be able to do to discomfort bloody Constantin of the Scots. I tire of his over-demanding ways. Perhaps, I consider, the English king might be a means of holding King Constantin at bay for a little longer.

# 9

# JULY 927, EAMONT, NORTHERN ENGLAND

### Constantin, king of the Scots

It's a sobering thought to realise my advanced age compared to this young king, Athelstan, who styles himself 'of the English'. I was a man grown before he was even born. He's courteous and treats me with respect, as he does all the other kings he's called before him, at this meeting place, high in the north of his lands but too close to mine for comfort. This place is not in Mercia but further north.

And yet, for me, his respect just reminds me of how very old I am compared to him and the other kings and lords he's summoned here. I'll list them all, just to mark myself amongst them. Hywel of the South Welsh, Owain from my puppet kingdom of Strathclyde and Ealdred of the independent kingdom of Bamburgh, the northernmost tip of the once mighty land of the Northumbrians, so called for they live to the north of the tumultuous river Humber. I do think the kingdoms further south should be known as the Southumbrians, but few seem keen to adopt that term.

So many of us all together in one place and at the behest of the young king, Athelstan. It's an unsettling thought and a remarkable achievement for how little blood has been shed to bring it about. We could have chosen war, but instead, Athelstan, with his vice-like grip on the kingdom of York, has achieved through the blood of marriage what the blood of battle could have brought about.

Are our people so tired of bloodshed and distrust that this meeting has been possible, or is it that King Athelstan is emboldened by the knowledge that our God blesses his every move and brings about his successes? I don't know the answer, but I hope I'm not too tired and old to fight. I've done nothing but battle throughout my long life. I wouldn't wish to stop now.

Athelstan's respect annoys me. My age should mark me as wise and wily. I've been able to hold my own against my enemies for more than twenty years, yet I can't help but think this young man thinks me too old, too weak to fight and too easy to subdue. I might have given that impression when I agreed to this alliance; I don't deny that.

Athelstan has gained much from the deaths of his stepbrother, Ælfweard, his father's chosen heir in Wessex, and Lord Sihtric of York. his brother-by-marriage. Athelstan now stands as king over the Saxon kingdoms of Wessex and Kent, Mercia and East Anglia, and the Norse kingdom of York. Now he looks at my kingdom a little too closely for my liking.

I want to assure him that I'll not be the next to give up my earthly crown for a more heavenly one, but he might just have a valid argument, for, of all of us here, I'm most likely to die next.

The intensity of his gaze annoys me. As does having to be here at all. Why should I bow to this king of the English? I'm king of the Scots and have been for nearly thirty years. I've governed well and kept my people safe, so why should I now submit to an 'overlord,' a man who thinks to be an emperor, in the guise of the great Charlemagne, who ruled Frankia? This island of Britain needs no emperor.

I've never feared to fight in the past and don't now, and yet I'm here, as are the other kings. We've determined to conclude a peaceful accord with each other, but I can tell from the shifting feet and sideways looks of my fellow attendees that this might all be a ruse.

Athelstan is not untried in battle, far from it, in fact. In the past, he's encountered the Welsh and Dublin kings. Alongside his aunt, Æthelflæd of Mercia, he's accomplished great deeds and secured more land for his kingdom of the English. But Lady Æthelflæd has been dead for many long years now, and he stands alone against us all. Gothfrith, and his failed attempt to claim York, has reinforced Athelstan's belief in his rightfulness to proclaim peace throughout our island.

I came to terms with Lady Æthelflæd once, over ten years ago. She was a wise woman, devout and assured in her powers, and she trained her young nephew well. That peace accord didn't last. Afterwards, I came to terms with her brother, King Edward. That peace accord didn't last either. They never did.

I met the young king's father once, Edward, king of the Anglo-Saxons. Seven years ago, when bloody Ragnall and his Norsemen were causing havoc along our borderlands, having claimed York, or Jorvik as he termed it, for himself following the Battle of Corbridge two years before.

Edward, Donald of Strathclyde, the previous king of that kingdom, and myself concluded an arrangement to curtail Ragnall's raiding activities on any of our lands. If Ragnall attacked one of us, we would all respond. Or so we said.

It worked, in a fashion, for later the same year Ragnall came to an independent agreement with Edward. Again, it was short-lived, for Ragnall had the audacity to die the following year. The shifting sands of allegiance and counter-allegiance run contrary to any agreement lasting too long. Perhaps the shifting feet have the right of it after all.

Since the alliance with Edward, Sihtric had ruled the kingdom of York. But the Wessex kings weren't finished with Sihtric. Athelstan proposed marriage to his sister, Lady Edith, and although the marriage went ahead, Sihtric cast her and her Christianity aside. But, as though punished by the old Gods, his death was not long in coming. That was all the pretext Athelstan needed to claim York for the English, and he moved swiftly before Sihtric's heir could mobilise and make his way to York from Dublin. The damn fool should have been more alert to the possibilities. And he should certainly have been victorious when he did battle the English king.

And my point in recounting all this? Athelstan's aunt and his father were more my age, and their respect was genuine, one contemporary to another, not as a son to a doddering father. I've sons enough of my own to know the bloody difference.

Still, Athelstan is a finely built man; long blond hair graces his head, and he's tall and well-formed, training each day so that he can wield his sword, shield, seax and spear as and when they're needed. For all that Athelstan wears fine clothing, I hear chosen and embellished by his second stepmother, King Edward's third wife, the lady of Wessex. The raw energy of his muscles can be seen flexing and stretching the fabric of his deeply dyed royal tunic.

Athelstan almost compels me to train as often as he does instead of passing the duty to my sons, who are more of an age with him. I wish I could feel fatherly towards him, but I don't. I can respect him, providing he respects me.

And so, this treaty. Why am I here? Is it because he swept into the Norse kingdom of York after his brother-in-law's death and effectively annexed the land to his kingdom, and I fear what he'll gain if allowed to push further north? Or is it because Athelstan avows himself a Christian king, and I too am a Christian king, of the old Ionian school no less, and it would be a good and Christian thing to live in peace with my neighbours?

I don't yet know, but what I do know is that few have died an untimely death to bring about this mutual understanding between the kingdom of the Scots, the people of Strathclyde, the lord of Bamburgh, the people of the southern Welsh kingdom and the English. All we need do is accept King Athelstan as our overlord. So, in the spirit in which it's offered, and provided it doesn't become too onerous, I'm prepared to accept the hand of friendship extended by King Athelstan of the English. It'll be easily done and can be just as easily undone. I risk nothing by being here, and I may even grow in acclaim if this union beneath the

English king is a success. Perhaps, we, unlike the fracturing kingdoms in East and West Frankia, can unite for a common purpose and remain united, after all. I confess, we do share a common enemy, the Norse of Dublin.

I'll wait with bated breath.

# 10

## JULY 927, EAMONT, NORTHERN ENGLAND

*Athelstan, king of the English*

It feels a little like my coronation again with all eyes on me, only here the eyes are unmistakably hostile and certainly not those of my family members.

Or are they? Perhaps there's a hint of approval in a few of those looks. I hope there is. It doesn't bode well if everyone is here against their will, grudging in their acceptance of my desires, even if so little blood has been shed to accomplish this momentous meeting of so many of the kings of Britain.

In the two years since my coronation, I know I've accomplished much and that some of these kings probably begrudge me that success, particularly when it's come at their expense. I believe that only by working together can we repel those who try to take our land from us. And anyway, my most recent acquisition has come at the detriment of none of these men.

Jorvik, or York as I'll name it, is mine to command. The man who thought he should succeed to Sihtric's throne, Gothfrith, the Norse king of Dublin, has fled, possibly seeking sanctuary from one of these kings before me. But for now, and in the interests of diplomacy, I'll not press the matter further. My new allies have assured me they don't shelter him in their kingdoms, and until proved as liars, I'll accept their word. As their overlord, I must show them some respect.

I've never been as far north as Eamont before. It's almost within the land of the Strathclyde king, but still part of England. As such, I've not left my kingdom, but have forced others to come to me. They're my visitors, and not vice versa. I have the greater power. I have knowledge of these men and have heard much about them.

Constantin of the Scots is the most recognisable. He's an elegant older man, more of my father's generation than mine. I know he and my father met in the past, just as Constantin met with my aunt, Lady Æthelflæd, as well.

Constantin watches me with interest from behind his wrinkled eyes and creased face. He's the most careworn of us all and possibly the most cynical of events here today. I hope to prove him wrong, but neither am I a fool. I know these men change their views with the wind, just as our Norse enemies power their ships with the selfsame winds.

Hywel of the South Welsh is a man very much like myself. His age falls between mine and Constantin's, and he's ruled his kingdom almost as long as Constantin. Rumour has it that Hywel's wise and well educated, an avid believer in the one true faith, and as such, someone I would like to know better. He was eager to reach this accord when my messenger first sought him out.

Hywel acknowledges me with a genuine smile on a face that's younger than his years as king suggest. I return the greeting. Here, at least, is a man who holds the same ideals as me. He wants the menace from the Dublin Norse contained as much as I do. His kingdom of Deheubarth has a vast coastal area, almost opposite the Dublin king's stronghold and separated only by the expanse of sea. The kingdom of the Manx nestles in the heart of that sea, and the Norse are not above claiming it as their own to rule. It's a handy place for them to launch their attacks against the Welsh.

I don't envy Hywel for having such close neighbours and imagine his problems are similar to mine in keeping the sea routes under close guard. There's only a limited supply of warriors and ships to watch the coastal lands, and they can't be everywhere at once.

Hywel is a warrior. I can tell from his practised stance and his steady observation of everyone. With his mop of unruly auburn hair, he's on edge and yet manages to appear relaxed.

King Owain from Strathclyde is someone about whom I've heard a great deal. Rumour has it he's heavily influenced by Constantin of the Scots. I consider the truth of that assertion. Owain is here with his retinue, and he seems kingly enough with his fine tunic, stitched with looping symbols, the shimmer of gold and silver at his neck, wrists and fingers.

Owain doesn't once look to the man who may, or may not, hold the true power behind his reign. But still, it's a perplexing problem and one I hope to get to the bottom of during my time at Eamont.

Ealdred of the old royal family of Bamburgh is a man about whom I'm fully conversant. He knew my father. Now that I've taken back York on the death of Sihtric, we're neighbours. As with all these men who live in the northern lands, he's a close ally of Constantin of the Scots, perhaps because it's better to be an ally than an enemy. Constantin, the king of all the Scots kingdoms, has many men who'll fight in his name. Ealdred of Bamburgh won't be able to claim even a third as many, but I've sent him a gift to show that we can be friendly neighbours towards one another. I hope he appreciated me parting with such a priceless relic, returning it to its true owners.

Ealdred is well dressed, his leather boots elaborately decorated with embellishments of gold and silver. I shouldn't like to have to walk any great distance in them. I'm sure they can't be comfortable, and yet they speak of his arrogance. A man with jewels in his shoes has the time, and the necessary resources, to think before meeting any attack from an enemy. Either that or whoever dressed him thought it better to speak of wealth than prowess in battle.

Ealdred and Constantin have fought against the Norse in the past. They share common goals and needs. Seeing them arranged in such a way makes me consider who'll be true to their word, and who won't, and whether, one day, I'll have to face their combined ire against my plans to expand the reach of England.

By rights, we should all hold much in common. It should be natural for us to unite against the Norse, whether they come from the lands of the Dublin kings, the Outer Isles or the homeland of the Danes and Norwegians. It's easier to name them Norse than try and determine their exact birthplaces. Their ancestors were the Viking raiders, and now, they're the Norse.

But I doubt we'll stand and fight battles if the other's land is attacked. It's more likely that we'll look only at our borders and assist only when incursions threaten our existence and property.

My purpose here is to prevent that from happening, to decide on a goal we can all agree upon, and to ensure our kingdoms are left alone by the Norse.

I hope we have a unifying force at our command. I'll remind these men of our love of the one true faith, and I'll have them visit my witan and see the strength with which I control my kingdom.

For now, I'll feast them and show them my wealth and extract promises from them that we'll act together against the Norse. For those who please me, I'll propose marriage alliances, and for those who displease me, I'll take their sons or grandsons as my hostages and raise them at my witan, under the watchful eyes of my stepmother.

Such hostages will be treated honourably as if they were my brothers. They'll return to their lands one day, in awe of my kingship, keen to emulate it and stay friendly with the English. While their fathers resent me, their sons and heirs will show nothing but love for me. I'll gain the support of the other kingdoms no matter what. What happened with York and my sister's marriage assures me that I should think broadly when planning for the future. I don't know what it holds, but I must do all I can to ensure England's triumph.

The day is fair and warm, the breeze gentle on my face. My household troops are close to hand, ever vigilant and armed well. The ancient archbishop of Canterbury is here too, a warrior clad in a holy man's clothing but no less devout for that, for all I fear he might fall if called upon to hold shield and sword. I've asked the archbishop of York to remain in York, with the aid of many of my household warriors. Together, they'll ensure York stays loyal following the recent battle outside its walls.

Surrounding our gathering, in a circle of my devising, are the men who look to these kings, including my own ealdormen: Wulfgar, Osferth, Guthrum, Ælfwold, Ælfstan and Ordgar. Osferth is, of course, related to me. He's named as my uncle for all none would ever say that my grandfather, Alfred, was crass enough to have a child born out of wedlock, although it is obvious that he did. Ealdorman Wulfgar has been to speak with the Scots king on my behalf, as well as Owain of Strathclyde. He thinks it's a punishment, but I sent him as a sign of my trust. Also, perhaps, because if my embassy wrong-footed itself, I wouldn't miss Ealdorman Wulfgar. Still, he lives and has excelled in the task I laid at his feet. I'll reward him for that.

My cousin's husband is also in attendance, supporting his brother, Ealdorman Ælfstan. He fought for me outside York. His reputation as a warrior continues to grow. Soon, very soon, I'll be able to name him as one of my ealdormen.

All those in attendance watch either with suspicion or with ease. After all, we're merely men and distrustful at that.

I've brought precious gifts for my allies, as they have for me. They've already been exchanged in more private arrangements, and we all know where we stand with one another.

Am I content with the gifts given to me? It would make me an unchristian man if I weren't, and yet, perhaps I'd hoped for some greater commitment to the cause here and some more substantial gifts from these men to show theirs, especially from King Ealdred of Bamburgh. The arm of Saint Oswald that I sent to him was no small gift.

But for now, I'll eat and smile and laugh and joke as best I can. Later, I'll scrutinise the actions of my fellow kings. Later.

# 11

## JULY 927, EAMONT, NORTHERN ENGLAND

*Hywel, king of the South Welsh*

The English king is smiling. Constantin of the Scots is smiling. Even King Owain is smiling, and so must I, Hywel, king of the South Welsh.

It's strange, this collection of men who hold sway over so much land on this island we call our home. We are, for once, amongst equals in rank and prestige, piety and warcraft, statesmanship and power.

Our lands may be vastly different, but we have the same hopes and fears. Will we keep our kingship? Will we die as embittered old men in cold and lonely beds or on a trail of glory on the battlefield? Will our neighbours remain our friends or covet our lands? Will our successors rule as well as we have done, or will they, heaven forbid, outdo us?

Behind our smiles, we plot and evaluate and consider our options about how to get the best possible outcome from this gathering of great men.

Beautiful drinking horns are passed between us as we toast each other and our accord. The wine is sweet and blood red. Perhaps not the best choice in the circumstances. Athelstan's archbishop will shortly present us with an elaborately written and beautifully decorated vellum upon which we'll place our mark, and with that mark, the bargains made here will be sealed. Possibly.

I, for one, am keen to make this agreement. I've more spiritual cares that I plan to turn my mind towards once the peace is concluded.

I've visited my lands and some of the English king's but I wish to set forth and journey further, see the religious wonders of this earth and eventually seek the physical embodiment of our Lord on Earth, the Pope, in Rome, as King Alfred of Wessex did as a child. If I can leave Eamont confident that my co-signatories will not invade my land in my absence, then I plan to leave as soon as possible. If.

The sun is warm on my exposed head. My heavy garments, suitable to show my wealth and power, are a little uncomfortable in the summer heat, and I'd welcome something more thirst-quenching to drink than the too-sweet wine.

We're gathered outside to take advantage of the warm weather, and yet, exceptional goods and valuable gems surround us. We sit on fine-crafted wooden chairs, before a large, well-built and functional table and, above our heads, a small half-tent flaps in the almost non-existent breeze, despite the river close by. Our followers are similarly arrayed on wooden benches, in rows, as if they sit within a great church, and they share drinking horns of the fine, sweet wine.

King Athelstan sits erect, listening calmly to the words of his archbishop while his eyes dance between the assembled kings and behind us, noting those who accompanied us here and no doubt calculating the strength of our fighting forces.

But I didn't come to fight. I support King Athelstan and his plans for this island.

I might be the only one here who does.

Athelstan has with him a small collection of the relics of the saints that he so avidly collects. I'd rather spend my time in discussion with him about those relics than listen to the droning of the peace accord that's being read to us.

It uses the language of the English king. I understand everything being said, for I'm fluent in more than my tongue, but the flowing words and convoluted sentences are unappealing. For those who don't speak the language, this must be a laborious process, and I pity their translators.

I wish the archbishop would just get to the point. Nothing he says will be unexpected. The wording of the document has already been agreed.

Diplomats have been busy working, rushing between the courts of all gathered here to ensure that this meeting runs as smoothly as possible. It may only have been a month since this gathering was conceived, but much has been done behind the scenes to make the actual meeting of the kings appear as flawless as possible.

King Constantin of the Scots sits as contentedly as I do. He's assured of his position and loved by his people, fearless in the face of his enemies. King Owain is more unknown. He's regal and proud but maybe just a little too proud.

And then there's the figure of the House of Bamburgh. Ealdred is younger than all of us, but his face wears a frown of thought as he squints in the bright sunlight. I'm not the only one to mark it. What must he think of his future with Constantin of the Scots on one side of his kingdom and this ambitious king of the English on the other?

Is it much different from when he had the Norse king, Sihtric, with the weight of Dublin at his back, to having this English king with the might of his united kingdoms? Time will tell, I suppose. As it will for all of us.

At last, the voice of the archbishop dies away, and King Athelstan looks at his guests expectantly. With a fluid movement, he rises first to add his mark to the peace accord with a flourish and no hesitation. I watch him as he reaches for the quill, long experience ensuring he holds his sleeves away from the ink, his hand raised high above the shimmering white of the vellum before he bends quickly to add his mark.

This is the only part of the proceedings not to have been preordained. Who will rise next? Who will rush to admit their submission to the English king?

I glance at the other kings with interest, and when none makes a move, I rise and bend to add my cross, where the archbishop indicates with his long, ink-stained finger. I'm a little surprised that this great man of God has clearly written this charter himself. Surely, he has others who could have done it for him?

With a flourish, I add my dash in the bright green ink, as King Athelstan has just done, careful not to stain my sleeves or my fingers. It's no lie that this ink can mark the skin as clearly as it does the scrapped parchment before me. And it burns as it does so, a sharp pain that nothing can dilute until it's done eating away at the flesh with which it comes into contact.

King Athelstan extends his hand of welcome to me as I step to his side, and we clasp, as brothers should, arm to arm, shoulder to shoulder. A faint word of thanks from the English king and I realise that he was worried that none would mark the agreement.

Again, I'm surprised. His supreme confidence in the face of possible rejection astounds me, and I reappraise him once more. He's a worthy grandson of King Alfred, a man I've heard so much about and whom I hope to emulate in his love of learning and law. King Athelstan is, after all, a man I'm pleased to call my overlord. He's fair, honest and courageous.

Behind us, a small skirmish breaks out as the other three men now vie to have their turn with the charter next, and I smile again, as does Athelstan.

There's a feeling of relief that the deed is done, a freely taken breath of the clean air. Now, we can celebrate our unity in the face of the Norse aggressors. We can drink as we please, and converse about holy relics as we like, for we are now allies, witnessed by God, each other and the remainder of the kings.

Allies, a word to mask many others.

## 12

## JULY 927, EAMONT, NORTHERN ENGLAND

*King Ealdred of the independent kingdom of Bamburgh*

My hand is steady as I sign the charter before me. It's a beautiful piece of statecraft, finely decorated around its edges, with emblems deemed to show the peace we've agreed upon, holy allusions to unity and tranquillity.

Even my rudimentary understanding of the written word is stirred to admiration, and I'm minded of some of the more elaborate designs I've seen within the walls of the monasteries that dot the landscape of my homeland.

My homeland.

King Athelstan needs to appreciate that while we may now be neighbours, I've no intention of gifting him my homeland. My family and I have held it against the ravages of the Norse, the pretensions of the kings of Dublin, Ragnall and his men and even against the forces of Constantin of the Scots' countrymen.

My family. Not Athelstan's, and I'll guard it as well as my ancestors have done. Not for us, the submission to Dublin Norse kings, not like other lands that once formed the mighty kingdom of Northumbria.

And yet, I'll come to terms with King Athelstan. His gift of Saint Oswald's arm was a threat or a promise, but it was certainly more than it seemed. For now, I'm content with this agreement. I'm not sure how long it will be to my benefit to do so, but that little concerns me today.

My mark made, I step away from the table, holding the quill out to King Owain of Strathclyde. He'll sign last, Athelstan, Constantin, and Hywel already having made their mark, and Owain is unhappy to do so last; I can tell by the scowl that mars his face. He's a man who truly wears his heart on his sleeve. Does being the last to add his mark make him the least of the five of us? Let him think about it, and perhaps next time, he'll be quickest to act.

Kings Athelstan and Hywel are conversing quietly amongst themselves, so I turn to Constantin of the Scots for want of anything better to do. He seems as comfortable with proceedings here as the other two kings who've already ascribed to the agreement.

'This is a grand plan,' I mutter softly, watching Constantin's wise eyes wrinkle in amusement. We're allies, and enemies of old. This is by no means the first time we've met in person. But it is perhaps my fault that Constantin is here. Had I held out against King Athelstan, then Constantin might not have acceded to this grand peace accord. I'm curious to see if he'll hold me accountable.

'Yes, it is, but these kings of the Angles and Saxons, or the English as they now like to be called, do like things to be grand. His grandfather, father and aunt were the same.'

'I knew his father, but I don't think his aunt, and certainly not his grandfather.' I furrow my brow in thought.

A loud chuckle of amusement. It seems that Constantin has decided to make the best of it, after all.

'And I, contrary to reports, did not meet the grand old man either. But I've heard much, and we can't deny, no matter how much we'd like to, that the House of Wessex stands and flourishes.'

'No, we couldn't deny that,' I mutter darkly as Constantin chuckles ominously once more.

'I know, don't tell me again about how long your family survived, marooned as you were between my lands, Strathclyde's and the limits of the Norse kingdom of Dublin and York.'

I bite down, realising I was about to say just that. Have I become so predictable? 'I wouldn't dream of it, Constantin. After all, I think you're only too aware.' My voice is light, the attempt at irony perhaps not quite as successful as I'd have liked.

'Yes, your father never tired of ensuring all and sundry were conscious of that. And I think when you came begging to my court for assistance to reclaim those lost lands from Jarl Ragnall, that you too might have made use of that same argument.' Constantin's voice is high with derision. It seems he does mean to rile me, after all.

'Ah, well, he was on occasion a little too sure of his family,' I reply, trying to ignore the jibe about my time at Constantin's court.

'And you'll not fall into that trap again?' Constantin queries, eyebrows raised, all joviality gone from his voice.

'The might of this king will not take my land. And neither will you. Nor the bloody Norse.' I fill my voice with hard resolve.

'Don't want it!' Constantin replies too quickly.

'Well, tell your retainers that then, will you?'

'Gladly, Lord Ealdred. And now, let's not mar the proceedings with an unseemly argument. Remember, unity is the key to success.'

As he says, Constantin and I aren't strangers. We're uneasy neighbours and often allies, with more in common than I have with King Athelstan and all his pomposity and sense of superiority.

Do I resent adding my agreement to this accord of his? Yes and no, all at the same time. The idea is a fine one, and yet, it seems unworkable. The lands around me push and shove, hoping to claw back my domain, and they do the same with all the other kingdoms around them. There seems to be a march to be as united as possible while all I see is a 'land grab'. The right to govern any land claimed by conquest is legitimised by reference to forebears who had no clear claim to the lands either, and so to my mind, it is all a little laughable, a little too much.

Not that I say this out loud. My kingdom is mine, and I plan to hold it well. Whether King Athelstan threatened me or tried to win me over with his gift, I'll be wary of his aspirations.

But would I like more? That's not easy to answer. I know my lands and my people, and I trust them with my life as they trust me with theirs. Why would I look to add people hostile to my regime to my command? And yet clearly, others have no problem in asserting claims over lands and people hostile to their rule.

I'm a warrior, never doubt that, but I don't look for unnecessary trouble. Security is more important than aggression, or so I tell myself.

# 13

## JULY 927, EAMONT, NORTHERN ENGLAND

### *Owain, king of Strathclyde*

I know a glare mars my face as I reach over and add my score to this ridiculous piece of scraped parchment before me. The grimace is more than skin-deep, running through my blood and penetrating as far as my churning stomach. I feel sickened by the blood-red wine and revolted by my presence here.

The smiles on the faces of the other kings do nothing for my aggravation and annoyance. Even King Constantin of the Scots, the old bugger, is smiling wildly and enjoying himself. Keen as a young squire, he leapt to add his name to this superfluous bit of parchment after only Athelstan and Hywel. I fear I've been played for a fool, and it doesn't sit well with me. Not at all. In years to come, when others look back at this bit of parchment, they'll know the order in which we signed. They'll take it to mean I was the most subordinate of all. That I was the weakest of all five kings.

When Gothfrith of Dublin came to me, after his defeat at the hands of King Athelstan over York, begging me for help and assistance, I offered it gladly. I was prepared to do anything to discomfort this upstart Wessex king who styles himself 'of the English'. Not for one moment did I think Constantin of the Scots would pull rank on me and demand that I send Gothfrith on his way back to Dublin. I thought Constantin might even support Gothfrith in his intentions to claim York after the unexpected death of Sihtric, but I was wrong.

Our relationship, until that point, had been amenable, and I'd almost forgotten that I owed anything to the king of the Scots. But now Constantin's not only reminded me, but he's also brought me into this laughable alliance with other kings, constantly under risk of attack from the Dublin Norse. I've done my best, speaking to the English ealdorman myself, but as Constantin and Ealdred capitulated so quickly, I hardly feel as though I've gained anything.

Now I seem to have two overlords, whereas only a month ago, I could think I had none.

The hearty laughter of the other men resounds too loudly in my head. I'd like nothing more than to call my war band to me and demand that they kill all these men here. Or perhaps take them as hostages. Then we could net ourselves some fine coinage and jewellery, and this journey to the far southern borders of my lands would at least have been worthwhile.

Turning to look at the gathering of my supposed allies, I note that Athelstan and Hywel are standing almost nose to nose, perusing some ancient text that the English king's holy man holds in his hands. In hushed tones of awe, they confer about it, the holy man earnest as he answers their many questions.

Besides them, King Constantin and King Ealdred stand a little more aloof from each other but laughing and conversing all the same. I imagine their fake good humour hides the truth from the English king about what they discuss.

I hope it's an idea to attack King Athelstan, drive him back from the lands of York, and send him back to Wessex and Mercia mewing like a kitten. I doubt it, but I can hope all the same.

As another holy man works to seal and store the parchment we've just witnessed, King Constantin gestures for me to join him and Ealdred.

I go, but unwillingly, and I'm right to be sluggish in my response to his command.

'Come, King Owain; a smile would look better on that face of yours. We do good work here today.'

A tight and sardonic smile touches my constricted face in response to his words. He's baiting me, or he knows me too well. Neither thought is appealing.

'It may well be good work, but I don't look forward to the repercussions from across the sea when Gothfrith of the Dublin Norse reacts to this.'

'I'm sure that you've little to worry about. Why would Gothfrith want to come anywhere near your kingdom? You know as well as I do that the Dublin Norse enjoy a land crossing from Chester to York that's now in the hands of King Athelstan. It's him who should be wary. Not you.' Constantin speaks too loudly. Is that a hint from Constantin that his intentions here are less honourable than they appear?

'Indeed, Owain. It's Athelstan and I who should be worried, not you,' Ealdred announces, no humour in his words. Perhaps Constantin shouldn't have reminded Ealdred about that.

'You don't share a coast with the marauding bastards,' I grudgingly counter.

'No, but I do have a coastline to protect, and it's just as open as yours. It might take a little more thought, a little more time and effort, but if they wanted to attack me, they could sail around the top or bottom of this island and cause havoc wherever they went. And anyway, what of King Hywel? He seems little concerned, and his lands are just as unprotected as yours from the Dublin Norse. In fact, more so.'

I turn to look at Hywel then and notice that Ealdred is correct. He seems happy with this arrangement.

'Hywel will probably just be pleased to get the Wessex and Mercian men off his border.'

'The English, Owain, you must get used to calling them the English. They're now one race under one king,' King Constantin offers, the disdain in his voice clear to hear, for all he rules over the united kingdoms of the Scots: of Fortriu, Dal Riata, Cait and Atholl.

'You can call them what you want, but I see them for what they are. The men of Wessex and the men of Mercia, and now the men of York, all looking to one king but only while he's powerful and winning this war against the Dublin Norse.' I know I sound angry, but I can't help it.

'Now, that might well be true, Owain, but you'd do well to accept it for what it is.' Ealdred's words infuriate me further.

'I would much rather it had stood for longer than a few months before I accepted anything,' I continue to complain. 'You'd do well to do the same, Constantin and Ealdred. He'll not be happy with what he has. King Athelstan wants all of Britain for his domain.'

'That might well be true as well, but this accord binds him as surely as it does us. He can't take our kingdoms.' Again, it's Ealdred who speaks. I detect some unease in his retort.

'There's nothing mentioned about annexing his allies' lands if the agreement is broken.' I can't stop myself. Constantin and Ealdred are fools not to realise the danger they're in. 'His sister was only married to the old king for a span of months, and then she was cast out on the wishes of Sihtric's retainers and lords. Somehow that still allowed him to exert his hold over that kingdom. She doesn't even share a child with Sihtric. Sihtric's sons are older and by another woman.' I rush my words, determined to convince the other two that they're mistaken to be so calm about this peace.

'Athelstan might have used the marriage as a basis for his invasion, but he won the battle, if you can call it a battle. Gothfrith's men deserted him. That's hardly Athelstan's fault.' Ealdred's face shows just how ridiculous he finds my argument.

'But Athelstan shouldn't have been there in the first place?' I try again, not wishing to attract the attention of the man about whom we speak.

'Are you telling me you'd have let an opportunity like that pass you by?' Constantin raises his eyebrows high in astonishment.

'No, I wouldn't if I'd had the men and the finances. But that doesn't make it right.'

Constantin is laughing merrily now, fuelling my anger further and only a quiet hand on my arm from Ealdred prevents me from stomping away in anger.

'Why do you let the old man provoke you so much?' Ealdred probes. 'You know what he's like. He enjoys seeing you outraged. Why give him the satisfaction?'

I turn to glare at Constantin's smirking face and take a moment to calm my anger. Ealdred's right. I always let Constantin upset me with his snide remarks. After all these years, I really should have learnt to control my temper more. I continually play right into the older man's hands.

'Why didn't you march on York?' I counter to Constantin, only slightly less aggressively than I'm feeling. 'Why didn't you send your heir, Mael Coluim? I notice he's not here with you now?' I look around as though expecting to see Mael Coluim. I know these words will wound.

'What, and upset my good friend Ealdred? I think not.' Constantin murmurs, for now, ignoring my comment about his heir. For Constantin's heir is not his son. That's not the way of the Scots rulers. Another must rule, from another line, Mael Coluim, for now, is that man, the son of the man that Constantin succeeded.

'What about your sons then? They could have gone in your wake.'

'Yes, but they're hot-headed and rash and more likely to cause additional problems than solving the current ones.' Constantin speaks with pride.

'I'd have thought that would please you,' I offer, raising the ceremonial drinking horn to my lips as I speak.

'The only thing that pleases me is keeping my borders safe. If that means keeping my sons well and truly tethered, then so be it.' Constantin's voice has lost its merriment, and I glance at him through narrowed eyes. Good, the old man is as liable to bad temper as I am. And still, he doesn't answer my jibe about Mael Coluim. While he speaks of his sons and their hot-headedness, we all know that Mael Coluim is just waiting for the opportunity to rule after Constantin. Constantin has lived a long life already and shows no signs of dying any time soon. If Constantin had sent his sons to defend York, then Mael Coluim would have gone as well. And just what might have occurred had Mael Coluim won a great victory there?

'Then I suggest we raise a toast to the future of our alliance. Long may it stand.'

At my words, Constantin grins once more while Ealdred's eyes dance with amusement as we raise our drinking horns high before sipping deeply of the too-sweet wine.

Only then do Athelstan and Hywel join us, and I'm not alone in smirking. It seems that Constantin and Ealdred are as keen as I am to see what happens next. Let the English king make what mistakes he must. We'll always be ready to take advantage of any weakness.

## 14

### 927, EAMONT, NORTHERN ENGLAND

*Athelstan, king of the English*

Now that the peace accord is signed by my fellow kings, it needs to be witnessed by the ealdormen and religious men that I've brought with me to this meeting before some of the kings call on their own followers to do the same.

When we return to Winchester, I'll also have my stepbrothers ascribe their names to it, even young Eadred, at only four years of age. I wish it to be known that the æthelings support my peaceful endeavours and that, should I die, they'll continue my diplomatic intentions toward my neighbours. My youngest stepbrothers, under my care, are being nurtured to be warlike and pious in equal measure.

My oldest stepbrother, Ælfweard, was an unpleasant character. He believed he had a right as the king's heir to be respected, regardless of his surly nature. It's perhaps to England's advantage that Ælfweard didn't long outlive our father. My other stepbrother, Edwin, Ælfweard's full brother, I find not to my taste at all. I wonder if he's more like his mother, but as I knew her so little before her death, it's hard to tell. I remember her spite towards me when I was a motherless child. I see it in her son, whether I will it or not.

I'm merely pleased that I'm the king and not him.

I know Edwin resents me claiming the kingship, but he'd done nothing to prepare when Ælfweard unexpectedly died days after our father. For all the little snippets of gossip that come my way, I don't seriously worry that any of Edwin's half-hearted efforts to oust me will come to anything. He's an annoyance to be tolerated. Nothing more.

As to my sisters. I hope they're pleased with their husbands or happy in their nunneries. Eadgifu is married to Charles III of West Frankia, yet she lives at my court following her husband's exiling and imprisonment by his enemy. That Charles lives is a miracle. They had a son together, Louis, who now resides at my court as my foster son, and under my care. What the future holds for Louis is impossible to tell.

Three of my stepsisters have elected to follow a life of religious devotion in the nunneries at Wilton and the Nunnaminster, and, of course, Edith has also chosen a life of prayer since the end of her marriage to Sihtric. But she'll remain in Mercia. She's not likely to enjoy sharing a home with her stepsisters in Wessex.

I think that perhaps it's Louis' presence in my court that attracted the attention of Hugh, count of the Franks, to ask for marriage with another of my sisters. Only after receiving excellent gifts and even finer relics did I agree to the union. I hope Eadhild fares better than her older sister and that her husband doesn't spend his time in imprisonment at the hands of overmighty ealdormen. The disintegrating kingdom of the West Franks is a violent place. My aunt was married to the count of Flanders. As such, while she's a dowager countess, her two sons are both counts in their own rights following her husband's death. The news I receive from my aunt assures me that both men are as bloody-minded as I can be. They'll cause problems or be instrumental in bringing peace to the region. They have their own Norse problem to contend with. I'm content to wait and see what happens in Flanders and this new kingdom, ruled by the Norse on West Frankish land. It's to be hoped that my cousins will aid my nephew to return from his exile, or if not, assist my stepsister and what children she has with Count Hugh to perhaps claim the kingship of West Frankia. Time will tell.

All the same, I'll look further afield for the next marriage alliance for my remaining stepsisters. Having my stepsisters, foster son and cousins as uneasy allies and, more often than not, outright enemies is the very reason I'd not allow my sisters to marry into the ealdormanic families within England. I want no war amongst my nobility when the external threat of the Norse is not entirely contained.

I'd not dare suggest that my stepmother, Lady Eadgifu, marries again, as it would remove her from my court. I need a strong woman to manage my domestic arrangements when I'm absent and to ensure my young stepbrothers receive all the attention they need.

But I digress again, and my fellow kings look at me a little expectantly. With haste, I instruct my ealdormen to step forward and add their signatures to the charter, a slight sheen of sweat sheeting their faces as the day grows hotter, not cooler as I'd hoped.

For future reference, I need to remember that looking resplendent and noble serves as nothing when the heat of the summer is at its fiercest. Red cheeks and sweat certainly detract from the regal clothing my ealdormen have chosen to wear. It's long past time that this ceremony was concluded.

## 15

## 927, EAMONT, NORTHERN ENGLAND

*Constantin, king of the Scots*

I glance unhurriedly away from observing King Athelstan and meet the troubled eyes of Ealdred of Bamburgh. He's not paying close enough attention to proceedings. No, it still rankles that he's even here. Ealdred pays no interest to the staging of the actual event. Ealdred means to show his face, make his agreement with the new king of the English, and then go home and protect his lands. Whether the attacks come from my people or the warriors of the Dublin Norse, Ealdred suspects deceit, and he's uneasy about Athelstan as well.

Owain, too, is paying scant regard, although I suspect from Hywel's surreptitious glances that he knows what the English king is planning.

I watch Athelstan carefully. He's relaxed now but still wary. Athelstan has what he wants but is that all he envisages for the future? Conceivably, I've been the fool here in agreeing to this peace. Unease dulls my enjoyment. Perhaps the joke is on me, after all. Maybe I should have taken longer to consider my response. Maybe I should have simply claimed Bamburgh from Ealdred and had done with it.

'Constantin.' Hywel says my name in conversation, and I focus once more on the convivial company of my fellow kings. They're discussing nothing of importance. No great matters of state weigh on their minds. I wonder, for a moment, if they even think of what may happen next week, let alone next year. Do these men plan for the long term, or do they think only of the here and now?

Perhaps it's only my longevity as king that makes me think of a year from now, ten years from now, maybe even twenty, by which time I'll be long dead and succeeded by another.

Hywel passes me the drinking horn. I take it and swallow the liquid, even though it burns a little on the way down. My unease will spoil the food about to be served to us, and that annoys me. It's been a long time since I last ate, last evening when I first arrived at the English king's camp, and I'd rather savour the delicious dishes of fish and pork than worry about the effects the food might have on my delicate stomach.

Swallowing once more, the rich wine settles more easily. Perhaps I'm looking for conspiracies where none exist, I console myself. But I've only lasted so long as king because I can read people well, I can almost see treason being plotted, and spot those who speak only to blacken my name.

King Athelstan is at my side now, beckoning us to where the table is set for us to dine before all our supporters. They'll receive food as well, but none will be as finely served as that which is now being brought forth from a local house commandeered for the purpose.

Again, there's an order of precedence in how we're seated at the long wooden table, with elegant carved wooden chairs to ease aching backs and legs. Before we signed the treaty, it didn't matter where we sat, for then we were all equals. Now that it's sealed and we've become subordinate to Athelstan, it matters greatly.

Athelstan sits proudly in the centre of the table and purposefully doesn't watch us as we try to sidestep each other to be seated as near to the king as we dare or as far away from the king as we'd like. It's almost as if sitting close to the king is a sign of our subservience to him, but sitting too far away could be deemed as a physical display of our unhappiness with events here. It's a difficult decision to make on the spur of the moment. I should have considered it instead of worrying about the king's intentions.

Eventually, I find myself next to Hywel, who sits beside Athelstan. On my left sits Ealdred, and on the king's other side sits Owain. He's clearly pleased with his place so close to the king, but I'm happier with mine. My men will see this for what it is: an acceptance of the treaty we've signed here, but also a show of defiance. Both stances will keep my supporters loyal and my options wide open. It'll also keep Mael Coluim guessing as to my true intentions. I've learned to mask as much from him as possible and to ensure I give him no excuse to purposefully countermand my decisions and wishes.

He's almost as slippery as Athelstan, but Mael Coluim has no kingdom from which he can summon household warriors, and I mean to keep it that way. If only I could do the same with Athelstan, the king of the English, and his conquest of York.

# 16

## 927, WINCHESTER, SOUTHERN ENGLAND

*Eadgifu, lady of Wessex*

News from the north is not slow in arriving. The scribe sent to Winchester when my stepson won glory in battle at York was buoyed by the successes of his king, and so was I. News of the peace treaty, formally signed at Eamont, quickly followed. While some may grumble at peace with the enemy of the Saxons, I prefer it to war on this island. I've lived through too much war. I wish to see the Saxons, the English as I should name them now, united against the threat of the vicious Norse.

Our men and women have known too much war in the past. It should not become a habit but rather something to be avoided unless it's impossible. Peace is not the dirty word that some seem to believe it is. It takes a strong man to forge a peace. It'll take an even stronger man to enforce it.

I could only wish that Edmund and Eadred were old enough to witness the submission of the northern kings in Eamont, as I should like to see it with my own eyes. More, I'd like to be a fly on the wall when the Dublin Norse hear of it. But my sons are too young to even recognise the importance of the peace of Eamont, and so I can't travel there to witness it either. My responsibility is to my sons and to those left behind in Wessex, the heartland of the House of Wessex.

But I know what will be happening in my absence. The Scots king's son will be baptised into the Christian faith once more, with Athelstan standing as his godfather, a sign of submission to Athelstan, and yet others will leave a hostage in their wake. They'll all agree to a tithe to support Athelstan's imperium. My stepson will emerge from the peace accord as a man rich in wealth and, hopefully, allies.

From there, King Athelstan informs me that he'll travel to Hereford, on the border between Mercia and the Welsh kingdoms, and receive the begrudging submission from those kingdoms of the Welsh not inclined to give it at Eamont. This is something that the powerful king, Hywel of the South Welsh, and my stepson have agreed on.

Hywel is a man I should like to meet. He seems more reasonable than some of the other kings; his eyes focused on growing his Welsh kingdoms to benefit all rather than just to raise his battle renown.

The kings of Athelstan's Eamont alliance should be strong enough to mount an attack against the lands of the English. They have resources and the wherewithal to defend their lands if they must, only they've chosen not to do so. Events outside York have proven that Athelstan has no problem taking the fight to his enemy when peaceful means are not enough.

But the scattered Welsh kings, with their tiny kingdoms, have no such luxury. They must submit to the greatest king, the king of the English. There's too much bickering between the myriad kingdoms of the Welsh to make them realise they would be able to counter Athelstan's threat through unity. Provided they don't discover that anytime soon, Athelstan will prevail.

My sons were too young to rule when their father died. Edward's death being so quickly followed by that of his son Ælfweard, has enabled me to build an alliance with Athelstan. This alliance will ensure that Edmund, my oldest son, will rule after Athelstan and not Edwin, Ælfweard's full brother. For now, Edwin, the 'spare' stepbrother, ferments trouble within the witan, and it's my primary role to undermine his attempts at destabilising Athelstan's kingship. If he were twenty years younger, as my sons are, it would be much easier. No one would support a child against the warrior's reputation that Athelstan built for himself fighting with his aunt in Mercia. But, all the same, Edwin lacks allies, and it must remain like that.

Now that Athelstan's kingdom has so outgrown what his father once ruled, there's wisdom in ensuring someone protects his interests while he's absent. Sometimes I'm that person, with the aid of Ealdorman Osferth, a kinsman of Athelstan, through his grandfather, though few admit it openly.

Athelstan's a wise man. Some liken him to his grandfather, Alfred, who held back the tide of Viking raiders when they threatened to engulf this land in a wave of war. I didn't know King Alfred, but my husband was his son. All I know of Alfred is that he was pious, determined and stubborn. Perhaps not the best attributes for a great king, but that seems to little concern those who write the history of that time. I smirk a little at the thought. Bishop Asser wrote the life of King Alfred. I've read it, but there's much there that I don't recognise from my husband's reminiscing. Perhaps, one day, I'll have someone write of my life and fill it with all the extravagances that only a king, or queen, can have assigned to them, regardless of the truth of those assertions.

Of course, the chronicle writers thought Alfred was great for his piety; they were all men of God, after all. But Athelstan is a religious man, too, collecting relics of the saints and fragments of the disciples' possessions. I wonder what the chroniclers of his reign will make of this moment of peace? Certainly, they make much of Alfred's treaty with the Viking raider Guthrum all those years ago and how it brought about enough of a peace accord to 'save' Wessex from drowning beneath the attacks of the Vikings.

I smile afresh. The chroniclers are religious men. They'll comment on Athelstan's piety, as they did his grandfather's, but I know Athelstan's devotion hides his fierce desire to win. I wonder if his grandfather was the same. Maybe Alfred was, and his religion is merely an acceptable mask for the holy men and chroniclers who wish to praise him. My young daughter, Eadburh, will be a nun, and already lives in the

Nunnaminster, although she has yet to give her vows. Her devotion is sincere and real. I'm not sure that others can say the same. Certainly, I know that I can't. The cloak of respectability that the Church can imbue a person with is merely that. It hides ambition, cruelty and much else besides.

But, King Athelstan, like my young daughter, is perhaps a deeply devout individual. If he's not, then he's a clever man, for he's learned the means to win the support of his nobility and his religious men and women. The bishops almost fall over themselves to be associated with him, and indeed, I'm not the only member of the nobility who's made their name by ascribing to the vision of England that Athelstan foresees. I only hope I've chosen wisely, both for the sake of myself and my young sons.

## 17

### 927, HEREFORD, THE BORDERLAND WITH THE WELSH KINGDOMS

*Hywel, king of the South Welsh*

The journey from the peace conference at Eamont was leisurely but not without adequate precautions for our safety. The English king may have chosen to hunt in the woodlands as he travelled, but Athelstan surrounded himself with his household troops, especially when we passed the borders with the other kingdoms of the Welsh, Gwynedd, Powys and Ceredigion, on our way to Hereford. Hereford is an English settlement, a Mercian one, really, but it's almost within one of the Welsh kingdoms. I'm unsurprised that Athelstan chose to go no further west. He didn't step foot in Strathclyde or the kingdom of the Scots, or indeed venture as far north as Bamburgh. King Athelstan means to keep his feet firmly in the kingdom he rules. For now.

But Athelstan did make a point of sending out scouting parties to ensure the old dyke built by Offa, king of the Mercians, is well maintained. It's an earthwork dividing the Welsh kingdoms from that of the Mercian kingdom. It stretches almost the entire length of the border with the Welsh and now the English. It's stood for well over a century consisting of a deep ditch and a steep embankment, which time is being unkind to. In places, the embankment has fallen into the ditch, and yet all regard it as the true border between two peoples. Athelstan is wise to ensure it continues to be regarded as such.

The kings from the northern lands took their leave from us at Eamont, contempt on their faces when they offered their farewells. They think I'm too much in the hands of Athelstan, but they don't understand my motivations. I'm not bound by the same desires as them.

Torn between hostilities from either the Dublin Norse or the English king and his pretensions to govern all the peoples of this island of ours, I'd much rather ensure my people's freedoms by turning to the English king without bloodshed. I can only protect so many borders and boundaries.

Athelstan has given me an assurance that he'll make no war against us, and that's what I want: peace for my people to flourish and my coffers to grow rich with tribute. King Athelstan possesses the honour of his grandfather, Alfred. He'll stay true to his words, of that I'm sure.

King Constantin and his newly baptised son were the first to leave Eamont. The old man was subdued in his parting words; for all that, they were respectful enough.

Constantin, Owain and Ealdred had all been in conference together. That was clear to see as they emerged from one tent to make their farewells. I couldn't tell the purpose of their meeting. None looked as though they plotted to undermine the treaty, but I don't know the men well, and it's possible that they were doing no more than discussing marriage alliances and exchanging family news. They all know one another far too well. Athelstan and I are outsiders to this northern grouping.

The relationships of the northern kingdoms are as complicated as those of my fellow Welsh kings. Family loyalties are there to be maintained unless they go against the opportunity to gain at the expense of others. I know the game well, and I've marked them all as complicit in it.

If I found it strange that Constantin left alone, without Ealdred, Athelstan didn't. Perhaps it's true and Athelstan has managed to split the alliance between Constantin and Ealdred that's endured for over a decade.

When Owain left, alone as well, Athelstan watched him depart with a puzzled expression on his face. It seems he'd been expecting more from him. I consider what the English king promised and has been denied. Perhaps, there, Athelstan thought to drive a wedge between the kingdom of the Scots and its subordinate, that of the kingdom of Strathclyde.

But when Ealdred sought the king for a quiet word, I knew of what they spoke. Ealdred's fierce determination that the English king will not invade his lands was evident to see. Athelstan was keen to give the reassurance, and his face glowed with his earnestness until he offered Ealdred a marriage alliance with one of his numerous sisters. I saw Ealdred's eyes narrow in annoyance while he was forced to mouth the words that he would consider the king's most gracious offer. No doubt, Ealdred's mind went immediately to events in York, where a king married a sister of the English king, only to die within a year and have the kingdom taken over by the English. Or perhaps, he considered the feelings of his own wife.

I know of the relic that Athelstan sent to Ealdred. I understand, despite Athelstan's earnestness, that it was as much a threat as a gesture of alliance. The arm of a Northumbrian saint, returned to that kingdom by a man who would overrule the independent kingdom of Bamburgh, can be nothing but a threat. An ancient relic. The offer of a new wife. Poor Ealdred. He's overburdened with options, and none of them are good.

All the same, I could have laughed to see Ealdred so outfoxed. It's common knowledge that his wife is barren now, having produced only one son for her husband. None would object to him taking another, more fruitful bride, even if she was an English woman. None, apart from Ealdred, so it seems.

On the journey to Hereford, Athelstan and I often spoke of day-to-day matters: the weather, the hunting, what was for dinner; but a note of civility touched him, and he never let down his guard. I'm yet to see the 'real' Athelstan.

Athelstan remained kingly all the time, or at least that's how it appeared to me. At Eamont I felt we were alike, but as we journeyed south, I think he wished to step aside from such familiarity.

I'm unsure what he was like when he retired to his travelling tent, surrounded by his most trusted ealdormen, his mass priests, his reeve and provost. I hope Athelstan let his guard down then and let his stiff back become slightly curved as he relaxed for the first time all day. But I remain to be convinced.

Our arrival in Hereford is heralded by a small display of the king's power when his household troops line the road, their byrnies shimmering beneath the bright summer sun, and his accompanying ealdormen also arrange their household troops to swell those ranks. Included amongst that number is Ealdorman Wulfgar, the man Athelstan sent to speak with Constantin and Owain when the alliance was first suggested. The ealdorman still seems unsure that he's accomplished a great thing for his king, despite the gifts and praise heaped upon him.

Watching his household warriors in their formation, I can't but think that it appears Athelstan has come to make war. I'm uncomfortably aware that Athelstan knows this place well. He was here during his time in Mercia, assisting his aunt in her fight for Mercia's freedom. I'm not sure I welcome that knowledge. Does he know the routes into the Welsh kingdoms? Was he involved when she overran Brecon Mere and took Welsh hostages to Tamworth? I rein my thoughts in. It's too late. I'm committed to this alliance.

The other Welsh kings have arranged to meet Athelstan at Hereford, on his orders, and having granted safe passage to them and their retinues. It's in Hereford that the situation between myself, Athelstan and the other Welsh kings becomes more complicated. Here, I could be as hobbled by family connections and alliances as the three northern lords, Constantin, Owain and Ealdred.

My cousin, Idwal of Gwynedd, eyes me unhappily from his place atop his horse as Athelstan and I ride into Hereford. There's nothing I can do to soften the far harsher terms the English king has chosen to exact from Idwal in exchange for being included in this peace accord and the promised protection from the Norse.

Idwal's submission has been begrudging, but not, admittedly, as begrudging as Owain, king of Gwent's. As I've told Idwal countless times in the last few weeks via mounted messenger, he should have contacted King Athelstan himself and arranged this peace when it was offered after Athelstan proved his worth in battle outside York.

If Idwal had sought an accord first, Athelstan, driven by his need to be a genuinely Christian king, would have had no choice but to accept the arrangement as it was proposed. These Welsh kings and their people will now face a far more stringent alliance with Athelstan. But an alliance with Athelstan they must have, if only to counter the threat of the Irish kings and the Norse who make Ireland their home. It's impossible for the Welsh kings to face enemies from the west and the east. I know that only too well. I might admire Athelstan, but necessity has played its own part in my decision to submit to his wishes for a peace. I might have affixed a smile on my face while I did so and presented myself as the most alike of his allies to him, but I did it with the intention of gaining.

Rumour has it that the Norse Dublin lands are rife with discord, but, as the court poets foretell, eventually, a Norse man will either unite the discordant factions in Ireland through guile or will simply ride roughshod over them and unite them anyway, in much the same way that Athelstan has united the kingdoms on our island. Then they'll turn their attention back to Britain, toward the lands of the Northumbrians and York. It's best to be united against that threat. It's safest to know that the English king has our back when the might of the Norse once more focuses on our kingdoms.

Cousin Idwal is of age with me. He's been king of Gwent for a decade, and in that time, he's governed well, if without flair or ingenuity. I'd rather see him under more pleasant circumstances than this, but it's still good to see him. As I slide from my horse, he does the same. We meet in the middle, smiles on our faces.

'Cousin,' Idwal greets me as we embrace. He's a tall man, firm and well formed. He has the build and stance of a warrior.

'Cousin yourself,' I reply, amused despite the situation.

'And what have you been doing consorting with this Wessex whelp?'

'Helping my people, and hopefully, perhaps, yours,' is my muffled response. I won't attempt to explain the true nature of Athelstan's extended kingship. I'm sure that Idwal understands it much better than he implies.

Stepping back, Idwal looks at me with interest in his deep blue eyes, a little more wrinkled around the edges than in the past but still bright and genuine. I've been told that we look much alike, the spitting image of our shared grandfather. I'm minded of how alike the Norse we are. Idwal and I claim descent from one grandfather, as do all these men who think to rule Norse Dublin.

Now I study him carefully, noting that he looks good. I hope that I age so well. It's acceptable to be a little vain. After all, I want women to desire me for more than just my position. I'm widowed and seek no new wife as I have sons grown to manhood, with children of their own, but a man can't survive without a woman to warm his bed on occasion.

Behind us, Athelstan has dismounted onto the stone-lined road that runs through Hereford, a remnant of a long-ago past maintained now by the people of this small town. I take it upon myself to introduce him to Idwal, hopeful that even now, Athelstan may be prevailed upon to make the terms of this peace a little fairer.

Athelstan is as regal as on the journey to Hereford. He doesn't wear his crown, not here, but he does have his ceremonial sword, and his clothing is richly decorated with embroidery and jewels.

When Athelstan stepped from his tent this morning, in all his finery, I understood why we'd travelled so close to Hereford yesterday and yet stopped short of it. Athelstan needed time to prepare himself for this meeting. He could not have travelled far in his stiff embroidered tunic and flowing cloak.

Athelstan greets Idwal coolly, and Idwal, after my nod to him, instantly descends to his right knee, while beside him Owain shows his disdain for such a show of subservience in the roll of his eyes and his refusal to follow suit. That Athelstan is pleased by such respect from Idwal is clear to see, and Idwal is only on his knee for a few moments before Athelstan graciously bids him rise.

Owain steps forward as one amongst equals, and Athelstan's face clouds. This isn't what he wants to see.

Idwal meets my eye, his face blank but his eyes dancing with amusement that his belated show of deference has worked so well. I've been sending messengers to Idwal since I met Athelstan at Eamont, trying to explain to him how to make the best of this situation. There are peace terms, and then there are more acceptable peace terms. I hope Athelstan will choose the second option. It'll make it easier for me if Idwal isn't discontented on my northern borders.

I don't want Idwal to be too belittled by the English king. After all, we share blood. But neither do I want him to be acceptable just because he is my kin. Idwal must make concessions and win the English king's trust, as I've done. I don't think it'll be an easy task, but he's started well.

Around us, Athelstan's trappings are rapidly being brought to order. The horses have been led away, and in the near distance, I can see a medium-sized wooden hall with its door flung wide. I assume that it's there that we'll walk and have our meeting.

The king's royal followers busily file inside while others dance attendance on my fellow kings as we arrive at the hall. A drinking horn is passed to me to quench the thirst of the road, and I share it willingly with Idwal, savouring the wine, which is less sweet than at Eamont and more palatable for it.

'Thank you for your messengers,' Idwal comments under his breath as he steps close to me once more.

'My pleasure, cousin, but the terms are still not going to be to your liking.'

'I know, but if they can be softened a little, then it's worth the charade. You were perhaps correct to recommend this course before.'

I chuckle at his rueful tone.

'I don't think "perhaps" is the right word, but as apologies go, I'll accept it,' I comment, glancing sharply at where Owain and Athelstan are still attempting a stilted conversation. Athelstan's face is far from relaxed. I'm overly aware of the band of warriors who stand at his back. I recognise two of them. They're not ealdormen, but they're often to be found with the king. Perhaps, I should determine their names.

'Now come, let's precede the English king inside. It'll be another way of showing our subservience.'

Trying but failing not to show his glee at such a simple task, Idwal walks beside me into the brightly lit room.

A huge table dominates its centre while a small fire roars away merrily, its heat not really needed for anything other than cooking. Around the table, the king's archbishop is already busy at work with parchment and ink laid before him, another watching over his shoulder as he forms the letters. I watch him for a moment, considering just what the king has decided to put in his treaty this time. It isn't to be the same terms as those agreed at Eamont. There's a reason I went to Eamont and didn't wait for Athelstan to come to Hereford, for all it would have stopped me having to traipse through the English kingdom to reach Eamont. I might have obtained a free passage, but still, the people who dwell on the borders were not likely to be eager to see me.

Unlike at Eamont, this submission of two of the Welsh kings hasn't been carefully predetermined. Here, the English king is the master. It'll be interesting to see how far King Athelstan thinks he can push them without the intercession of his messengers and their gifts to grease the wheel. I've heard outrageous numbers for the tithe to be demanded from the two subordinate kings. I only hope, for Idwal's sake, that Athelstan has shown more caution than that. There's little point in me bending the knee if my brother kings aren't going to do the same.

## 18

### 927, HEREFORD, ENGLAND, THE BORDERLANDS WITH THE WELSH KINGDOMS

*Athelstan, king of the English*

I've been to this place before, with my aunt when I was a youth, and she was busily reinforcing the boundaries against the Welsh. I think my father and I have come a long way since then, no longer on the defensive against the Welsh kings but firmly on the offensive.

Some of those kings have appealed to me now, asking for an alliance without bloodshed. Pity, it's only after I've made my mark and taken the lands that my dead brother – by-marriage – Sihtric of York, once reigned over, and when I've proven that I can beat these men from Dublin Norse, descendants of Viking raiders, who crawl over our lands like ants.

I know they plague the Welsh kings as much as they did my grandfather, father and aunt, but I'll not let them again. No chance. They can't beat my desires for a united land that's the envy of the people who occupy the Frankish kingdoms, where two of my stepsisters have married into the warring royal families.

My father, for all his apparent antipathy toward me, knew how to govern and rule well. He may not have intended to, and he certainly didn't act like my grandfather regarding his relationships with women, but my father emulated his father in almost every other way: in matters of learning and in his relentless march against those who'd taken the lands of the Mercians and the other Saxon kingdoms.

I'm proud to continue my father's legacy and that of my grandfather, but I'll do more as well. Take back more land, either through war or peace and if, in the process, I exact some revenge for past actions, then I'll do so willingly.

And grandfathers and fathers have much to answer for here. Hywel and Idwal are cousins, I know this, and I also know that my grandfather Alfred was responsible for their grandfather's death. The great Rhodri, whose dynasty has tried to dominate the Welsh lands ever since his death, has left his mark on these realms. But without Rhodri, they can't be held by just one man. They've fractured back into individual kingdoms. And that's their weakness and one I plan to exploit. That and pushing back their boundaries so that my people gain at their expense.

From now on, the River Wye will demarcate our lands. In peace, I'll gain more than through the wars of my grandfather and father. Provided, that is, the Welsh kings agree to sign the peace accord.

I suppose that Idwal and Owain could change their mind, even this late in the day, if my terms are too harsh. But with my household troops on display and my ealdormen's warriors as well, I hope to discourage them with a show of force.

As demanded, they don't have many men in attendance upon them, and so I would win any battle that took place here. That's good. I'd rather not fight. I'd rather have these kings as my friends and a further ally against the might of the Norse, should they attack again. The more obstacles in the path of the Norse when they set foot on this island, the better.

Idwal has bent his knee before me. Owain will not. Hywel didn't need to because he came willingly to make his peace. These men rule small territories. I liken it to the lands of the individual Saxon kingdoms, which fell such easy prey to the Norse menace.

I wish these men would realise that only by allying with each other do they stand a chance of beating the Norse. And yet, I can't blame them.

The kings of Northumbria, Mercia and the other Saxon kingdoms didn't realise that only through unity could they defeat their single enemy. My grandfather understood the truth of this, and I'll strive to prove he was correct. I'll hold my realms and keep them whole and bequeath them to my successor, my stepbrother.

But I stray from the here and now. As I say, Idwal has bent his knee and now speaks with Hywel. They're much alike, but their terms will be different. Owain. He's another matter entirely. His very bearing makes it clear that he doesn't want to be here. I wonder why he came at all. Other Welsh kingdoms, such as Ceredigion, haven't sought peace with me. I respect them for that but know I'll have to try and undermine them differently if my future overtures of peace are also turned down. Owain of Gwent is the king of a territory that almost encircles part of England, here, on the borderland. I could crush Owain or befriend him. Only time will tell as to which option I choose but why he's here when he doesn't want to be is a mystery to me. Unless, of course, he knows it would be more damaging not to be here.

Within the hall being prepared before us, my archbishop is completing the treaty. The long days and nights of my journey here have been spent thinking and plotting. My closest advisors, the ealdormen, the holy men and my intimate friends and advisors have all suggested how we can gain the most without losing the friendly overtures of these men. I only hope I've shown enough caution. I should have run the terms past Hywel, but I'm still a little unsure of his ambitions. He reminds me too much of myself, and I know what that could portend.

With Owain beside me, Hywel and his cousin, Idwal already inside, I walk into the hall. I feel a little apprehensive, more so than with the northern kings, even though I'm in the most domineering position.

I offer a silent prayer to God that I've acted as I should and that my quest for unity against the Norse won't falter here.

# 19

## 927, HEREFORD, ENGLAND, THE BORDERLANDS WITH THE WELSH KINGDOMS

*Hywel, king of the South Welsh*

Even I'm surprised by the terms being laid out before Idwal and Owain. They're harsh but fair all at the same time. My admiration for King Athelstan increases once more.

Athelstan demands a tribute, a massive toll; only it's for things that are abundant in the lands of Idwal and Owain, and myself, if I must participate as well. The gold and silver weight will be easy to accumulate, and the oxen, hounds and hawks even easier. The numbers might be huge, but they're manageable, and beside me I feel Idwal relax a little knowing that the number is only twenty-five thousand and not fifty thousand as it might have been. Even Owain looks a little pleased, a half-smile playing around his lips.

The only sticking point, and this does concern me, is the idea that the great River Wye should now act as the border in the southern lands between the English and the Welsh kingdoms.

Owain and I both shift uncomfortably at the thought that the English will be so close to our heartlands. I know this is a punishment for Owain, but I'm unhappy about it too. The English king and his well-disciplined troops are all well and good, provided they're more than a day's march from my homeland.

Idwal smirks a little at his good fortune, for he still has Offa's Dyke as the boundary, and I return his smile, although it grates on me. The lucky bastard. Bend his knee only now and be left almost alone! I'm outraged by his fortune. I just hope that in private, King Athelstan has some reassurances for me, and they must not revolve around a marriage agreement.

I've long had my sons arrayed around me. Perhaps when I journey to Athelstan's English court, I'll take them along with me, or at least one or two of them. I need no more wives, and I'll not gift an English wife to my sons. I know the double-edged blade that would be.

Once more, we go through the motions of having the treaty's terms spoken out loud by the aged archbishop of Canterbury before we must sign our agreement to it. Again, I plan on being the second behind Athelstan to do just that, but out of the corner of my eye, I can see Idwal preparing to scamper to his feet, and my need fades away. I'll not play the game of favourites with my cousin, and he knows it. The sneer on his face makes that clear for me to see.

Instead, I sit back and work hard to relax my tense body. I want to appear as nonchalant as King Athelstan about the whole thing.

The voice of the archbishop drones on and on, rising and falling with the nature of the demands. Loudly, he proclaims the greatness of King Athelstan, king of the English, and quietly the treaty's terms, almost as if he's a little embarrassed by them.

The king's closest advisors remain in attendance upon him. I muse as to who governs their lands in their absence, but I know they wouldn't be here if they feared any problems. Ordgar, Ælfwold, Osferth, Guthrum, Ælfstan and Wulfgar: the king's ealdormen. I've still to determine who rules where but understand that Athelstan holds much of the old kingdom of Wessex himself, for all that he was raised in the Mercian lands of his aunt. Wessex is the heartland of his family's holdings, and he guards it jealously.

I wonder why the king doesn't use his stepbrother to govern the old kingdoms. And then I grin at my stupidity. What could be worse than having your family rule in your stead? Just because they share a father, or a mother, or both, it doesn't mean that they're alike.

I do pity King Athelstan having so many close contenders for his crown. There are three already named as æthelings, throne-worthy: his stepbrothers, Edwin, Edmund and Eadred. And yet, I also know there are others who might have more than half an eye on his crown. The son of Æthelwold, his great-uncle. And also the sons of Æthelweard, his uncle.

Finally, the archbishop finishes his recounting of the treaty, and with a look first left and then right down the line of kings, Athelstan rises and places his mark on the agreement.

Besides me, Idwal makes to stand but then sits again and allows me to go first, his face creased with delight at his trick. Ignoring him and grateful he's only my cousin and not my brother, I rise and mark my name.

The treaty is a beautiful piece of penmanship, and I hesitate just for a moment before I lean forwards. I wouldn't want to drip my ink where it shouldn't be.

With a flourish, I add my mark and step toward King Athelstan. He stands a few paces away, watching my fellow kings with interest, a drinking horn in his hand. He passes it to me with the first genuine smile on our journey south.

'Your cousin?' Athelstan queries, nodding towards Idwal.

'Yes.'

'You look alike.'

I laugh, swigging from the drinking horn as Idwal places his mark on the treaty, trying not to let my frustration with Idwal show.

The last few months have been difficult, and now I know the work and thought I've put into everything is ending. Soon I'll be able to travel to my home, see my children, bed a woman and relax.

Idwal joins us, looking from the English king to myself in interest, no doubt aware we speak of him. Idwal is no fool, although he often acts as though he is.

Behind us, Owain stands and saunters to the treaty. He's handed a quill to add his mark, but before he does so, he hesitates and peers through the open doorway to where his small force of supporters is milling around. Noise filters in from outside, the bark of laughter and cough of amusement combined with the shuffling of the horses' hooves. A loud clang of metal on stone resounds within the hall, and we all jump at the piercing sound and look behind us to see what's happening. I don't miss that Athelstan reaches for his weapons belt. I don't miss that two of his ealdormen move even closer.

The cook looks our way apologetically as the heavy cooking pot tumbles onto the hearthstones, spilling the contents onto the small fire. Liquid sizzles in the heat, and a delicious smell wafts my way.

Owain curses loudly, and I turn back to him. Clearly, he's defaced the treaty with green ink, and the archbishop shakes his head in dismay at the mess before him.

King Athelstan merely flicks his hand towards his ealdormen, his warriors and the cook, and a new cookpot is immediately in place as though it had been waiting for just such an event. Perhaps King Athelstan has planned this far better than I thought possible, foreseeing all eventualities.

'We may have to wait a little longer to celebrate our agreement,' the English king offers by way of explanation as a young lad, dressed in a smart uniform festooned with the Wessex wyvern and the Mercian double-headed eagle in close proximity, winds his way through our small group, refilling the drinking horn as he goes, almost as though nothing's happened.

'My lord King Athelstan, I apologise for my accident,' Owain calls across the small space, now that he's hummed and hawed and finally added his signature. His words lack sincerity, his eyes flicking from the archbishop to the cook, an unfathomable expression on his face. What has he been up to?

'The archbishop will do all he can to preserve the contents. Now come, we'll retire outside until our meal is ready.'

King Athelstan leads the way back into the bright daylight, and Owain leers my way.

'I hope I've not obscured anything of importance,' he whispers, and I suddenly realise that this little act of defiance has been choreographed. Owain's pettiness annoys me, but it's nothing new. He can be devious when he wants to be. I look forward to the day that I can, hopefully, take the land he rules over from him or his descendants. If I have to take his life in the process, then I'm content to do so.

It makes sense to me that, like the lands of the Saxon kingdoms, the lands of my fellow Welsh should be united, as my grandfather, Rhodri, thought. Pity that King Alfred killed my grandfather, and his Welsh empire crumbled. But I'll bide my time and see what happens. I can act just as quickly and decisively as King Athelstan if the opportunity presents itself.

I hope it does and at Owain's expense, or my cousin's, or one of the other kings who've not come here today. I don't mind who has to die or be deprived of their kingdom, provided my influence expands.

For now, I wonder how Owain convinced the king's cook to drop their cookpot. And then I look again. The cook, now busy at work, is different to the man who was there before, and his face is flushed an angry red.

Clearly, the other man was an imposter, and this is the real cook. The English king needs to be more careful. The borderlands that divide the Welsh and the English are a hotbed of conflicting and contradictory allegiances. Here more than anywhere else on our journey, it's important to be circumspect and mindful of his safety. I thought he had been, but all the same, something has managed to get past his careful guard.

The commands coming from the king's men assure me that the risks are currently being taken more seriously. As we step into the dull summer's day, I watch the pretend cook being led away between two of the king's household troops.

The smug expression on Owain's face has disappeared but has worked its way over to mine. The man is a fool, after all. He might well have obscured his agreement on the charter with his antics, but his name is there all the same, and Owain of Gwent is just as much a part of this treaty with the English as Idwal, or I am. If he thought anything different, he's going to be very disappointed.

## 20

### 927, WINCHESTER, ENGLAND

*Eadgifu, lady of Wessex*

The king has finally returned to Winchester. He comes in triumph, and my young sons watch him with unadulterated devotion on their faces as he rides into the palace grounds to the acclaim of the residents.

King Athelstan might look more like a boy on his first horse, but no one has the heart to remind him of his position. Certainly not me. Rather, I bask in his reflected glory.

For now, the borders with the Scots king and the king of Strathclyde are secured, as is the border with the independent kingdom of Bamburgh, and many of the Welsh kingdoms. The Dublin Norse have no foothold on the island we all share, and the Norsemen are quiet as if they sleep in their winter beds already. The Danish Five Boroughs are almost entirely reconciled with the king, and he holds York as well.

But, as with all things, peace in one place does not mean peace in another.

I meet the king with my young sons in the courtyard of the palace complex. They bow to him, the pair of them smartly dressed. Eadred rouses a smile from the king's lips as he stumbles on his bow, a steadying hand from his royal brother keeping him upright. I dip my knees and curtsey, wishing the fabric that enclosed me was more forgiving, grateful that Athelstan doesn't allow my son's exuberance to embarrass him.

With our welcome made, a sly look in Edwin's direction where he struggles to bow, but not because he's young and high-spirited, but rather drunk, and together we attend a small religious ceremony in which Athelstan's favourite priest offers prayers for his safe return, unharmed and victorious. We ignore the sniggers coming from the wobbling Edwin. He's been drinking since waking and is intent on making himself out to be an arse. I'd hoped he'd have drunk himself into a stupor before Athelstan's return, but there's been no such luck.

Athelstan somehow lets the incident pass him by, but it's a bad sign of things to come. I'm sure that Athelstan will not always allow such disrespect from his stepbrother. I fear that Edwin will continue his insolent behaviour until he pushes Athelstan too far. I wish his sisters would bring him under control, but they seem to enjoy Edwin's antics too much.

I'm not sure what Edwin hopes to achieve with his attitude towards the king. Edwin has little support amongst the men of the witan, apart from the disgruntled bishop of Winchester, Frithestan. Athelstan doesn't trust Edwin, and sidesteps Bishop Frithestan whenever he needs to accomplish something that involves the support of the Church. It's not as though Athelstan doesn't have holy men on whom he can rely. Frithestan's dismay that Athelstan is king is similar to Edwin's. While some might not have liked it at the time, most realise how lucky we are that Edwin isn't king.

I pity Edwin a little. His father pampered him and his older brother. With Ælfweard's death, he's lost his place as the heir's heir and doesn't know how to behave. He's bitter and resentful, especially of Athelstan's success and military prowess.

By rights, Edwin should retire to his estates somewhere in the heartland of Wessex, marry, have his children and forget that he was ever an ætheling, and considered throne-worthy. But he won't do that. Edwin thinks far too much of himself. Instead, he'll cause trouble and do everything he can to unbalance the king's power. I wish him luck with that.

'Athelstan has accomplished a great deal.' Ealdorman Osferth speaks with me after the religious ceremony. We're seated in the king's hall, and a feast has been prepared to welcome Athelstan back to Winchester. Ealdorman Osferth looks a little worn by his travels, as though he's content to have the floor stable beneath his feet. In the candlelight, he looks so like my dead husband. I struggle to understand how the fact that he's Alfred's bastard son can ever be overlooked.

'Indeed. He's resolved to uniting the old kingdoms of Mercia, Wessex, the kingdom of the East Angles, Kent, the Five Boroughs and York,' I confirm, the names tripping from my tongue. How much easier it is to simply say, 'England', the land of the English.

'He's set his sights on the south-western areas as well, some might call it Dumnonia, but it's easier to say the area west of Exeter.'

'But they look to him anyway,' I state, my forehead furrowed, a quick glance ensuring that my sons are behaving themselves at the table directly opposite to where I sit. They have permission to attend some of the feast but not all of it. Edmund, I notice, keeps glancing at me as though to ensure I'm content with his decorum. I'm proud of him. Eadred, I'll need to speak to him, but he's doing his best, and here, in the king's hall, people will be more forgiving of his age.

'When it suits them, they do look to Athelstan as their lord. He wants to make it a more permanent arrangement, have them accept him as their king as well.'

I nod in understanding, reassessing Athelstan's ambitions once more. And then Lord Osferth changes the subject.

'Edwin is as difficult as normal.' Osferth's words drip with disdain. Together, we often comment on the behaviour of the rest of the king's court. Osferth has always been one of my allies. He, I know full well, didn't like my husband's second wife or any of the children from that union. Now, our gaze moves to rest on Edwin. He's a part of this feast, sitting with his sisters on a separate table from that of my sons. Edwin, slouched between two of his sisters, Queen Eadgifu of West Frankia and Eadgyth, can barely sit upright, his goblet never allowed to empty, and I see how his sisters glare all around. They mean to support him. No matter what he does.

'He's a fool, and he makes himself a bigger fool every day. He's lost the respect of the few who did see him as a possible heir, and that's just made him even more unbearable. I'm glad he's not my son,' I add with satisfaction. I'm inordinately pleased that my young sons know how to behave so much better than their much older stepbrother. 'I'd be embarrassed to call him my son, and if I could, I'd disavow him altogether. He's a disgrace to the royal family, and your nephew should have dealt with him far more firmly.' Lord Osferth hardly seems to notice that I name him Alfred's son. There are few who would dare to do so. 'Edwin tries to intercept every messenger who arrives and leaves the court. He works actively against the king.'

Worry crosses Lord Osferth's face. He's a survivor of family rifts. He knows as I do that Edwin needs to support the king, not try and undermine him. After the treaty of Eamont, and the peace accord with the Welsh kings, Athelstan is held in higher regard than his warlike father or preaching grandfather. There are few, if any, who would wish to face the might of his military power. And yet, Edwin is certainly one of those.

'I'll try and speak with him.' But there's little hope in Lord Osferth's voice, and I wonder why he even takes the time. But then, Lord Osferth is blessed with his father's need to unite the family, not divide it. He might not like his nephew, but neither does he wish to see the same discord that saw the Wessex royal family divided after Alfred's death, when Lord Æthelwold, Alfred's nephew, tried to wrestle the kingdom from Edward's hands. We all know how that ended. With the Norse battling my future husband and my father, a man I have no memory of, dead at the hands of our enemies.

# 21

## 927, ST DAVID'S, THE KINGDOM OF DEHEUBARTH

*Hywel, king of the South Welsh*

I sink gratefully into my chair before the huge, blazing fire, although the night has yet to start drawing in.

Home.

There were times I doubted I'd see it again. Times when I resented being away so much that I almost decided that the sacrifices I was making for the future of my kingship and my people were just too much to take any more.

Home.

My small grandchildren rush around me, gleeful to have me home. My older children watch me intently. I've been away nearly the entire growing season, and no doubt, they've become used to governing in my place. The harvest is almost complete, and the fields of grains safely stored against the coming shortages of winter. The cattle and sheep, perhaps, sense that their time has come to an end as their lowing and baaing can be heard even behind the walls of my palace.

There's a bite of cold in the air. The fire is both warming and welcoming. Soon, I'll have to hunt out my thicker cloaks and wear more layers. I allow my new woman to approach me, and she bends to kiss me. She's not my wife. I won't marry again, but she smiles to see me. No doubt, she'll be pleased to return to my bedchamber and earn some respect from my sons, who will, I don't doubt, have done all they can to ignore her in my absence. They don't believe a man of my age should have need of a woman's warm embrace.

'Welcome,' she offers breathlessly. She smells of the summer, and even that warms me.

'It's good to see you,' I confirm and then turn to survey the state of my court as she settles on a low stool before me. She can't sit at my side. She's not my wife. She's not my queen.

I'm proud of my sons and plan for them to govern when I'm dead, but still, this is my land for now, and I'll have it returned to my control now that I've made my way back to St David's.

Home.

Away from King Athelstan of the English, at last, I feel that I can breathe more freely. Of all the kings who've bowed low to him, accepting his overlordship, I'm the only one, the only one who's not let his true feelings show. Of them all, it is I who Athelstan thinks stands closest to him and his plans for the future.

That's not to say that I don't agree with his desires and wishes. I, too, wish to know the Norse will never trouble my borders again, that should they, my neighbours will come to my defence and fight at my side to protect my kingdom. And that they won't use it as an excuse to attack me. But it does mean that I've decided to mask my true intentions a little more. I'll wait to see just how this new alliance plays itself out before I fully commit.

King Constantin of the Scots, the wily old git, has made his reservations felt, and Owain of Strathclyde too. Even Ealdred of Bamburgh with his fears that Athelstan will marry him into the Wessex king's family. And the other kings of the Welsh? They could barely be civil for long enough to sign the alliance into effect, especially Owain. It's confusing that Owain of Gwent and Owain of Strathclyde share a name. I'm sure it'll cause misunderstanding in the written records of our times.

King Athelstan, although he consulted me only a little on our journey to Hereford, did avail himself of my opinion. He's not given any of the others such an insight into his hopes and fears. And I'm pleased with how relatively easy it's been to gain his trust.

Not that the alliance doesn't assist me. I'd not have agreed to it if there hadn't been something in it for me. I need the peace as much as Athelstan does, and I need him to ensure it remains in place while I travel.

I'll give it the winter and some of the early summer, but then I plan on journeying far afield and seeing places that other kings and, indeed other people can only dream of doing. I want to visit the Pope. I want to see the soaring mountains of the Alps and to see with my own eyes where the Romans, who once inhabited England, if not my kingdom, originated from.

My oldest son Owain ap Hywel approaches me first, a wide grin on his face and a new bundle in his arms. I chuckle. Just another Owain. That'll be three for the men and women of future years to struggle over. There'll be Owain, my son. Owain of Strathclyde. And, of course, Owain ap Rhodri, who made his peace with King Athelstan at Hereford. Perhaps we should expand the names we use for our children and heirs. Perhaps.

'Another son?' I ask, the corners of my mouth tugging with joy at the sight of his safely delivered child.

'No, a daughter of all things,' Owain mutters, a little aggrieved. 'What will I do with a daughter when I have only sons and only experience of boys?'

I grin at his obvious discomfort. A girl would flummox me as well, but I'm not about to share that with him. It'll test his abilities, and I look forward to seeing how he manages.

'And does she have a name?' I query, taking the bundle into my arms and looking down at the sleeping face of the child. She smells of milk and farts gently in her sleep.

'Of course she does, after my mother, Elen. What more could I do?' My son looks at me as though ensuring I understand his decision.

I'm immobile at his words. The mother of my older sons has been dead for more than a decade, and still, I miss her and yearn for her gentle touch each day. Her loss goes almost hand in hand with my renewed interest in God and His saints. I pray for her as fervently as I can. She shouldn't have gone so soon. There was still too much life in her while she was crippled by disease and pain. When I wake each morning, I think of her, as I do before I close my eyes and settle in sleep.

'My thanks for thinking of her,' I manage to choke, forcing the smile back on to my face. Perhaps this is what I need. All that talk of not giving children the same names as their fathers and grandfathers, but at that moment, I feel a thin tendril of peace. I welcome the chance to see young Elen grow to womanhood.

My son looks a little less smug now.

'In all honesty, it was the child's mother who had the idea, not I. I'd not even considered the baby wouldn't be a boy.' His words are rueful.

I examine the bundle in my arms. Big blue eyes stare at me and meet my gaze. I'd not realised the child had woken. I hazard that his mother stares at me through those untried eyes. It might be fanciful, but I won't dismiss it as impossible.

'She's a pretty little thing. Your mother would have doted on her. She was always keen to have a girl of her own.' My voice catches a little at the swirl of memories rushing through my mind, and I cough to mask my emotions. My son doesn't need to be reminded how much his mother's death still troubles me.

'And other news?' I ask loudly, hoping to drive the grief from my voice.

Owain does me the honour of ignoring my emotional stutter.

'Little and nothing. We've had no overseas visitors. By that, I mean no Dublin Norse incursions. The other Welsh kingdoms have been quiet too. This alliance of King Athelstan's is not attractive, but none have yet come before me and openly condemned it.'

I absorb the information, all the time watching my other two sons as they make their way toward me. Owain has always been the most faithful of them, but all three boys have been my most loyal supporters since they've been old enough to play a part in the royal court. They'll inherit my land one day, and hopefully, if the other Welsh kings prove as useless as I think they will, for all that Idwal is my cousin, they'll inherit a larger area than they should. Then it'll be easier to divide it amongst them, as is the way of our laws. Then they'll have a kingdom worth fighting and defending as opposed to a small square of space that's more effort than it's worth to keep.

Rhodri and Edwin greet me next. They look just like their older brother, but their temperaments couldn't be more different. Rhodri is quiet and introspective; Edwin is outlandish and almost always nearly drunk. As I understand it, he shares the same temperament as Athelstan's stepbrother. They decline to marry but have many children. I make no comments on the way they live their lives. I'll be long dead by the time all these children decide to vie for the crowns of their fathers. That the children are all boys only adds to the problem.

'Father.' Rhodri greets me warmly, a smile on his face, his words gentle and soft. No wonder he can charm any woman he wants into sharing his bed.

'Son,' I respond, smiling at my thoughts and his welcome greeting.

'Father,' Edwin snaps out, staggering a little, even so early in the evening. I can smell the mead on his breath but hold my tongue. We've had this argument too many times in the past. He's a man and must make his own choices and live with the consequences.

'You've been away longer than we thought,' Rhodri mutters, drawing a stool so that he can sit before me and we can converse in the relative quiet around my kingly chair.

'King Athelstan was keen to take the submission of all and sundry who would come before him.'

'So we've heard,' Edwin growls low in his throat.

'But did you get what you wanted from him?' Owain queries. He doesn't share my deep religious beliefs, but he'd like to travel through the lands I hope to visit nonetheless.

'Yes, we've reached an accord, and I hope that this time next year, I'll have visited the Pope and will be travelling home for a winter with you all.'

The boys, well, men really, nod as they absorb my words. It's as we discussed before I left.

'And I take it I can trust you all to govern in my name when I'm gone, but give me back my kingdom when I return, as I do now.' There's a threat in my words, but it's not needed. Owain and Rhodri both vigorously gift me back my kingdom, and Edwin swoops his arm around the hall.

'It'll give me more time to drink and enjoy the women,' he offers, a manic grin on his face. 'This governing plays havoc with a man's sex life.'

I laugh along with my boys, aware that he doesn't mean it but also grateful that he can be so generous in giving up his position of power.

It's good to be home, but soon, very soon, I know I'll feel the need to journey from my homeland, and now I know I can do it without fear of any problems in my absence. That, if nothing else, was worth bending my knee to an upstart Saxon who calls himself the king of the English.

# PART II
# THE ROAD TO WAR

## 22

## MARCH, 928, SCONE, THE KINGDOM OF THE SCOTS

*Constantin, king of the Scots*

The wind's fierce so early in the morning, screaming outside my royal residence. It makes it all seem possible that my God's devil could be the vengeful spirit I always imagine him to be. The screeching has woken me from a fitful sleep, and now I lie wide awake.

Settling back into my warm bed, I caress the warm body at my side and consider the future and the past. They should be easy to differentiate, but instead the past flows into the future with no seeming end, and likewise, the future flows back towards my past. Once a decision is made, its impact seems to reverberate throughout my past, present and future. It rankles that I can never cut the ties between youthful indiscretions and wiser decisions only possible with age.

I recall my summer meeting with the English king at Eamont last year and growl a little. Although the warm body beside me promises oblivion for some time, the chance to feel truly alive during the deepest storms of winter, I can only think back to the warm summer's day of my submission.

I've been doing the same ever since returning home, with my youngest son, newly baptised in the English king's Roman-based faith, and the English king as his godfather. I've been lingering over the decision to send my son, Alpin, to Athelstan's southern court ever since. I don't want him gone from my side. He's too precious to me. I shouldn't have so willingly agreed to that condition of the peace treaty. Never before has a decision caused me so much internal grief. It doesn't help that sometimes I believe my son wants to go to the English king.

The men of my royal council are rational in their approach to the English and always have been. This, my third alliance with the Wessex ruler, well, the English ruler really, is correctly interpreted by all as just another part in the dance of politics our kingdoms must make with one another. But not for the first time, I find myself regretting the decision and my part in the submission of my countrymen. And my son. It's not as though my son wasn't already a good Christian, and yet, it's the way of the English rulers to subjugate those they control with their Roman-Christianity, as well as their superior warrior strength. The same is happening in York. The archbishop is keen to ensure all of the Norse convert to his particular version of the Christian faith.

Not that the effect of the peace treaty has been far-ranging yet. In fact, most of my people will know no different. They tithe to me, as their king, as they should. What I do with the funds once I've received them is my prerogative. But the anguish burns deep within me. I know I'll not be able to contain it for long.

'Be patient,' my councillors have advised, as has Owain of Strathclyde. 'Just give them a year or two, and they'll forget all about us. They always do. The Dublin Norse will come and fight for York, and we'll be forgotten about.' I want to believe that; after all, that's what happened to my alliance with Edward, the English king's father, and with Æthelflæd of Mercia, his aunt. I've always relied on my enemies in the past to distract the English from their attempts at coercing me and my kingdom.

Only the news from across the sea is not the best. The Dublin Norse engage in battles amongst themselves and with the many, many tiny Irish kingdoms that dot that landscape. I can see no way that the Dublin Norse will be able to leave their lands to disturb the English. Not anytime soon. Gothfrith is once more in Dublin, but his failure to supplant Athelstan from York has done him great harm. If he loses all his possessions in Ireland, then he'll come across the sea, but his homeland is as important to him as mine is to me. He'll not leave it without a good fight. He, and his followers, would rather die than cede what they've held for over a century.

This knowledge keeps me awake at night when I should still be sleeping. That and my age. I blame my age for many of my ailments. I feel like a young man when I sleep, but when I wake, my muscles ache, and my back twinges. Everyone pretends not to notice, but I'm aware that they know, which annoys me. What point is the wisdom gained at my age if my body's too crippled and weak to make use of it?

Sighing loudly, I roll on my side, ignoring the shot of pain that streaks down my back like a red-hot brand. Reaching out, I fondle my sleeping partner's breast, hoping to wake her and, for a while, forget my worries, but deep snores greet my attempts at arousal and, frustrated once more, I roll back over. I know better than to wake her.

The shadows from the fire play across the roof of my bedchamber, and in the images, I see portents and futures denied to me. I predict that the coming year will be a painful one for Gothfrith and the Irish clan chiefs. I can see no possibility of the Norse attempting to attack York when they'll be so busy fighting each other.

And that leaves me with the dazzling possibility that I should be the man to claim it and threaten King Athelstan and his peace accord. In the flickering shadows, I can see riches and wealth, a kingdom bigger than any before held by my ancestors, and that thought stirs me to try and grab it, reach it and make it real.

If only I'd not allied with Athelstan. If only Ealdred of Bamburgh wasn't quite so firmly in the way and quite so determined to hold to the peace with the English, and with the Scots. And of course, those Saxons who look to Ealdred as their lord are a wild bunch, proud of their ability to stand against the Norse invaders while every other kingdom, apart from Wessex, has, at one time or another, fallen to them.

Beside me, a small sigh escapes the lovely woman in my bed, and my excitement mounts. A sleepy, warm body slides alongside mine, and I brush the hair back from her face to look at the woman who's been my bed partner for many long years now. She's a beauty, lacking wrinkles around her eyes. I could have had any woman in my court, but I fancy myself a little in love with her, and so I keep her close. Never my consort, for that would bring more trouble than it's worth, but as my lover, she's an excellent choice, soft, warm and pliant, and barren, for in all our years together, she's never produced a child. Thankfully. I have sons and daughters enough, and now grandchildren have started to appear, a further reminder of my age.

I sigh again, and a lazy blue eye locks on my face.

'What troubles you, Constantin?'

'The usual,' I reply despondently, knowing that her pity will drive her to greater heights to pleasure me.

'Then I must distract you, for a time at least.'

Her hands slide across my flat chest and provocatively lower, and I gasp in pleasure. But this is only the beginning. I'll need to wait far longer to reach the height of my desire. A half-bite on my lip and a soft, throaty chuckle, and I submit to her soothing touch. No time to think of the English king now, or York or Lord Ealdred. Or my bloody age. In my bed, I'm a hot-blooded young man once more. I'll enjoy it.

## 23

### MARCH, 928, BAMBURGH, NORTHERN ENGLAND

*King Ealdred of the independent kingdom of Bamburgh*

I pace backwards and forwards in my great hall, the messenger from bloody King Athelstan dismissed from my presence. He was as pleased to be gone as I was happy to see the back of him.

The gall of the man. I'll not be summoned like some hound to his master. I'm a king in my own right.

The messenger arrived with the burgeoning warmer weather, almost as if he somehow knew to wait those few extra weeks so that my land would have caught up with the balmier southern lands. I hear that in the southern kingdoms they speak of four seasons, and not just summer and winter. But here, there's no need for those two additional seasons. Here, there's winter and summer, the one becoming the other in a matter of a few days, not months.

All winter, I've brooded on my submission to King Athelstan. Far more than when I accorded his father the same honour, but there's something about Athelstan that worries me far more than his father ever did. More than likely, it's the intent behind his words and the meaning of the holy relic he sent to earn my agreement to the peace at Eamont. When Athelstan speaks, he means what he says. His words are weighted and reasoned. With Edward of the Anglo-Saxons, I wasn't always sure, but then Edward was older by the time I knew him, more secure in his kingship and acutely aware of its limitations with regard to Bamburgh. He never, not once, summoned me to attend upon him at his witan in Wessex.

The messenger, a smartly dressed man on a horse more likely to be mine than reserved for a mere messenger, spoke the words from King Athelstan carefully to ensure that I understood them all as if somehow our shared language was my second language. His eyes showed no emotion, and his respect for me was impeccable. It was the content of the message that was less than acceptable.

My rage already fired, he then continued with his list of demands from the English king. I've heard the reports of the huge tithe that he's forcing the Welsh kingdoms to pay to him, well, all apart from Hywel, but I didn't realise that he'd also be making exactions upon my wealth.

As I pace, I wonder. Has he sent the same message to King Constantin of the Scots? Is Constantin as angry as me? Or will Constantin dutifully make his way south to Winchester or wherever it is we're supposed to go?

Rumours have reached me of current affairs in York. It seems to me as though Athelstan treats those under his control with far more respect than he does me, his fellow king. Surely it should be the other way around? He should want to entice me with gifts and pledges of his goodwill. Instead, I hear that he taxes them as little as possible, not wishing to add to their burdens as they attempt to readjust to life under their English master. Of course, he's asked for some changes to take place. The coins must now be of his devising, difficult in a place where those of the Dublin Norse have long held sway. To melt the coins down and replace them with those not only showing Athelstan's face but to a new standard weight as well, his moneyers exact a cost. Still, and to my annoyance, few have spoken against their new king. Athelstan doesn't disrupt trade and, indeed, allows those in York easier tariffs should they turn their business towards Mercia and Wessex.

I'd hoped for an uprising, another battle, anything to make Athelstan less confident, to make him dance around me instead of stomping his way into my hall with his ridiculous demands that I realise, inadvertently, I've already agreed to.

The messenger didn't even do me the courtesy of remotely looking dismayed by the news he carried, reminding me of my responsibilities, willingly agreed to at Eamont.

Damn the bloody English king.

The winter has been long, cold and hard, and I was looking forward to the warmer summer months, the chance to relax in the knowledge that Athelstan would be busy enforcing the peace between the Scots, his kingdom and mine. Now I'm not so sure. Perhaps a late snowstorm would allow me to ignore this command completely, coached as an invitation.

A chuckle emanates from behind me, and I turn to glare at my wife. She's a strange creature, alluring and repugnant in equal measure. Even now, she sits wrapped in furs and adorned with jewels, but she has refused to bathe for much of the long winter, and while she looks appetising enough, her smell has driven me firmly from our marriage bed. I believe she's done it on purpose and not because, as she tells me, she believes that her belly will quicken if she carries out this revolting penance. I have but one son, Ealdwulf, from this union, a lad now, almost a man, and I doubt I'll ever get any more. There's no hope I'll share my bed with her until she bathes, and she'll not bathe until I share my bed with her. A tense situation and one I have no intention of capitulating on.

'I see this King Athelstan must be a mighty king to command you as he does.' Blood boils in my ears. She's voiced the words that I know everyone else within my hall is thinking. I'll not appear as a weak king. I'll not be seen as a place filler until Athelstan grabs our land.

'Athelstan forgets that I'm a king in my own right, owing little to him.' I try to speak evenly and not be stung into showing my fury.

She laughs at my words, a desultory sound that angers me further.

'Athelstan seems to forget nothing. He remembers that you met him and agreed to his terms and that you've had a winter of peace and harmony.'

I temper my angry response, knowing that she's trying to make me speak without thinking. She'd probably like nothing better than to see me impaled on another man's spear, and if this peace lasts, that's increasingly unlikely.

'My dear,' I begin, and instantly, her face clouds. She knows that I'm not going to let her win this argument. 'Athelstan has done nothing but shake some hands and obtain some signatures. The peaceful winter has had far more to do with the terrible weather and blistering storms that have kept everyone by their fires.'

Disappointed, her face turns away from me but not before I see the contempt in her eyes. Why the woman hates me, I'll never know. She hasn't always, and I wonder if it's her own bitterness that she's turned around on me. I'm not to blame for her barrenness, or at least I wouldn't be if we'd had any form of close relations during the winter. The birth of our one son was difficult for her. She almost died, but she doesn't see the joy in her survival, only the bitterness of the failure since.

My initial anger diminished, I return to my original seat at the head of the hall, where my men and my warriors will converge if needed. There are few within it today. Most are seeing to their crafts, their farms or their wives. It's a warm day after such bitter cold, and there's a spring in everyone's steps. I'll not let this messenger hamper my good cheer. I'll think of a way to put Athelstan off. I've no intention of running to do his bidding as soon as he asks.

Moodily, I stare into the fire, wondering what excuse I'll send to explain my absence. After all, I can't refuse without a valid reason as to why I'm not attending his witan; that goes against our agreement at Eamont, and neither can I do as I'm 'requested', for that goes against my intentions when I signed the agreement. There must be something for me to gain here. I just need to decipher what it is and then calculate how I'll achieve it.

In the meantime, Athelstan's messenger can await my pleasure. I'll feed him, I suppose, and I might even give him a space to sleep for the night. And then, when I'm good and ready, I'll bid him return to King

Athelstan, denying as many of his requests as I can. But – and a small smile spreads across my face – perhaps I might suggest that a union between my house and his is now acceptable. Certainly, when my wife hears word of that, it'll wipe the humour from her face.

If it makes her bathe, then that will be even better. Perhaps the English king might have some uses after all.

## 24

## MARCH 928, SCONE, THE KINGDOM OF THE SCOTS

*Constantin, king of the Scots*

A smirk crosses my face as I watch Ealdred of Bamburgh strut in front of me. His ire is a welcome sight, and I can't deny that it pleases me. The more King Athelstan of the English pushes, the easier it'll be for this farce of an alliance to crumble around him.

Back home, safe and sound within our fortresses and protected by our household warriors, none of us should fear the English king. After all, what can he do? March into the land of the Scots and confront me? My religious men and keepers of the historical records assure me that the English, the Mercians or the Northumbrians, or even the Welsh, have not dared to enter our lands within our lifetimes. Even before then, all they met was their death and defeat. My people are wondrously strong and arrogant warriors. We'd not let anyone take us unawares.

The Norse. Now they're another matter entirely. They sneak and slide their way into my kingdom, but their violence is often repelled unless they reach an accord with us. And even then, my people are likely to wait until they sleep, or are too drunk to care, before they slit their throats, steal their treasure and forget the whole incident ever happened.

King Ealdred continues to vent his anger and frustration, and I'm amazed, as I always am, that one man can be capable of talking non-stop for so long. I thought only the holy men could wax lyrical at such length, and only then because they were repeating a passage from a religious text that they'd memorised.

Ealdred swept into my hall with the evening wind, and since then, no matter the food and refreshments offered to him, he's not paused, not once. All I need to do is nod my head every so often, and he seems content. He doesn't expect me to counter anything he says. He wants my agreement, my acceptance that Athelstan is unreasonable, and without saying a single thing, I'm giving that impression.

At my right hand, my eldest son watches Ealdred with amusement. He, too, can't believe that the man can speak for so long, and yet, he's intrigued as well, listening to every word that drips from Ealdred's down-turned face. Every few words, Ealdred spits with his vehemence, and I only wish that Athelstan could see what trouble he's caused.

I, too, received a summons to the English king's Easter witan, but I dismissed it as of little import, not even deigning to send a reply saying I wouldn't be attending. My kingdom needs my full attention after the upheavals of the last few years. If Athelstan weren't such a cocky young upstart who knew how to run his kingdom, he'd know that it was unacceptable for me to be away from my lands this year. I have too many sons and Mael Coluim to boot, and all of them think they should sit on the throne of an old man. I must stay here and show them all that my age is a blessing, not a curse. I've served my people well, and I'm not finished yet. And, of course, if I don't venture south, then my youngest son, Alpin, can stay by my side.

And still, Ealdred shouts and stomps and moans and whines, more like a child than a grown man with a kingdom to manage. His rush to ask me my opinion about Athelstan amuses me and excites me in equal measure, almost as if he thinks I'm his overlord, not Athelstan. I can use that to my advantage.

A sudden silence has fallen, and belatedly I realise that Ealdred has finally finished his diatribe and is sitting, eating and drinking, without so much as waiting for an answer or my agreement that Athelstan is excessive in his ultimatum that Ealdred attend upon him and all the other slights that Ealdred has against the English king.

Ildulb leans towards me, a smile still on his face, his hand raised so that none can see what he says to me.

'I thought you said the message from the English king was merely a request to attend his witan,' he queries, puzzled by Ealdred's heated response.

'It was, and his words were simpering and respectful of my position.'

'So why is King Ealdred so incensed?' Ildulb presses.

'God above only knows,' I muse. The same thought has crossed my mind. 'It little matters what the message said; the result is exceptional. Athelstan is on the cusp of losing an ally he's only just gained.'

Ildulb fixes me with a serious stare. 'Are you telling me that you classify yourself as Athelstan's ally?' He's shocked by my choice of words.

'Better to be an ally than a subordinate,' I mutter darkly, and the grin slides back on to his face. He's the kind of person who finds fun in everything and takes little of life seriously, apart from his three children. Those he watches more protectively than a mother wolf, almost keen for people to threaten them so that he can step in and flay the perpetrator. I was never as protective of my children, and I'm glad I wasn't. I fear it'll bring him heartache in years to come.

'That's true,' Ildulb offers consideringly. 'Are you going to take any action now that Ealdred is so upset?'

'No, nothing. I'll make the appropriate noises and maybe add some more oil to the flames, but other than that, I intend to sit tight here. I'll not be crossing the border anytime soon, and I'll not be sending your brother to the English witan either.'

'I could go on your behalf?' my son offers slowly, and I look at him with my piercing eyes. Why would he want to do that? Why would he want to visit the English king's witan? Does he fancy himself my successor? I'd thought more of him. He sees those fears flash across my face.

'Only out of curiosity,' Ildulb hastily amends. 'I'd like to see what royal splendour surrounds this supposed king of the English. Such an elegant title makes me think he lives in a castle of gold and silver and eats from plates encrusted with jewels and drinks from a drinking horn made from the horn of a mythical unicorn.' The smile returns as Ildulb continues to let his mind wander as to the spectacular palace the English king may live within.

I smile now, too, seeing the dour-looking, God-fearing king, with his yellow hair and bright clothes surrounded by so much flashing gold and silver.

'Aye, but there'd be no women,' I offer as the only slight reservation. 'He's determined to live the life of a celibate monk and will take no woman to his bed. And so, the only way to do that is to have no women near him, I imagine.'

'No women,' Ildulb ponders, 'a strange way to live one's life.'

His tone is wistful, his eyes watching the graceful curves of a young woman as she sashays across the hall before us. My son, like his father, enjoys a good woman.

'But it does do away with pesky offspring,' I offer seriously, although my lips are curved upwards.

'A man should have children to care for him in his old age,' Ildulb offers as if to counter that argument there and then.

'If he's lucky enough that his sons don't see their advancement in the early death of their father.'

'Perhaps amongst the English and the Norse,' Ildulb counters. This is an old argument that we have at least once a week, and our responses are always the same. 'We Scots are a little more civilised.' The thought of the civility of my successor-in-waiting makes my eyes narrow as I pick him out amongst the men sheltering within my hall. He's been waiting far too many years to become king, or at least that's what he tells anyone who'll listen. I need to keep Mael Coluim close to me while allowing him to learn how to govern. It's a treacherous line I walk, and yet the comfort of knowing that my sons don't pray for my death is a soothing balm to my soul.

Ildulb is always keen to highlight the differences between our race and the others on our island. The Welsh kingdoms fascinate him. Strathclyde, more my kingdom now than Owain's, is the one he knows best and often visits on my behalf. But the king we met at Eamont has aroused his curiosity, and he's had my scribes and holy men finding out all they can about Hywel, king of the South Welsh.

Hywel's the grandson of a great king and the cousin of another king who rule or ruled the diverse lands wedged between the sea, the mountains and the encroachments of the English. And yet, for all his grandfather's accomplishments, Rhodri was murdered at the behest of the Wessex king, Alfred. Rhodri Mawr's kingdom disintegrated at his death, the rules of their land making it impossible for one man to inherit the hard-won regions completely. It seems a little strange to me. Why work all your life to unite people and land if it's all to be lost at your death, divided equally amongst sons? I suppose it takes all sorts of men to populate our island. I try to understand those who are very different to me, but it's not always easy.

And Ildulb is convinced that Hywel intends to rebuild his grandfather's kingdom. Hywel presents himself as a holy man, a man who acts with God's blessing, and Ildulb says that coincides with his desire to take the land from his cousin. I think Ildulb correct in his assessment, but I've not told him so. I want him to pay attention and watch those around him, for I hope that one day, when my successor is dead, Ildulb will govern in my stead. He needs to know the motivations of the men who also rule the people of our island. He needs to know what they're going to do before they even do it.

As I did. I knew that Athelstan would not be able to ignore the opportunity to show off his new allies to the people he rules over in England. I knew he'd summon us to attend upon him. What he didn't know, but I did, was that I'd not be doing so, and nor would Owain of Strathclyde, at my request, and nor Ealdred. Ealdred vowed many, many years ago that he'd never step foot in the lands of the southern Saxons. They may well have a shared ancestry, but the men of the far northern lands have always been a little bit different to the softer men of the south. After all, they must face us Scots on their borders all the time. We're not a group of men or women to be forgotten about or ignored.

Ealdred, full of food and mead and devoid of his rancour, comes to my side, his face softer now, his anger spent for the time being.

'We're not bloody going, are we?' he asks, more a statement than a question.

'No, we're not going.'

'Good,' Ealdred mutters before turning his attention back to the fire and the mead, 'I didn't want to give the jumped-up bloody little upstart the satisfaction of having even one king turn up to bow before him.'

'And we won't,' I offer softly, thinking about my next word with delight. 'Ever.'

## 25

## EASTER, APRIL 928, EXETER, ENGLAND

*Athelstan, king of the English*

Easter is a grand religious feast, one I'm always happy to both celebrate and mourn in equal measure. I like to visit with all my relics and spend time praying with the artefacts from the holiest of men, women and places, but this year, I feel aggrieved and struggle to find the peace that I seek. Perhaps, it's grief for the death of Ealdorman Wulfgar, during the winter. I find I will miss him, for all he took a great deal of time to convince of my right to rule Wessex.

Three of my kings from last year have reacted to my eloquent requests, delivered by my messengers, to attend upon me at Exeter for the season of Easter. All three of them are from the Welsh kingdoms. Constantin of the Scots, Ealdred of Bamburgh and Owain of Strathclyde have not responded. I suspect that there's treachery afoot. And I'm bitterly disappointed. Of all the men I treated with last year, at Eamont and Hereford, my higher hopes were that it would be my allies from Hereford who played me false, and that's why my demands on them were so great. I was wrong to think so; a fool to believe the peaceful intentions of coming together in such a way would be upheld by everyone.

Hywel of the South Welsh, Idwal of Gwynedd and Owain of Gwent have come, the last two against my greatest expectations, keen, I think, to meet with Constantin, Ealdred and Owain of Strathclyde. That they're not here shows me as weak, and I must do something to demonstrate that's not the case. I should have pushed Constantin to send his son to court. I should have insisted on a marriage alliance with Ealdred. I should have assured Owain of Strathclyde that I'd be a kinder master than Constantin of the Scots. I shouldn't have allowed Constantin to take his son home with him after the baptism.

I'd planned to show them the splendour of my witan, to gift them with holy relics in tribute to the season, and I've arranged for great feasts in their honour. Now I'll need to hold these feasts in the esteem of others, my brother Edmund perhaps, and maybe my stepmother, anything to save face.

The three Welsh kings didn't arrive together. First came Hywel of the South Welsh with his larger-than-expected retinue. He apologised and explained that, from here, he'll be taking his leave, with my blessing, to travel overseas, leaving his sons in control of his kingdom. I was genuinely pleased for him and a little in awe. The things we spoke of last year and which I thought were mere heated words on a hot day meant more to him than that. His conviction and his deep faith are a wonder to behold. I would be jealous of his journeying to meet the Pope, but for now, my eyes are firmly focused on securing my expanding kingdom.

The next to arrive was Idwal of Gwynedd. He came hoping to be amazed by the grandeur of my dwelling at Exeter. My stepmother has worked for many weeks to make sure the palace is correctly decorated, and the finest furnishings are available for our intended guests. I feel as though even I inhabit a palace more magnificent than I deserve. New tapestries, threaded with bright colours, have been completed to adorn the walls, and every scrap of dust has been vigorously expunged from the tiniest corners. The servants worked so hard and so often that I was, on occasion, concerned that I'd be treated to the same punishment if I stood still for too long.

Idwal and Hywel are similar but different in important ways. They care deeply for each other, as cousins should, but I don't think that a familial relationship would stop either of them from harming the other if it should prove beneficial. I'll watch with interest to see if Idwal respects Hywel's borders when he's gone. Hywel has assured me that his three sons will govern for him, but even so, Idwal may try to gain the upper hand.

And finally, and almost when the festival of our Lord's resurrection itself was being celebrated, Owain of Gwent made his appearance. He apologised profusely for his delay, his eyes taking in all he could see and turning to me with an amused tilt of his lips when he asked where Constantin of the Scots, Owain of Strathclyde and Ealdred of Bamburgh were. I couldn't help but think that he had intelligence that they'd not be attending even before I knew. Perhaps then, he didn't come to see them, but instead to observe my failure.

And that's the exact opposite of what I'd hoped to achieve with my peace treaties last year. I wanted to be the one who knew everything, the one who held as much power as possible. Not the one that all the others were plotting to overthrow or harm. For the briefest of moments, a cold dread seizes my insides. Have I, unwittingly and without intent, managed to unite every kingdom on the island against the English? Will they turn my intentions inside out and work to undermine all that I accomplished?

Only with my relics do I find the courage to pray to my God that I've not harmed with my actions. Only to him can I admit that I have even the smallest amount of fear, and even then, these admissions only come to my mind. I won't even voice them to my priests, men I know to be above suspicion.

We'll all feast together tonight, Hywel, Idwal and Owain, Edmund, Eadred and my stepmother and my unmarried stepsisters. The great men of my land are also in attendance, the ealdormen and their sons and wives. And before them all, I must sit and enjoy myself, even though my hopes are more than dashed. I must hope they don't realise how much I needed this show of submission by the men from Eamont to cement my hold as their overlord.

But, the feast will be fine; the food will be excellent. Hywel has with him a poet who'll perform tales of long ago. I've arranged for music and singing, and Idwal informs me that one of his men has the blood of the Norse in his veins and will share stories of great adventures down mighty rivers and of trading with men and women very different to us; from the frozen lands in the north to the sun-kissed expanses of the south. I look forward to the chance to learn something new.

Tomorrow, my poet will perform the great legends of our homelands, and if I press him enough, he'll speak aloud the great poem Beowulf. It had been intended as both a warning and a compliment for the northern kings, but it should serve as well for the three who've come.

Perhaps I'll ask my poets to construct a new poem, one that tells of my deeds, or perhaps my father's, or my grandfather's. Maybe all three. It's time I made it clear that I'm the king of the English, that my father was the king of the Anglo-Saxons, and that my grandfather was the king of Wessex. All three of us, men of great talent and religious conviction and great in our desire to unite this land. These kings of Bamburgh, the Scots and Strathclyde had best be warned. I'll not be made a fool of by them.

## 26

### EASTER, APRIL 928, THE WITAN, EXETER, ENGLAND

*Eadgifu, the lady of Wessex*

I can tell that Athelstan is disappointed that Constantin, Ealdred and Owain of Strathclyde have refused his invitation to the court. I can tell in the sharpness of his jaw and the tension in his shoulders. I've made it a pastime to learn as much as I can about my stepson.

I've worked long and hard to make the Easter festival, held in Exeter, a place I've never visited before, as spectacular as possible. I've had the huntsman out, chasing down venison, the gamekeeper bringing pheasant and the fisher people bringing delicacies from the depths of the glorious blue sea. I've had boughs of sweet-smelling wood hung in the rafters of the hall, and I've had refreshing herbs placed in bowls and over every surface.

The winter has been bitter, and yet in the last month, it feels as though summer has arrived early. Even the storms that I was warned about when visiting Exeter for the Easter season have so far kept away.

Now, I sit, and I observe all that happens before me. Once more, Lord Osferth joins me. He's dressed in a brightly coloured tunic, a reminder that the warmer weather is on the way, and he smiles with delight at the scene before him.

'Lady Eadgifu, you excel in this task. I've never visited an Easter festival that was so wondrously decorated. And the food is delicious.' I know that Lord Osferth is particularly partial to crabmeat, and so he's been presented with a dish of his favourite meal. It's in recognition of the good he does for me and my sons. I think he knows that well enough, for all his words are ripe with thanks.

'I hope the king will be pleased,' I offer, smiling with delight all the same.

'King Athelstan would happily hold his feasts in a canvas on the side of the road. And yet you still outdo all previous efforts. As you know, your predecessor was not known for her attention to detail.' His voice is filled with the warmth of a confidant. I smile, all the same, pleased at his appreciation for all I do.

'Your sons are growing,' he continues. My eyes roam over Edmund and Eadred. Eadred is still very much a bundle of overexcitement and often to be found with muddy knees or a scraped elbow. Edmund is less exuberant.

'They are, yes, and I saw my daughter only a month ago. And she's becoming a fine young woman.'

'But still determined to take her vows?' he questions.

'Even more so. She doesn't wish to be, and I use her words, "distracted by events beyond the walls of the nunnery".' I raise my eyebrows at that. Those are not the words of a child not yet ten years old, but they speak of her wisdom. And, in all honesty, I'm content with my daughter. I'll not have to part with her in this life. I'll not have to send her overseas and into a marriage alliance with those of West or East Frankia. That knowledge pleases me.

I watch Athelstan, where he speaks with Hywel. The two, I notice, are much alike in mannerisms. Perhaps, unknown to us all, Alfred killed Hywel's grandfather and had an affair with his grandmother. Looking at Osferth, it certainly wouldn't be the first time that Alfred strayed. I believe that Athelstan is far more serious about keeping to his vow of chastity than his grandfather ever was.

'What do you make of them?' Osferth asks me with his chin pointed towards the Welsh kings.

'Hywel is earnest. Idwal is merely bidding his time. And Owain? Well, I don't know what he is other than as troublesome as Edwin.' My tone sours as I'm reminded of Edwin. My eyes sweep the room, resting on him, settled between his sisters. They, it seems, are permitted to the king's feast but aren't encouraged to play any part in his diplomacy.

'Yes, Edwin. Still causing trouble,' Osferth confirms. He's lowered his tone. Perhaps he means to tell me something I don't already know. 'With Ealdorman Wulfgar dead during the winter, I'm aware that Edwin fancies himself as able to take his position.'

I startle at that, almost spilling my wine. 'Truly?' I counter.

'Aye, the damn fool. Does he not realise that to become an ealdorman, the king would need to name him as one? I understand he means to win the support of Wulfgar's family, who have no son. I've even heard rumours of a marriage accord between him and Wulfgar's daughter.'

'They wouldn't be so foolish.' I remonstrate, trying to convince myself. Ealdorman Wulfgar had only just redeemed himself in the eyes of King Athelstan when he was killed, falling from his horse on a hunt. The bloody fool. If his family thinks of making an alliance with Edwin, they'll soon find themselves on the wrong side of the king once more.

'I don't believe they would, no. They need Athelstan to confirm the lands were held not for only the duration of Wulfgar's life, and aren't due to revert to the abbey. Without them, they'll be almost destitute. The king knows that. It seems Edwin doesn't.'

I nod, my good cheer evaporating at the reminder of Edwin and the problem he poses. I'm working hard, as young as my sons are, to ensure they don't battle one another for important things. They must learn to work together. It's a hard lesson for me to teach, just as it's hard for them to learn it. It seems that we all believe we're better alone.

'And what damage will the failure of Constantin, Ealdred and Owain to appear do to the king?'

Lord Osferth shrugs. 'I think very little. Apart from Edwin and Bishop Frithestan, Athelstan has won over much of the court. I even believe Queen Eadgifu of the West Franks is close to reconciling with

Athelstan. It seems most unlikely that her husband will ever be free again. If she doesn't support Athelstan, her son will never take his father's place as king of the West Franks. We share a glance. We both know far too much about events in West Frankia. We could write our own annals on the double-crossing and court politics that take place over the Narrow Sea.

I nod. I confess I've been coming around to this way of thinking as well. For all Lord Osferth has showered praise on my endeavours for the king, Queen Eadgifu of West Frankia has done little but pour scorn on them. I saw her face when she entered the room for a brief moment. I saw the surprise on it. A pity she won't allow herself to enjoy her position a little more. A shame she's forever tainted by supporting Edwin against Athelstan.

And then there's no more time for talk, for the entertainment has arrived. I listen, delighted, as one of Hywel's skilled poets begins his performance. I've observed the lamentations of the Welsh before, and they're as mournful and uplifting now as when I first heard them.

When the poet finishes, bowing deeply, I call him to my side, place a small bag of coin inside his hand, and offer him a smile. 'Tell me,' I ask softly. 'How is Bishop Asser thought of these days in your kingdom?' I think the man most skilled at artifice, but even he's startled by the question, and for a brief moment, I see the truth laid bare. Bishop Asser, the man who wrote of King Alfred's life, who was made a bishop by Alfred, is, it seems, little lamented since his death, tainting himself by his association with the king of Wessex. I think it's a sign that Hywel, Idwal and Owain all need to be careful. Their accord, I perceive, is not at all popular with the people they rule over. Trouble will come. It's only a matter of time. I hope Athelstan is alert to it as well. I wouldn't be surprised if Edwin made much of this disappointment in his quest to replace Athelstan. And there will be someone, somewhere, who'll listen to him.

## 27

## EASTER, APRIL 928, EXETER, ENGLAND

*Hywel, king of the South Welsh*

My poet is good, but I notice that Lady Eadgifu beckons him to her side. What, I consider, is that all about?

Athelstan absorbs the majority of my attention, and yet, I still find myself tallying up the men and women who've come to the Easter witan. I realise, quickly, that Athelstan's summoned all of his ealdormen, their wives and families, as well as the holy men and women. The hall is about ready to burst. The servants, in their smart tunics showing the wyvern of Wessex and the double-headed eagle of Mercia to either side of a holy cross, struggle to slip between the tables and the exterior walls to serve food, mead and ale. There's also good wine. Athelstan knows how to show his wealth to the men and women he commands and also, to me, Idwal and Owain. It's a great pity that the absence of the northern kings is so noticeable.

Before us, my poet bows his way from Lady Eadgifu's side, a perplexed expression on his face as a scop takes his place. This man will tell stories of the Norse and their ancestors. These stories, even more so than those of my Welsh poet, will be riddled with hyperbole and exaggeration. It amuses me that the Norse name their ancestors as Gods, and yet no Christian king would dare the same.

'I understand Ealdorman Wulfgar died,' I murmur softly, thinking of the man who was so instrumental in bringing about the peace of Eamont.

'Yes, a bad fall from his horse. A shame. I'd finally won him round,' Athelstan admits wryly.

'Who'll replace him?' I question. 'His son?'

'No, he had no son. And the ealdordom is mine to gift. If he had a son who was my enemy, I'd not give him the ealdordom,' Athelstan confirms.

'So, it remains vacant?'

'For now, yes.' Athelstan doesn't seem to object to my questions.

'Your brother?'

Again he shakes his head, sitting forward on his wooden chair, and fixing me with a firm look. 'The æthelings, the throne-worthy sons of a king, are never gifted with an ealdordom. Too much potential for them to cause problems. My father would never have given me one,' Athelstan concludes, his voice neutral. I'm not sure why he added that in his answer. 'Tomorrow,' he continues, beckoning for the scop to begin his piece, 'we'll worship in the church, here, in Exeter. Bishop Eadwulf will preach to us. He's also keen to speak to you about your forthcoming visit to Pope John X.'

'I'd welcome such a conversation. But, I might perhaps have more to say on my return,' I admit. The thought of my journey to meet the Pope fills me with enthusiasm.

'Indeed, that's true. But, please pass on my sincere thanks to the Pope for all he's done to try and restore my sister's husband to the kingship of the West Franks. I believe that there are some who've not appreciated his involvement.'

I laugh now, for Athelstan speaks to me of matters about which I know very little.

'I'll do as you request, but I hope he doesn't say anything to me about it. I'd rather see the places that I've heard so much about and pray under his guidance.' Sudden understanding fills Athelstan's face, and he nods.

'Of course, of course. It's not for politics that you make your voyage.'

With those words, Athelstan turns aside, Idwal calling on his attention. I listen to his voice but not the words. I know that Idwal means to renegotiate his settlement with Athelstan. He's come here, filled with firm resolve, that his kingdom should be treated as lightly as mine is. It seems he'll never fully reconcile the knowledge that I eagerly entered into the agreement with Athelstan and that he did no such thing.

Aware Idwal says nothing I've not already heard, I look to the assembled men and women, my gaze caught on the two women who prop up Edwin, Athelstan's drunkard stepbrother. I shake my head at the sight of him sloshing wine down his tunic. I'm minded that my own son, also called Edwin, is not dissimilar. I must speak to him when I return from my expedition.

My attention instead turns to the two boys, Edmund and Eadred, Athelstan's younger stepbrothers and the sons of Lady Eadgifu, whom I saw speaking with my poet. The boys have the look of their mother about them, a brightness to their eyes, and of course, they comport themselves with the gravitas of a true member of the ruling family, unlike Edwin.

As the words of the scop fill the air, I consider the strangeness of the children we breed. King Edward had three wives. I can't yet see that the children born from the second union are worthy of their father, but clearly, Athelstan, and the children from Edward's third marriage, are. How bizarre. But then, my sons are very different, and they have the same mother and father. Smiling to myself, I listen to the tales of the Norse. I'm always intrigued by the stories they tell of their origins, of how they see their place in the world, and equally, how often they can mention wolves, blood, ravens and, of course, their bloody Gods in any one story or poem.

I lower my head and grin. There's been no sighting of the Norse on my coastlines during the last year. Gothfrith of Dublin is, I'm informed, once more returned home and battles no end of opposition to his rulership, including from his sons, who thought they would keep Dublin for themselves while their father ruled in York. Gothfrith's return to Dublin hasn't gone smoothly. His loss of York to Athelstan has, I believe, done irreparable damage to his reputation. I'm not convinced that anything other than reclaiming York will allow him to retain his position, and that suits me just fine. While the Norse and the Irish chieftains bicker and fight, the Norse have no need to sate their warlike tendencies elsewhere. I hope it continues while I'm away on my journeying. I don't want my sons to face our enemy, and not just because, if they do, they might make themselves a reputation that surpasses mine, and no matter how much I love them, I can't allow that to happen. I won't have my kingship questioned by my children. Not for many long years.

## 28

## EASTER, APRIL 928, EXETER, ENGLAND

*Cousin Athelstan of the English, King Athelstan's ally*

Bishop Eadwulf rose to the occasion, but now I'm pleased to once more be in the king's hall. Fervour in our Lord God doesn't make for warmth when the bishop determines to speak at great length on King Athelstan's glories, ably assisted by the archbishop of Canterbury, who, of course, couldn't allow Bishop Eadwulf to have his moment of glory without getting involved as well.

I know I won't be alone in correctly interpreting the bishop's words as I have. He extolled King Athelstan's victories and glorious faith in God making it a slight against the kings who've attended Athelstan's Easter gathering in Exeter.

It's a pity that not all of King Athelstan's allies were present to hear the words of the bishop and archbishop. I can't help but think it might have caused some difficulties. Now that the Mass is concluded, I know that King Athelstan will wish to turn to the more mundane matters of this gathering. There are some land grants that need witnessing before the assembly. Just as at Eamont, this will give Athelstan the opportunity to have his subordinate kings mark their presence at his court; their names permanently written on to the charters they'll witness while here. I smirk, lifting the heated wine to my lips, keen to inhale the fragrance and the warmth in equal measure. The taste is almost irrelevant.

I've been busy, watching all around me, and now my wife, Lady Ælfwynn, joins me. She's been deep in conversation with her cousin, the king, and a rosy glow touches her cheeks.

'I truly never thought it possible,' she confirms, her words only just audible to my hearing as she whispers into my ear. 'That he'd accomplish so much.'

I nod. I share her surprise and admiration. Athelstan, the all-but-abandoned son of King Edward, is now king of the English. It's written as such on the charters to be witnessed today. He's praised as much by the bishop in his sermon. And yet, none of us, and I include the king in this, are blind to the problems that his successes might bring. The refusal of King Constantin and his allies to attend upon Athelstan is just the most obvious way these are making themselves manifest. There are also other problems: niggles from his stepbrother, Edwin, that might become more pronounced; a feeling, difficult to nail down, that the Norse are too quiet; that the West Frankish kingdom might once more erupt into war at any moment as well. Athelstan's aunt, the dowager countess of Flanders, keeps Athelstan well informed of matters there, as do her sons. We heard of Charles III's freedom being granted by his captor, but it was short-lived. By the time we knew of it, he was once more under lock and key at the hands of an overambitious ealdorman, Heribert of Vermandois.

It's a balancing act. It behoves the English to have discord in West Frankia, especially between the Norse leaders who hold land in Normandy. It certainly keeps those Norse leaders occupied. But equally, if peace is never achieved, then Charles III can never resume his place as king, and that will leave little Louis without the means to claim his birthright. For those who think that England is an island, they're very wrong. Events in Ireland, events in West and East Frankia, and also in the northern countries, of which young Hakon, another of the king's foster sons, hails, can have a huge impact on what happens in England.

For now, it all feels as though, at any moment, the careful placing of pieces on the *tafl* board could come awry. It might be through the manipulation of the pieces. It could be because it gets overturned entirely.

'My lord, my lady.' I turn and rest my eyes on Lady Eadgifu of Wessex. I smile at her, pleased that she seeks us out. Her gaze settles on Lady Ælfwynn and they share a knowing look of mutual respect. It will never be love, not after what Edward did to Ælfwynn, in depriving her of the rulership of Mercia on her mother's death, but all know that Lady Eadgifu wasn't responsible for what happened.

'Edmund and Eadred are becoming fine-looking boys,' my wife offers. It's always easiest to divert by talking about the children.

'Yes, they are. I'd hoped your son would be with you.'

My wife shakes her head, although her smile remains in place. 'He's teething and a menace. Unlike most children, it seems that a long ride by a cart doesn't soothe him when he's fractious. It was better we left him at home for fear no one would get any sleep during the gathering.'

Lady Eadgifu shares a rueful smile at this admission. 'It's a difficult time for them. I don't envy them. When my teeth ache, they make me want to cry as well.' The two women, united over such matters, don't notice as I move aside. I'm keen to speak with King Hywel.

He notices my approach and offers me an incline of his head. I return the gesture. It is problematic knowing how to act around a man who is a king but not my king.

'A delightful sermon.' Hywel speaks first. That at least saves me from having to wait, awkwardly, until he does.

'Indeed, yes. The bishop is a man filled with love for his God, and his country. But I would speak with you of other, more delicate matters.'

'And what would they be?' Hywel's face is immediately more guarded. I shake my head, trying to reassure that it's not something to be wary of.

'The borderlands, with the Welsh kingdom of Gwent.'

'They're not my lands,' Hywel interjects quickly.

'I'm aware of that,' I confirm. Hywel seems a little too sharp at my words. 'I merely wanted to seek your advice about whether you thought it would hold. My brother, as you know, is keenly invested in the governance of the region. I've reassured him that there's no cause for concern, but I still thought I would ask your advice.'

Here Hywel nods and then sighs deeply, the tension in his bearing bleeding away.

'King Owain can be a hot-headed fool, but there should be no more than border skirmishes. He doesn't have the warriors he would need to do anything more than that. But,' and here Hywel is firmer, 'don't approach him about it, and certainly not here. He's determined to seek some reduction in his tithe to your king. If he doesn't get it, he might think to lash out, perhaps even bring the agreement to an end. It's better for you to tell your brother, Ealdorman Ælfstan, to have a trusted war band close to the border. If they're there, then it will...' and he pauses, seeking the word he wants, '...dissuade Owain from doing anything he might regret.'

'My thanks for such frank words,' I offer, and he smiles in return.

'It can be difficult, turning old hatreds into friendships when there have been so many years of unrest between us all.'

'It can, yes,' I agree, but our conversation ends there. King Athelstan takes his seat, and the witan is called to order as I return to my wife's side. There are many men and women within the witan. As this is a holy festival, bishops have come from far and wide. I do note Archbishop Hrothweard of York and his counterpart, Wulfheard, the archbishop of Canterbury. Equally, Bishop Frithestan of Winchester also elicits my attention. I consider whether he's finally reconciled himself to Athelstan's kingship or whether he was merely not prepared to allow any decisions to be made in his absence had he chosen to remain at Winchester.

But my eyes turn once more to Archbishop Hrothweard. I'm curious to know how York is doing. I fought there for my king, and I was proud to do so, but I'm yet to be convinced that York is a valuable holding for King Athelstan. And, I consider, just what is Gothfrith doing with himself now? There are reports that he faces difficulties at home. Affairs in Ireland are complex to understand. There are many kingships and chieftains, and there is much unease.

Archbishop Hrothweard has picked a difficult path while the Norse have had control of York. I consider whether he finds it easier now, with Athelstan as king, or if it has actually made it more problematic.

The Norse have their religion, and the Saxons who still live there have theirs. How that impacts the archbishop's actions and influence is something about which I'm not entirely aware. Indeed, the very fact that Hrothweard has managed to journey all the way to Exeter is intriguing. Is he confident of his welcome when he returns or has he brought Athelstan news of unrest in York? Or is he, as the Welsh kings are, here to show his allegiance to King Athelstan? Is Archbishop Hrothweard, despite Athelstan's deep religious conviction, just as subservient to him as those who ascribed their names to the peace accords at Eamont and Hereford? Time will tell whether my king was right to take York or whether it will prove problematic. I hope it will not cause more shedding of blood, should the Norse determine on claiming it back.

## 29

### 929, ABINGDON, ENGLAND

*Athelstan, king of the English*

Once more, my palace is refreshed and emblazoned with as many illusions of my great wealth and prosperity as my stepmother can fit into one wooden building, stretching over two levels. Not one speck of dust is out of place, and I'm in her debt. I'm pleased she didn't remarry. I'll have to find a suitable gift to express my thanks.

While I've been making overtures of friendship to the Welsh kings of Brycheiniog, Tewdwr ap Griffi ab Elise and Glywysing, Gwriad, on the advice of Hywel of the South Welsh when we met last Easter, my virtue and esteem have been travelling far and wide.

With the changing year I've been asked to accept an embassy of men and women from East Frankia. I'm honoured and humbled in equal measure, while likewise, I think that the king of East Frankia, Henry the Fowler, should be just as flattered that I'm prepared to barter with him for my stepsister's hand in marriage. We'll both gain from such a union.

And that's why my stepmother has spent so much of her time in recent weeks ensuring the palace is decorated as it should be. For my part, I've arranged for my holy relics and riches to be displayed.

My priests have vowed to bring me the best of my collection and place it in my great hall, and my provosts have arranged for previous gifts to be put on display. I've many from the marriage Eadhild made to Count Hugh, but I also possess precious items that were bequeathed to me when I became king.

I could name many such articles, but for now, I'm expectant about my new visitors. I consider if they'll speak my language or rely on interpreters. Will they have specific instructions from their king? Which of my remaining stepsisters will they decide upon?

As of yet, there are still two who are unmarried and haven't chosen to live in a nunnery. Three years ago, when Count Hugh of West Frankia sent an embassy to ask for the hand of Eadhild, he ensured that within the entourage was a member of my extended family, an aunt I'd not seen since I was a small boy, Ælfthryth, wife of Count Baldwin of Flanders. However, it was her son who led the embassy, as her husband had been dead for many years. I've recently heard of her death as well. She did well, to travel so far at her age. She's the last of my grandfather's legitimate children to die. Lord Osferth yet lives.

Aunt Ælfthryth eased any difficulties between the two parties that arose due to differing expectations and customs. I'm curious to know what advantage it gave to her and her sons, but I'm not a fool. I'm well aware that members of an embassy must gain from it. I hope she got what she wanted from Hugh, count of the Franks. Eadhild happily left the comforts of my court to start a new life with him. I've heard little from her since, but I hope she's well. Affairs in West Frankia are complex and difficult. There are too many who think to be king there, and too many who don't want to be king but don't want someone else to be king either. I think of Louis, my nephew and foster son combined. One day, he'll need to disentangle the threads of his patrimony, and I'll do all I can to assist him.

It's a pity that no one hopes to win the hand of my stepbrother, Edwin. I keep Edwin close because I can't trust him when he's out of sight. Younger than me by five years, he resents everything about me: my birthright, my kingship, my faith, my religion, and more than anything, my success. He'd have made a weak king, a feeble king, too self-centred, too keen to cause trouble, but he sees none of that. He thinks he'd have united all the kings on this island, as I have done. He's deluded to think as much. It's more likely that the Norse would have united with the men and women of the Five Boroughs and overwhelmed his kingdom than vice versa.

All the same, I've attempted to keep Edwin in my counsel and offer him what small roles of power I can, but he refuses to cooperate. Edwin thinks he should be king, and that drives him every moment that he's awake. It's better when he's drunk, although it's even better when he sleeps. Then the whole court can breathe a sigh of relief and get on with their day-to-day chores. I've had many conversations with my stepmother and Lord Osferth about what the future holds for Edwin.

If he'd only enter a monastery, or marry, or join the household troops, it would be easier, but he'll do no such thing. He wants to drink all day and have any woman who comes within three steps of him. He'll be kept as far away from the marriage delegation as possible for all that it will be one of his full sisters who marries the East Frankish prince. I'm only grateful that few in my court are keen to be seen as allies of Edwin. I think that even his sisters have abandoned him, including Queen Eadgifu of the West Franks. I never thought she'd tire of her brother, but it seems he tests the patience of everyone.

'My lord king.' A voice breaks into my reverie, and I turn to see my young stepbrother. I smile at his brightness and buoyancy, for all a dark smudge of mud covers his nose, and one side of his tunic has been torn. His mother won't be impressed with him. But he's a boy. No doubt, he's been in the stables or playing with the hounds. I haven't seen him yet. I only arrived late last night, and he was already abed.

'Edmund, you're well?'

'Of course, my lord king, always. The weather is turning warm, and the night's long. I think it's my favourite time of the year.' His words are formal, but his smile is infectious. I share Edmund's joy of the coming summer. The winter has been extended and cold, although I think that every year. I hope that this year the summer is long and slow and the harvest excellent.

'A messenger has reached us,' Edmund continues. 'The delegation is less than a day's journey from here.'

'Have you informed your mother?' I ask, and Edmund does me the courtesy of not meeting my eyes. He's young and filled with enthusiasm. And yet, he's keen to perform tasks for me, and so I allow it. I'm training him, as I should, for the day that he'll assume the kingship of England, although I hope it'll be many years in the future. He's only eight years old. He can't yet wear the crown of England on his head. I shudder at the thought. If I should die, with Edmund still a boy, all of England would be lost. I don't say as much because I believe no man can rule as well as I can, but rather through the surety of knowledge. If I were dead, all our enemies, most notably the Norse, would overrun our kingdom.

'Not yet, my lord king, but I will now.'

'She'll have much to prepare,' I press, and Edmund shrugs his young shoulders. Even now, he isn't aware of how much effort his mother has put into ensuring the embassy from the East Frankish delegation runs smoothly. He, too, hasn't been here for long. He and his brother attend the school at Glastonbury Abbey. There they learn much under the guidance of the monks, taught in a similar way to how I had been before I was sent away to my aunt in Mercia.

'I'll tell her when I'm finished speaking with you.' Edmund is stubborn in his resolve. I admire that in him. In all honesty, I see a great deal of myself in him. When I was his age, I lived with my aunt. I was aware that my father had cast me out of Wessex, but it was far more enjoyable to be with my aunt than my overbearing stepmother, Lady Ælfflæd. And my uncle and aunt were keen to teach me how to be a warrior. My father, and grandfather, were only eager for me to learn how to read Greek and Latin.

'And what do you wish to speak to me about?' It's rare for us to have time together like this. I should probably be doing a hundred other things, but I give him my full attention, and those waiting to speak to me, my provost and seneschal, incline their heads and move aside to give us the impression of privacy.

'Edwin.'

I stay my frustration. Edmund might be young, but he's more than aware that Edwin, his stepbrother, just as much as he's my stepbrother, is a liability for the House of Wessex. 'What has he done now?'

'I hear rumours from my friends, and they hear them from their parents.' His voice is haunted. I take a moment to pity him for having to come running with half-whispered fears.

'I know that, and you and your friends, and their parents, have nothing to fear from me.' I regret seeing the relief that flashes across Edmund's face at my words. I'd have hoped by now that he knew he could trust me with anything that concerned him, but clearly, that's not yet the case. I should make more time for him.

'He intends to sabotage the embassy. He hopes to waylay them on the final journey here and make a case for organising the marriage himself. He plans on saying that as the bride will be his sister, he should be the one to speak for her, and he'll exact a cost for doing so; they must support him in becoming king in your place.' Edmund's words rush from him in a torrent. It must give him some relief to inform me of what he knows, for all I will now have to contend with the knowledge.

I suppress my annoyance at Edwin's absurd ideas. Does the fool not understand that it's my standing as the brother of the potential bride that makes the match appealing to the delegation? Doesn't he understand that they'll not even know his name? If anything, if Edwin gets involved then it will probably destroy his sister's chance of a marriage.

'My thanks, Edmund, for coming to me with this. Instruct my household troops to ride out and meet the embassy before Edwin can cause problems. You may go as well once you've spoken with your mother. But only to observe and not to interfere.' As I speak, I catch the eye of Sigelac. He'll know to go with Edmund and ensure that my instructions are carried out, even though a child gives voice to them.

'Of course, brother.' Edmund bows low, perhaps not realising that he's alluded to our blood relationship. I'm pleased he has, for, in this, there's a matter of family honour at stake. As Edmund turns to walk away from me, he pauses, one foot in the air, and I know he's considering his words.

'Thank you, brother,' I say softly so that he knows I heard him, and without further thought, he's dashing from my presence, his youthful vigour reminding me that I'm old to be his brother.

I summon my stepmother to me when I've left enough time for Edmund to have spoken to her first. She deeply curtseys to me, and I bid her rise. Her lips are already twisted, and servants rush hither and thither to carry out her instructions, even as she waits to hear my final wishes. 'I'll arrange for a welcoming feast. I assume you'll deal with Edwin?' she asks, but she's stating a fact, not a question. Edwin is my problem. She and my stepbrother have never spoken a civil word to each other, as far as I'm aware.

'Yes, Edmund, Sigelac and the household warriors will stop him.'

Her eyes flash dangerously then, and I realise I may have erred. 'I don't think Edmund should be overly involved. Edwin can far more easily turn his discontent on Edmund than on you. You should have considered that before you involved your brother. He's still very young.'

Immediately, I realise that she's correct, and before she's left my presence, instructions flowing from her lips, I've called Ealdorman Guthrum to me. 'Guthrum, my brother Edmund and Sigelac have gone to retrieve Edwin before he makes a fool of himself with the delegation. Can you race after them and, if possible, pull Edmund aside and make yourself responsible for Edwin?' Guthrum, not needing to be told more, nods his acceptance and quickly leaves my palace.

He's a solid member of my royal court, keen to prove himself, even in my family matters. His massive size is why I've chosen him for this errand. Edwin is a dirty little fighter, keen to use his fists when he can, and Guthrum has the power to pick him up and crush him in his arms. As Edwin didn't wish to be a part of my household troop, he's embraced more brutal forms of violence. It's probably for the best that he's not overly skilled in using weapons.

I could pace a little now, show my irritation, but instead I do as I should: retire to my room and prepare myself for the people who'll be anticipating meeting the great English king, Athelstan. I'll hide my unhappiness at Edwin's behaviour behind my mask of kingship.

I've had my crown removed from its safe box for this meeting, and I ask my priests to set it on my head. I'm pleased it still fits as well as it did at my coronation. I've not worn it since the Christmas feast, and I worry, just a little, that my head will have grown or shrunk. My priest always berates me for my concerns, assuring me that once a man is full grown, his head is unlikely to do either of those things.

Now, as he rests my crown on my nest of blond hair, he smirks a little, and I know he's thinking about my usual question. In amusement, I refrain from asking. By the time there's a disturbance at the gate to my palace complex, I'm attired, as I should be, in beautiful clothes crisscrossed with embroidery, with my crown upon my head and a cloak of fine purple silk across my shoulders.

I feel regal until I step into my hall and spy the twisted faces of both of my stepbrothers. I curse my father for his precocious ability to produce children. It would be so much simpler if I were an only child! Edmund, although holding his annoyance in place, is less than pleased that I had him recalled and replaced by Ealdorman Guthrum. All the same, I'm impressed by his restraint.

And Edwin? Well, Edwin is spitting and angry, his face showing where Guthrum enforced my will. I wince a little at his eye. It'll blacken, bruise and puff, and while it remains like that, he'll continually cast dark looks my way and blame me for every ill that befalls him and to every man and woman who'll listen to his bitching. Which, luckily, isn't a great number.

It's a pity Edwin has become an object of scorn to most. They'll nod and grunt, but not one person within my palace will agree with Edwin when he tries to blacken my name. Sadly, that won't stop him from trying. At least the family of Ealdorman Wulfgar saw sense and didn't contract a marriage alliance with Edwin.

Ealdorman Guthrum, as placid as ever, bows before me, and I beckon him forwards to report. He's a little dishevelled, his clothing rumpled, and a streak of mud smears his lower chin. No doubt this is the work of Edwin.

'Edmund was happy to be called away,' Guthrum confirms, and I ignore his glossing over of what must have been an awkward interview between him and my young brother. 'Edwin was less happy, and I'm afraid we got embroiled in a little fight.' Once more, he downplays what must have happened.

'My thanks, Ealdorman Guthrum, for accomplishing a less than pleasant task and promptly as well.' He bows again but doesn't speak further.

'Did you catch sight of the embassy?'

'I didn't, my lord king, but one of the outriders did. I'd say they'll be here for mid-afternoon.' And so spoken, Ealdorman Guthrum leaves my sight to clean my brother's blood from his fists and to make himself respectable for the men and women from East Frankia.

Edmund doesn't come any closer to me, but with a slant of his head indicates that he, too, will withdraw, and with my permission granted, he slides out of the door, leaving me alone with a foul-tempered Edwin. Edwin's hooded eyes glare at me angrily, his mouth twisted into a grimace of disgust.

'She's my bloody sister,' Edwin spits, swigging from a drinking cup given to him by one of my most trusted servants. She begged me for the honour of keeping an eye on Edwin, claiming that she could exert her power over him and make him see reason on occasion. Willingly, I agreed to her request, and in all honesty, she's served me well. Edwin grudgingly accepts her near-constant presence, and I consider just what exactly this power is. Not that I ask. Some things are best left unknown.

'No, she's the king's sister, and I'm the king. I'll negotiate on her behalf.'

'It's not your responsibility,' Edwin counters angrily, and I breathe deeply through my nose to calm myself.

'It's my responsibility. She knows it, and so do all your other sisters. You have no part to play in these negotiations. You didn't when Eadgifu and Eadhild were married, and you won't now.'

Edwin glowers at me sullenly. 'My father organised Eadgifu's marriage.'

'Our father arranged Eadgifu's marriage,' I say, stressing the 'our'. He'd do anything not to share a father with me. Anything.

'Yes, he did, and without you even being at court,' Edwin counters, trying to raise my ire by reminding me that my childhood was spent away from my father. We've had this argument before, and I grow tired of it.

'How I was raised is no concern of yours. I'm your older brother and your king as well. You'll listen and honour me, as you should. I'm the head of your family, whether that pleases you or not.'

Edwin spits out his wine at my words, and I feel my temper start to fray. Now isn't the time to deal with his feelings of inadequacy.

'If you wish to serve your king, that can be arranged. If you want to serve your family, that can be arranged too.'

'I wish to do neither,' Edwin chuckles maliciously, swaying on his feet. 'I'm happy with my life as it is.'

'And that's why you drink all day long and whore all night long.' A pleased look spreads across his face at my words.

'Just because you do neither doesn't make my life choice wrong, dearest brother.' His use of the word 'brother' angers me. The irrationality of accepting it from Edmund, but decrying it from Edwin, isn't lost on me.

'No, it doesn't, but it's not acceptable at my court. If you wish to stay here, you'll change your ways.'

Abruptly sitting on one of the benches around the tables already laid for the coming feast, upsetting the early summer flower decorations placed there by my stepmother, Edwin sloshes wine down his ripped tunic and across the table. Walking toward him, I notice how his entire body shakes.

'Brother,' I begin, the single word burning my lips. All the same, I hope that an appeal to him on such a basic level will work. I'm unsurprised when it doesn't.

'You're no brother of mine,' he slurs, raising his hand to rest his shaking head on it. His eyes are glazed and wavering as he tries not to meet mine. I don't remind him that he named me 'brother' first.

'As you will, brother. I banish you from my court. You'll go to your estates, and I'll have some of my men stay with you and ensure you plan no rebellion.'

Edwin's eyes flutter as I speak, and before I know it, a snore emanates from his open mouth. How he manages to drink himself into such a stupor day after day is a mystery to me. Three of my servants quickly surround his lifeless body and lift him between them. I'd like to say they've not done this before, but I'd be lying. They carry Edwin away, and I wish I hadn't sighed with relief as he went. At least I'll be able to meet my guests without having to worry about Edwin interfering.

Rubbing my hand across my face, I fix a smile upon it and turn to greet my real guests. Thank goodness they've arrived after Edwin drank himself insensible.

My stepmother, a hostess to the end, beckons the group of twenty into my hall, and I'm all smiles and excited. I'll think about my stepbrother later. Much later. Something must be done about him. Perhaps, after all, I might send him to West Frankia. There must be someone there in need of a husband. Sooner he was there, causing problems, than in England. They might not even notice amongst the bickering already taking place, and if it came to weapons, then alas, Edwin would meet his death.

# 30

## 929, ABINGDON, ENGLAND

*Prince Edmund, ætheling of the English*

I seek my mother as soon as I return from my aborted journey to find Edwin. My initial anger has dissipated, but still, I need to speak with her. That she shares my feelings of anger towards Edwin helps a great deal.

I find her dressing within her room, surrounded by servants and issuing instructions to members of the household. When she sees my face, she quickly dismisses everyone.

'It was I who asked for you to be recalled,' she volunteers once there's no one else in the room. 'King Athelstan needs to realise that he can't include you in this feud. Edwin will find it much easier to undermine you than King Athelstan. To most people, you're little more than a child.' I hear the caution in my mother's words. I feel my fury dissolve. It wasn't then that my stepbrother thought I was unable to carry out his request. It was my mother. Now I understand why Ealdorman Guthrum was so insistent when he caught me on the road from Winchester. He's both a keen supporter of the king and the king's mother.

'You have my thanks, I suppose,' I mutter a little grudgingly. 'Still, I was only to watch, and that was all I intended to do. The king sent Sigelac with me, and of course, the household warriors know that they're to truly ensure Edwin behaves himself.'

'I know, my son,' she murmurs. Her voice is calm and reasonable. I understand why she informed Athelstan of her unhappiness. Still, it galls me to know that my stepbrother would have allowed me that semblance of command, whereas my mother would not. I'd rather my mother hadn't interfered. One day, she'll have to realise that I'm going to be king. Then, she'll have to take directions from me, just as she does from Athelstan. I can't see that it will be easy for her to accept them from her son.

'Come on, son, the embassy will be here soon, and I'm keen to meet these men and women from across the sea. Dismiss Edwin from your mind. Athelstan will ensure he's not at the feast tonight and maybe not here for the foreseeable future. You need to change,' she almost squawks, taking in my mud-splattered clothing. I feel myself relax at such a mundane thought. I bat away her hands as they try to pry my clothing from my body.

'I'm going, I'm going,' I counter, trying to escape her clutches. All the way around the small walkway that flanks the individual rooms of the royal accommodation I can hear her chastising me. One day she might think of me as more than a child. One day. I wish I could tell her that at the age of eight winters, I'm quite capable of acting as the king's acknowledged heir, of knowing who my allies are, but a part of me is grateful that Athelstan wears the English crown and not me. I wouldn't like to be encumbered with such burdens as his. All I wish to do is to grow strong enough to fight beside him in the shield wall when I'm older.

Suitably attired and smirking at my mother's earlier outrage, I present myself to King Athelstan. He eyes my clothing with approval, and I wonder if I'd feel comfortable in clothing quite as rich as his. I think not. The embroidery is stunning, the work of my mother and her women, but it's too tight for my liking and far too restrictive. I'd feel unable to breathe, sneeze, move or even eat.

'My apologies for earlier,' Athelstan murmurs, but I grin at his contrite face. He was right to send me, and my mother was right to demand my return. It little matters now. Edwin shouldn't mar this happy event when he's not even in attendance.

Ealdorman Guthrum, his work on collecting Edwin done, has ridden back to meet the embassy, and I hear his authoritative voice coming from outside the building and announcing his return. I wonder what the East Franks think of him.

A huge fire burns in the centre of the hall, and to either side of it, the men and women of the royal court are expectantly waiting. Not as many as might attend the witan itself, but enough to do honour to the king's name. My stepsisters are amongst them, although my mother stands close to the king, and I stand beside her. The hall is resplendent in finery and early summer flowers; the smell from the coming feast is heavenly to my empty stomach. Somewhere amongst Edwin's exploits, and my mother's dismay, I've eaten nothing all day.

No fanfare greets the arrival of the delegates, but Ealdorman Guthrum escorts them inside with much ceremony, and then, all eyes on them, they're before the king. I watch with curiosity. Their travelling clothes are the same as ours, but underneath cloaks and hoods, I glimpse brightly coloured fabrics. I imagine they're all as well-attired as Athelstan.

There are at least twenty within the group, mostly men but some women as well. They look a little cold and fraught by their journey and exclaim with delight on seeing the welcoming fire.

Athelstan greets them respectfully but quickly, a young priest acting as their interpreter. He introduces himself as Brother Bruno, and Athelstan introduces himself, his stepmother and me. Eadred isn't a part of the welcoming ceremony. He's even younger than I am and more likely to be found playing with his wooden toys than bowing before regal men and women.

Brother Bruno announces the names of those he's accompanied on the journey.

'I'm honoured to introduce representatives of the great king, Henry of East Frankia.' The party is mainly made up of men who look no different to every other man in the room. Amongst them all, a young woman steps forward, introduced as Gerbega, a relative of the king, although I can't quite work out how, as here the priest seems to muddle his words. I hear a soft sigh from my mother and consider what that means. The woman is beautiful, even I understand that, as she bows low before the king. My mother emits a soft chuckle.

Gerbega curtseys prettily before the king, and then her hand is light on mine as I offer her an arm-clasp of friendship, and then she's gone in a swirl of dresses.

'It seems that Henry of East Frankia hopes to tempt the king to take a wife,' my mother murmurs behind her hand, and I know my eyes open wide at the thought. Would Athelstan take a wife? Should he do so, then I'd no longer be his heir. My heart sinks at the thought, but I know my stepbrother better than that. He's a man as cold and calculating as a sword in his every movement. A pretty face will not sway him.

I notice another three women within the group but none as beautiful as Gerbega, and two of them older than my mother. The other woman is more a girl, perhaps not yet even ten years of age. I wonder who she is and what possible part she can have to play in whom the king of East Frankia's son should marry.

Beside me, my mother mutters under her breath once more. I fix a smile on my gleaming face and turn to do my duties for my stepbrother. I must sit beside one of the embassy members, alongside my mother, and make what conversation I can with the stranger. The marriage isn't yet assured. Everyone here is testing each other, or so my mother has warned me, as she bid me behave, watch how I ate, and generally try not to embarrass myself.

I sit beside one of the men, my mother to my right, and only then do I realise I've forgotten the man's name. Sensing my predicament, he speaks first.

'My name is Eberhard, and I'm one of the king's chieftains, or as you would say: ealdormen.' He speaks our language with hard edges to the words. And yet his smile is genuine. If he's dismayed to find himself seated next to the king's younger brother, he doesn't show it. 'I'll tell you of those amongst the embassy,' he offers. 'I'll start with Gerbega.' I feel my mother lean over to listen carefully, and Eberhard pauses but then continues to speak. 'She's the daughter of one of the king's greatest ealdormen, and she's here at the bequest of King Henry as a surety for her father's good behaviour. It's no mark of respect for her to be here. She's an outcast,' Eberhard mutters softly. I focus on him as he speaks, noticing his beautiful beard and even more elaborate jewellery that flashes at his throat and the cuffs of his sleeves.

'The king thinks highly of you?' I ask, confused by his words, and Eberhard smiles.

'He tolerates me and often sends me on these short journeys for him. He knows that I enjoy travel, and he enjoys not having to worry about any trouble I might cause.'

'Then,' my mother speaks, 'Gerbega must be your daughter, and you must be the troublesome ealdorman,' she queries, her lips raised in a smile. I feel my forehead furrow. There's much at play here that I don't understand.

A slight guffaw of laughter from Eberhard, and I know my mother is correct. This should make for some interesting negotiations. Eberhard will want to please his king to win back his favour, whereas he must also appease King Athelstan. I don't envy the man for such a task. I imagine it'll be more difficult than trying to stop Edwin from saying things he shouldn't.

# 31

## 929, ST ANDREWS, THE KINGDOM OF THE SCOTS

*Constantin, king of the Scots*

The church is silent; all have fled from the extended service I asked my priests to perform in this holiest of places, the church of St Andrews, or Cennrigmonaid as it's also known, where the land touches the sea.

In this holy location, I feel my earthly cares slip away from me, and I'm free and young again. Not an easy thing for an old man to accomplish when his knees ache, and his back thrums with every movement he makes. I'd curse my old age, but I can't. I'm grateful for it. To see my sons grown to men, my grandchildren scampering around the royal palace. It does an old man's soul good to see that his endeavours on this earth have not been for nothing.

My country is strong, and my people united. Athelstan of the English is an annoyance, like a summer fly when the cattle are brought in for slaughter, desperately trying to crawl over the shit and happy to feed when they can. A smirk crosses my face. Oh, to think of the jumped-up English king being compared to a fly on shit.

I shake the thought aside. I came here for peace of mind, not to dwell on the affairs of state that prey upon my thoughts. Athelstan of the English has ascended far higher in the estimation of everyone, both within our island and in the lands of the East and West Franks, in the homelands of the Norse, and on the island of the petty chieftains of Ireland and their Norse neighbours. I worry I may have underestimated Athelstan. He's more than a wasp sting; more than an irritating fly come to feed on shit. He is, although I loathe admitting it, a man grown in reputation. Perhaps, after all, I should have been keener to submit to him. Perhaps, he shouldn't have had to force me to send my son to his court. Maybe, I should have gone to Exeter when I was invited.

I have a man close to the English king who keeps me informed of all that happens in his kingdom. I know of his negotiations with all the tiny kingdoms of the Welsh; I know of his marriage alliances with the East Franks; and I know that poets and scholars and religious men vie for his special attention. He loves learning, seeks holy relics wherever he can and, above it all, he remains a man of his word. Celibate, and devoid of heirs of his body. He's an enigma. But all love him, and I mean all.

He's to be feared and little trusted, which is why I came here today. My thoughts mull over his intentions, his wants, his needs, and I think myself a fool for incurring his wrath by not attending upon him as a friend when he so willingly offered it to me.

Owain of Strathclyde thinks me a fool too, not that I tell him his words are true. Never. In public, I hold firm to my refusals to bow my knee further, laughing off the growing menace of the English as something about which I'm too old to worry. After all, my knees bend unwillingly at the best of times. Why would I want to force them to my will?

Not that Athelstan's even threatened my land, or me directly, or my people indirectly, and yet, I have a feeling in my gut. It's not helped that I know he's reinforcing York. He's made his mark on that kingdom with the aid of the archbishop, Hrothweard. He's a great king, and such kings must always seek ways to make themselves even greater. He's bested his father in military prowess because of his love of diplomacy. Now he must aim to beat his grandfather, and no matter where I look, I see no enemies as great as the Norse for him to face in battle. No, I fear, or rather I know, that he'll look to the north. Athelstan will want my lands, and I'm a fool for not bowing my knee to him.

And yet, for all my self-recriminations, I know that my people stand by me, agree with me, and salute me for my firm resolve. They see the men of the English, the Saxons, as they insist on calling them, as weak-minded men, surviving on our island only by chance and the persistence of a few. They respect them not at all.

Ealdred of Bamburgh sends me messengers on an almost daily basis, informing me of the English king's movements and his attendant fears. He jumps at every rumour and scuttles to me when the fear and worry become too great. I wish he wouldn't. It sends the wrong signals to his people when he so callously abandons them to their fate, running to the apparent safety of my northern kingdom.

I fear that one day, Ealdred will simply bring all his people and his great hall with him and beg for some little plot of land to call his own within my kingdom. But I'll have no other realms within mine. My people are only recently united, and still, I cast my eye covetously on the lands of the Strathclyde king, a king in name only, for he rules at my command. His position was mine to gift, and it'll be mine to give away. Soon, soon, I'll make my move and add Owain's kingdom to mine, forever, but not at the moment. Not when the English king is so close. I feel his breath down my aching back, and turn, as though expecting him to be standing there, a sword in his hand, a satisfied smirk on his face; 'I have come to take your kingdom,' the words on his lips.

The only consolation in all of this is that my contact at the English witan tells me all that's discussed and all that happens. The king has many great ealdormen whom he trusts implicitly, and to them, he gives the governance of the ealdordoms, the majority of them determined by the ancient boundaries that were once kingdoms in their own name. One of these men, I hope, will prove false to him and come to my side, but who? Whom should I attempt to steal away from their fervent allegiance to their king? My contact tells me that all love the king, apart from his stepbrother, Edwin, and he's a drunken sop and no use to me at all. Edwin will blab if I approach him, his mouth running away from him whenever he's had too much to drink, and I understand that's a daily occurrence from my son, who I've unwillingly sent to the English king's court. It seemed easier to let Alpin go than continue my defiance. For the time being, it's stopped Athelstan from being more insistent on other terms of our peace accord.

Edwin grows wilder and more belligerent. He has no words of thanks for his brother. I even hear rumours that Athelstan has attempted to make a marriage alliance for his stepbrother, far from England's shores. It doesn't surprise me that none will have him. None would wish to welcome someone who already plots and schemes against his king into their own family or kingdom.

Athelstan's patience with his brother grows ever thinner, and I think that something will happen to Edwin. I believe the king will snap, tire of his constant attempt to incite rebellion when none wishes to rebel. I don't see a very rosy future for Edwin. Still, Edwin distracts the king enough that Athelstan makes no move towards me. He sends me friendly messengers and asks for his tithe and little more, now that my son resides at his court. In the spirit of our peace accord and following my refusal to attend upon him last year, I've sent my son to soothe Athelstan's wounded pride.

I know I disappointed Athelstan when I didn't rush to accept his invitation to Exeter last year. For now, I hope it'll only remain a disappointment. There's much I must put in place to counter whatever Athelstan eventually resolves to do with the fracturing peace treaty of Eamont. The loss of my son, for the time being, is something I will have to tolerate. Alpin will return to me. One day.

Perhaps, after all, I should send a representative of my kingdom to meet with the English king? Offer apologies. It could be one of my older sons or, even better, my successor in waiting. I wouldn't mind if the English king sought his revenge on Mael Coluim. Although, it might upset those men and women who've been vying for his patronage throughout their lives while longing for my death. That makes me smile again. Staying alive is another way to thwart Mael Coluim and one I quite enjoy. It makes up for the aches and pains, stiff limbs and loss of desire for women to see his twisted face every time I preside over my royal court.

Or perhaps it should be Owain of Strathclyde. It's about time he did something to earn his position.

Rising stiffly from my stool, my arse numb and my hands a little frozen in the chill of the church, I walk forward to lay my hands on the altar under which I know the holy relics of the church's name-saint rest. I know little about him other than that he was brought here by a man who fled to St Andrews, from lands much more temperate than mine. I think him a fool for leaving the warmth of the southern territories, but then, if it was death or a bit of discomfort, I think he probably made the correct decision. And I'm pleased he brought the relics.

And in that respect, Athelstan is no fool. He understands the power of the holiest men's bones. They legitimise his kingship and his pledge to rule the English, and everyone flocks to him. Even the rulers of the Welsh kingdoms. Defiant for hundreds and hundreds of years, ever since the words of that great man, Gildas, an ancient monk with a grudge against his military leaders and the incoming Saxon raiders, found their way into their people's thoughts. But now they've started falling at Athelstan's knees as though all is forgiven. The Welsh kings are practical men; their people not quite so much, and this once more is a weakness to exploit. The Welsh like a good fight, and they fight dirty, using the natural environment to give them an advantage over any who trespass there. So the Norse have learnt to their detriment, and so too could the English, if I just use the right words, the correct incentive to incite rebellion against the treaty of Hereford.

Perhaps a sermon, as Gildas once wrote? Maybe a poem. Something to worm its way into the psyche of the prideful Welsh.

Calmer than I've felt for the last six months, I turn away from my saint's relics, leaning on my elder son for support in those first awkward moments of taking steps after sitting for a long time. I take a moment only to compose myself. And then I'm all king again, mighty, powerful, old and wise. I have a little job for a poet I know and trust. His secrecy and discretion will be bought with trinkets of gold and flashing red rubies, and then he'll infiltrate the kingdoms of the Welsh so that Athelstan will be a little less sure-footed. Somewhat less magnificent and munificent.

It feels bloody good to be alive.

## 32

### 929, ABINGDON, ENGLAND

*Athelstan, king of the English*

I smile broadly, keen to ensure all know that I'm delighted by the success of the East Frankish embassy, as I return inside my hall, having bid my stepsisters farewell. It seems strange to think I might never see them again. Before the embassy arrived, I had two stepsisters in need of a husband, but now, I have only one. It's slightly unfortunate that I don't yet know which one it will be. The East Frankish king has requested both sisters return to his kingdom to allow his son to choose the most compatible one from the two. I would be outraged at the suggestion, but both Eadgyth and Ælfgifu begged me to allow them to go. Who was I to deny them their requests? Both are intelligent enough to know there'll be no English husband for them. And, I imagine, they might even fear that I'll find them a Norse husband, as I did Edith.

Now, I have no sisters left at my court other than Queen Eadgifu of the West Franks. My stepsister weeps for her husband's imprisonment, of which he's been released and then chained once more too often for my liking. Their son doesn't weep for Charles. Louis has no memories of his father. He was barely a babe in arms when he arrived here, with his mother, fleeing from the overmighty West Frankish subjects. Now he's a lively child, just like Edmund and Eadred, his closest friends.

I might be disappointed at the failure of Eadgifu's marriage to the now deposed king of the West Franks. But Eadhild is wed to Count Hugh, brother by marriage of the current king, and he, I'm sure, will be most useful when Louis is older in resecuring the kingship on Louis' young shoulder, should the worst befall his father and he not live to become king once more. And, of course, with another of my stepsisters wed to the East Frankish prince, there might well be assistance for Louis from there as well. I am resolved that one day, Louis will be king of the West Franks, not matter the current confused situation.

'My lord king.' I turn and meet the eyes of Ealdorman Guthrum. He inclines his head and offers me a wry smile. 'Sent on their way,' he murmurs. I think he's as pleased as I am. Edwin has been dispatched to his estates. There are few left to undermine the peacefulness of my court now.

'Indeed. All gone,' I agree. I confess I do feel somehow lighter without the spectre of sisters to wed on my shoulders. Once more, I could truly curse my father for his prowess in the bedchamber. It has certainly made me determined not to follow in his footsteps.

'I bring news from the Dublin Norse.'

'Are they still fighting amongst themselves?' I query. I'm happy to admit that events in Ireland have far exceeded my wildest expectations when I took York from Gothfrith. There's no need for me to do anything. They're all content to fight amongst themselves. And until one emerges as a victor, none can look to York.

'It seems so, yes. The Ui Neill clans, from the north and the south, are engaged in a war against the might of Dublin and Waterford. That keeps both Gothfrith, and his son, Olaf Gothfrithsson, busy.'

'Good. And in the kingdom of the Scots?'

'All seems quiet. King Constantin is being careful. Now that you have his son, Alpin, he's less eager to displease you.'

'That's to be expected,' I confirm. I like Constantin's son. It was very clear he didn't wish to come to England, but now that he's here, he's more content than bloody Edwin. Perhaps I should send Edwin to Constantin? But no, that would cause me twice as much trouble.

'And the Welsh kingdoms?'

'I hear that Hywel will return from his travels this year. In the meantime, his sons have ruled well, and all seems calm in the other kingdoms. There have been no attempts to take advantage of Hywel's absence.'

'Then all is as it should be?' I question, wondering why he's sought me out.

'Perhaps, my lord king, but there are rumours from Bamburgh.'

'What's happening at Bamburgh?'

'We're not really sure, but certainly, all is not as it should be. Perhaps, I might lead an embassy there, on your behalf, of course.' I consider this. King Ealdred has not proven to be the closest of allies; that's a surety. Perhaps, it would be worthwhile having an insight into events there. After all, York is mine, and much of the lands that used to be a part of the kingdom of Northumbria. Bamburgh is a bastion of an ancient lineage, but it doesn't have much going for it at this time. Ealdred has but one son, and as he turned down my offer of a new wife, I don't believe he'll have more heirs.

'Yes, I think that's a good idea. And, along the way, ensure all is well in York. The archbishop has been quiet of late,' I offer. 'Perhaps refresh the men left on duty there. It's possible they've become too close to the Norse of York. They might be plotting something.'

'My lord king.' Ealdorman Guthrum's bow is quick in following. I can tell, from the speed of his steps, that my idea for him to visit York as well, alongside his request to journey to Bamburgh, pleases him.

## 33

### 929, ST ANDREWS, THE KINGDOM OF THE SCOTS

*Constantin, king of the Scots*

'Now, my friend.' I bring the scop closer to me. The words I have to share with him are not for the ears of all. This must be our secret. None must know of my intentions, for all I must give him my commands in front of those feasting within my hall. All must be seen to be normal, without malice. I want no one to determine my purpose in having the poet brought to me.

'My lord king.' The man is obsequious. I imagine he thinks I'm about to offer him a hoard of coins for writing of my military prowess or some such. But that's not my purpose here.

'I have something that I require you to both compose and then disseminate throughout the many kingdoms of the Welsh. It's not to be rushed but rather devised carefully. And, of course, none should know that the instructions came from me.'

'My lord king.' A question forms on the man's face. He's not young, but neither is he as old as I am. With poets and scops, the measure of the skill is the ability to give voice to the true meaning of the stories they share. This man has a voice that can dip low and ring out shrilly, one that can urge men to war on the battlefield, and one that can make them weep in the mead hall. I can't imagine it hurts that he can make women squeal in his bed, either. There have been many husbands cuckolded by this poet. Of course, I'm not one of them. I would have killed the man had he tried it with my wife.

'It must be a tale, akin to the Welsh legends, that one day they'll rise up against and defeat the English who stole their land.'

'My lord king.' A smile touches the man's cheeks. He's closely shaved, and I wonder if that's what the women like. I rub my hand over my own coarse beard and moustache. I know it's no longer the rich brown of my youth, but perhaps it's not just the colour that's so unappealing. Perhaps it's also the fierceness of it. I think I could groom my horse with the bristles of my beard.

'It's to be done well,' I urge him. 'You're to think long and hard about it. Visit the Welsh kingdoms if you need to, and listen to their scops and poets. Ensure that once it's complete, I never see you again.'

'Then how will I be paid?' the man questions, his enthusiasm dimming at the prospect of the loss of a bag of coins I've not yet offered to him.

'I'll have arrangements put in place. None need to know what I'm paying you for, and you're to let no one know. If you're questioned closely, then you'll be working on a poem about me. Telling of my mighty battles and long life.' I smirk at that. Should a man be praised for living longer than his allies and enemies? Unbidden, I look to where Mael Coluim sits, brooding. I should really give the man some land where he can sit and drink himself sodden, but if I do so, I'll not witness his attempts at undermining me. No, I must keep him close as I seek to cause chaos for Athelstan. I find it typical that the one time in my long life I'd welcome the intervention of the Dublin Norse, they're all too caught up in matters of internal politics and trying to outfight the Ui Neill clans. Still, there's always more than one way to secure a victory, as I've learned during my long reign.

'My lord king.' The man bows again. I wonder if he knows more words than just that. But, of course, he does. He's a man of great skill and wit. He can keep drunken men and women singing on a bitter winter night. He can tell tales that have even me laughing until tears run down my coarse-bearded face. I know he'll do what I command.

'And remember. If you succeed in this, I'll forever be in your debt, and more, your name will be known as well as that of Beowulf's. Think on that, my friend.' I smile and wave Ildulb closer. 'See that he has a good, warm bed for the night. And in the morning, introduce him to my treasurer. They'll be seeing a great deal of one another.'

I see the flicker of uncertainty on Ildulb's face, but he bows and leads the poet away. I wonder if my most clever son has even the smallest idea of my plans. If he doesn't, I think that, in time, he'll come to understand them. Even that makes me smile. Only then my gaze slips over Mael Coluim. He watches me, eyebrows raised. I lift my goblet and drink to his health, although I'd sooner I could rid myself of him more easily. Sadly, the words of a poem will never undermine Mael Coluim and his righteous claim to my kingdom. More's the pity.

## 34

## 931, KING'S WORTHY, ENGLAND

*Athelstan, king of the English*

The messenger looks nervous, and I wonder what news he carries that would make him cower quite so much before me. I'm a Christian king, never known for having reacted angrily to any news brought to me. After all, it's not the messenger's fault if the news they carry is unwelcome or unwanted.

The man has come from the lands of the East Frankish king, the man to whom only two years ago I sent not one but two of my sisters in the hope that one of them would prove acceptable to his son, Prince Otto, as a future bride. I'd hoped to hear last year that one of the girls was happily married and that the other was on her way home. But no news came, and I only hoped that meant that nothing untoward had happened. Even my bishop, sent to escort them, has been delayed in returning to me. I'd like to hear tales of this new kingdom, being formed at the same time as mine, shaped out of disparate petty chieftains and made whole.

The messenger's evident unhappiness makes me worry, and beside me, my stepmother shuffles unhappily, for all that the girls were not her flesh and blood. We've discussed the matter at length, both assuring the other that all would be well even though we weren't convinced.

Finally, having drunk his fill and eaten a hasty mouthful of bread, the man steps hesitantly forward and begins to speak.

'My lord King Athelstan of the English and overlord of the island of Britain, I bring word from Henry, king of the East Franks. He's pleased to inform you that Otto, his son and heir, has married one of your sisters in a grand ceremony.'

'That's excellent news,' I speak into the sudden silence, for all within the hall are listening to the words of the messenger. 'And which of my sisters is destined to be a queen?' I query, watching the messenger's face with interest.

'Eadgyth, my lord king,' he stutters, and beside me, Eadgifu stands less tense, pleased that one of the girls was accorded the opportunity of marriage. It would have been a great dishonour if Otto had rejected both of my sisters.

'And what of my other sister, Ælfgifu? Is she travelling home now?' I look behind him, almost expecting her to be there. It seems that, after all, I have a stepsister who still requires a husband.

And this is where the messenger won't meet my eye, and I glance at my stepmother warily, praying that she's not perished on this journey. I might have too many sisters, but I wouldn't wish any of them dead. And yet the roads and seaways can be dangerous places.

'It was Lady Eadgyth's wish, and Lord Otto's, that she remains with them, a source of comfort and a friendly face from home,' the man finally spits out. I relax my tense posture. This was not an unexpected development and, provided the East Frankish king looks after my sister, as I would have done within my court, I'm happy that she's found a new home.

'And is she happy to remain? I wouldn't like to think that she's being held against her wishes.'

The messenger's face clears at my calm acceptance of his words. I consider what terrible rumours are circulating about me throughout the lands over the sea. I have no temper. Perhaps my sisters have filled the poor man's head full of false tales. I would chastise them if they were here. The messenger has carried his task with more trepidation than excitement.

'Oh yes, my lord king,' he exhales, 'most pleased.'

'Then that's also excellent news. Now, if you wouldn't mind, could you please talk in more privacy to my stepmother about how my sisters fare? She's keen to know everything about them.'

Almost falling over himself with relief, the messenger looks to my stepmother, who nods her thanks, and then regally walks towards him. They'll find a more intimate setting to discuss what she needs to know.

I settle back in my chair to think about the implications of this far-from-unexpected development. I now have one less sister to worry about, provided she either marries into a noble Frankish family or remains as a companion for Eadgyth. I'm pleased for her and for myself. This family of mine is huge, with tendrils reaching across the lands across the sea. My nephews will be kings, and my nieces will marry well. My grandfather would be pleased with our wide range, as am I.

Only then Edwin enters the hall, and my mood sours immediately. He's still a constant thorn in my side and one I'd much rather not have to contend with. I've not seen him for some months, while he's remained at his own estates, but it's the witan, and he'll come, as he always does, to glare at all those who refuse to rise against me at his whim.

He's an unwelcome guest, but I have other guests who are also coming, and they're far more welcome. For the last two years, I've worked hard to cultivate the kings of the smaller kingdoms of the Welsh. Not an easy thing to do when I was forced to exact such a high price from Idwal and Owain after they initially refused to accept me as their overlord four years ago. But I've done it, and they'll visit my witan, as Hywel, Idwal and Owain did two years ago, and present themselves before me, and all the men and women of my kingdom will see that I'm the king of more than just the English.

Along with Hywel and Idwal, I'm also expecting to see Morgan ap Owain, king of Gwent, son of Owain, dead this last year, and it's to be hoped that Owain of Strathclyde will also attend. I've expended some time and effort on enticing Owain of Strathclyde to my cause. It'll amuse me if I can undermine Constantin of the Scots on the borders of his land. His arrogance still chaffs. Not one word of apology did I receive from him when I invited him to my witan three years ago, and barely a word since. He sends his tithes and ignores everything else I do. Even his son rarely hears from his father. Hopefully, and if Owain of Strathclyde arrives, Constantin will see that my alliance is not optional.

Morgan ap Owain is a similar character to his father before him. He didn't wish to continue the alliance forged at Hereford, but I left him with little choice. The treaty was not signed to last only the lifespan of a man. It was signed in perpetuity. It's taken my messengers some time to convince him of that fact, and this will be my first opportunity to meet him in person.

I'd also like to see Ealdred of Bamburgh, but news reaches me that he's ill, sick, and worn out with the worry and stress of governing his kingdom. I don't know if the rumours are correct, but certainly, little of import has reached me from his kingdom for some time, in fact, not since Ealdorman Guthrum ventured to Bamburgh. It's to be hoped that if he should ail and die, his son and successor will be more open to my plans for the future and less under the thumb of Constantin of the Scots.

I should very much like to isolate Constantin. He's an ancient man, as old as my father would have been had he still lived and not worn himself out with too many women and too many battles and his scheming ways.

Edwin stumbles into my musings, and I glare at him, but he raises only an insolent eyebrow and belches his feisty breath into my face.

'Brother,' he exhales, and I curb my irritation. He uses our familial connection when he most wishes to annoy me and ignores it when he thinks he should be king in my place. 'I hear our sister is happily wed, and the other bitch is staying behind as some ealdorman's whore.'

His tone is accusatory and insulting all at the same time. When the embassy came, he begged me to let him leave with his sisters and pleaded with me to let him marry the beautiful girl amongst the entourage. I refused on both counts. There was no chance that I was going to allow Edwin to be rewarded for his treasonous activities against my rule. I would have sent him to be a husband somewhere else, but not where his presence would have upset the fraught negotiations still taking place.

Even now, a month does not go by that I don't hear murmurs that Edwin plans to set sail for lands across the Narrow Sea. I only wish he would go now, perish, perhaps in a shipping accident, drown his worthless body in the salty tang of the sea. It would be no different to the way he lives, drowning in mead and the best, and often the worst, of the wines.

'Don't speak of your sisters in such a way,' I admonish quietly, noticing with relief that no ire can be detected in my voice, no matter Edwin's accusatory nature.

'You approve of your unmarried sister living amongst those barbarians?' he tries again.

'They're our ancestors, as you well know, no more barbarian than me. I'd have said you and I, but I don't know what you are,' I say a little provocatively; only, for the first time in years, Edwin laughs at my attempts at rancour.

'Well, well, big brother, I see that you're not all quite as sweet as you portray yourself. I'm impressed to hear some barb to your voice.'

'Edwin, it is, as ever, my only intention to amuse you.'

Now he laughs out loud, and I watch him with narrowed eyes. What is this? What new trick has he devised in his drunken stupor?

'Brother, I'm bored and wretched. I've decided to outlaw all drink from my house and live a faithful and chaste life. If I succeed,' and here he pauses and takes a deep breath, as though he's trying to believe his words as he says them, 'will you allow me back into the family?'

I'm amazed at his words. I'd no inkling whatsoever that he'd even considered changing in such a profound way. Not that I think he's capable of giving up his debauchery and drinking, but I cannot, in Christian conscience, detract from his plan. With only a moment of pause, I nod slowly.

'If you can stay sober for more than six months, with no hint of a rebellion or a woman in your life, then yes, I'll consider allowing you back into my more intimate circle of family and friends.'

His hooded eyes alight at the answer I give, and he reaches his arm out to clasp mine, a means of sealing the bond.

'Then Athelstan, my brother and my king, I'll see you in six months when I'm free from my vices.'

Without another word, he stumbles from my presence, and I watch him go with narrowed eyes. I'm uneasy; I see treachery everywhere for an excellent reason. I'll need to ensure that my servants in his household are even more vigilant than normal. It's clear to me that Edwin is busy plotting something, and this time he's put far more thought into it than ever before.

I summon Edmund to my side, his eyes watching the swaying back of Edwin as he ambles from my hall.

'He's planning something,' I murmur, barely opening my mouth as I speak.

'When isn't he?' Edmund asks sourly, his words mirroring those of his mother. Our stepbrother causes rancour amongst all his surviving stepbrothers and sisters. 'We must arrange for someone to attach themselves to his household and report back to you.' Again, these are Lady Eadgifu's words, for all Edmund speaks them, but I heed them all the same.

'Yes, I believe now is the time to do so. He informs me that he'll sober up and that he wants to become part of the family again.'

Edmund's eyebrows rise in surprise at the words, and I share his disbelief.

'My mother hears he's been entertaining men from the north,' Edmund offers. Perhaps it's for this reason that he came to find me.

'From the north of the English, or men from Constantin's lands?'

'Both,' Edmund answers ominously, and I look at him pensively. This is an unwelcome development.

'I'll send two men, or maybe a woman.' I reconsider and then speak again. 'A woman, yes, but also two men. A woman will instantly arouse his suspicions, but if she's married and with one of the men, he'll see it as a challenge before he considers anything else.' It feels strange to speak so openly to a youth of no more than ten winters, but Edmund has eyes, and he sees what happens at the royal court, as does his mother.

Edwin's departure will cause me no discomfort now that I know he'll be watched for any sign of treachery. All I can hope is that he leaves quickly, today if possible. My allies are on their way, and I want to make a good impression on all of them, and one not marred by Edwin's presence.

## 35

### 931, KING'S WORTHY, ENGLAND

*Prince Edmund, ætheling of the English*

The day passes without any difficulties. Athelstan seems content with the success of his witan, as is Hywel of the South Welsh and Idwal, Hywel's cousin. Morgan ap Owain of Gwent is a more recent ally, so I have yet to decide what I think about him, although he's an improvement on his father. Owain from Strathclyde is also in attendance, and I've not met him before. Now, they're being feted and feasted. With or without the tacit support of Constantin of the Scots, Athelstan sits as king above all others, and I marvel at all my older brother has accomplished.

I'm seated beside Owain of Strathclyde at the feast alongside my mother. She's here to ensure I don't misspeak as I'm tasked with entertaining a slightly nervous-looking Owain from Strathclyde. It's not that Owain's uncomfortable or shifty with his looks, but there's something that makes me feel all is not as Athelstan may have hoped.

My mother and I have discussed Owain at great length. She believes he's here at Constantin's command. Rumour has reached her that Owain met with Morgan and Idwal before arriving at King's Worthy. She warns me to be careful and to listen carefully. More and more, she allows me to converse with the visitors to Athelstan's court.

As always, the palace has been spectacularly decorated to my mother's exacting standards. Hywel and Athelstan have already announced that they'll be spending tomorrow morning examining some of Athelstan's newest relics and religious books. Both my brother and Hywel are avid collectors. I can appreciate the poignancy and legitimacy of the relics, but if I was in his place, which I hope not to be for many years, I don't think I'd enjoy spending quite as much time with the odd bone fragments he's amassed. Not that I say those words to him. It would be inappropriate if there were any perceived rift between us. I'd sooner spend my time with my friends and training to become a warrior. Of course, Athelstan no longer needs such training. He's made his name in battle, fighting for Mercia, and for England. I can only hope to do the same when I'm older.

The entertainers for the feast noisily work their way into place before our feasting table. They'll share epic tales from all of the kingdoms of our land, and then a scop from the Five Boroughs will recount stories from the culture of the Norse. I queried the wisdom of such a move with my mother.

'It's important to understand the motivation of men who've been enemies and who might be again,' she offered by way of an explanation. She's wise to the way warriors think, for all she's never fought a battle.

There are also other men and boys amongst the witan who don't stem from our island. Athelstan has long been foster father to Alain of Brittany and Louis of West Frankia, our exiled nephew. But Athelstan also welcomes priests and poets from the continent. As I glance around the bustling hall, I can't help but be struck by how many different languages flow around the wooden walls. The voices of those speaking in the tongue of the Norse, or Welsh or those from Frankia. Athelstan indeed presides over a multilingual and multinational witan.

Many of those he's named as ealdormen, or king's thegns, also speak with a slight tinge of an accent, some heralding from the Five Boroughs. I've met some of the men. What Ealdorman Scule, or as he prefers to be called, Jarl Scule, lacks on the top of his head, he makes up for with a huge beard and moustache. Inhwaer has enough hair on the top of his head for both men.

It's from these men that the scop has made his way to Athelstan, filled with tales and stories. The scop is aware of Athelstan's close link with the king of Denmark, through his fosterage of Hakon, the son of the Danish king. He's come to seek my brother's pleasure and to perform before such a culturally diverse audience.

Owain watches everything through narrowed eyes, his shoulders set and his mouth stretched in a thin, flat line. He's ill at ease and uncomfortable with everything he sees, although he tries to mask it.

'My lord Owain, do you have many visits from over the sea?' I enquire, thinking he'll be pleased to speak of something, anything, other than the delicious food or the weather, but instantly, I know I've erred as he chokes a response. I shift in my chair, hoping my mother hasn't noticed that I've upset one of the royal guests.

'Not too many, lord Edmund,' Owain stumbles, but I can't help thinking that he probably has a court filled with men from the Dublin Norse and the land of the Scots. 'We do often have visitors from the Outer Isles,' Owain continues.

'They travel entirely by ship or over land as well?' I ask, keen to extend the conversation.

'Entirely by ship. They're men who live and die by their ships. A strange mixture of the indigenous race that inhabited the islands and the Norsemen themselves. Much like on our island,' Owain offers, seemingly as an afterthought.

Instantly, I wonder what he means by such a comment. I realise that I shouldn't press the man further about his thoughts. After all, he's a king in his own right, unlike me. I'm merely the brother of a king, a much younger brother, although I'm an ætheling of England. I shouldn't presume to have Owain answer my every question and whimsical query. My mother would berate me for such impertinence. Instead, I must draw Owain into making conversation.

I determine to think about Owain's words some more. Owain may, after all, be a little more slippery than I expected. Certainly, Owain thinks about the people of the island of Britain more than I ever have.

After the meeting at Eamont, Athelstan went to great lengths to discover all he could about the men who'd met with him. The relationship between Constantin and Owain has given him the greatest pause for thought, and he's spoken of it openly to his ealdormen and even to me. He's made extra efforts to meet with Owain and have him as a close ally. I think, if he could, that Athelstan would entice Owain away from Constantin of the Scots. He's told me that he'd like a partner in the northern lands, as he doesn't have one. Ealdred of Bamburgh looks to the northern kingdom of the Scots, and Owain is currently allied too closely with Constantin.

'Do you trade with them then?' I ask Owain, keen to continue the conversation about the Outer Isles, or the Orkneys, as others name them.

'Yes, for precious stones and furs. They like our furs. Apparently, the Outer Isles are not rich in trees, and they don't have bears and wolves as we do. And yet, their islands are dark for half of each year, and then for the other half, the sun rarely sets.'

This is all news to me, and I find it fascinating, and can't stop myself from asking for more details.

'Then how do they sleep when the sun never sets?'

'They sleep when they think it's night-time and wake when they believe that it's daytime. I would find it confusing,' Owain confirms, and I laugh along with him. I'd find it confusing as well.

'Does that mean that in the winter, it's always dark?'

'I assume it must do. No wonder they're a strange race,' he jokes. Owain seems more relaxed now, and his eyes sweep the room with interest, taking in the many men and women invited to attend the king's feast.

'The king has many sisters,' Owain queries, a question for all that it sounds like a statement.

'We do, yes,' I reply, although I wonder why. It's not as though Owain will have forgotten I also share Athelstan's sisters. 'But four are now married,' I hastily continue, keen to cover my words of correction. 'One of our sisters is a widow, Queen Dowager Eadgifu of the West Franks.

Her husband died two years ago in captivity, and another four have decided to retire to nunneries and devote their lives to God.'

Owain glances at the table where the royal women sit with interest.

'Are any of them here today?' he asks, and I wonder what interest he has in our sisters. But as I still can't think of anything else to say to him, I point out my sister, who shares the name of my mother, Eadgifu, which confuses everyone. I'm not sure why. My sister, the Queen Dowager Eadgifu of West Frankia, is haughty and older than my mother.

My mother, also Queen Eadgifu, but of the Anglo-Saxons, is younger and dresses with less formality. She's more likely to have a ready smile on her face. My mother says I should be kinder to Queen Dowager Eadgifu, but she's often ill-tempered, unlike her son, Louis, who's another of my friends.

Owain is very intrigued by the youths who sit with the royal woman.

'They're your brothers?' he asks, and I nod and then explain.

'One of them is.' And I indicate Eadred, my younger brother, as he fidgets on his hard chair. He'd sooner be beside me, but my mother said he was too young, at only nine, to entertain one of the guests at the feast. He must sit with his stepsister and stepbrother. 'The other two boys are Louis, my cousin, the son of Queen Dowager Eadgifu and her dead husband, Charles III, and Hakon, the son of the Danish king, my foster brother.'

'So, King Athelstan fosters others' children but has no children to call his own.'

'Yes, King Athelstan has decided not to marry. I think my father left him with enough sisters and brothers to contend with without adding to his familial obligations.' I say the words lightly. My father is a stranger to me. I have no memory of him. None at all. But this is how my mother and Athelstan have explained the situation to me. I assume Owain must know who Edwin is, for he doesn't ask about him. Edwin sits beside Queen Dowager Eadgifu, drinking sparingly, which surprises me. I thought he was to leave before the feast, but it seems he didn't accomplish that.

'Your father married three times, I hear,' Owain smirks. 'He was either an unwise man or one who liked women too well.' I think he forgets how young I am when he speaks in such a way. Not that I don't understand all the same, because I do.

'I think the latter, but I could be wrong,' I reply, not enjoying the turn of the conversation. I might not have known my father, but I struggle to hear him spoken about in such a flippant way.

'Three different women,' Owain muses, 'he was happy to cause discontent in his home if he had three different women to please at the same time.'

I want to point out that my father didn't marry all three women simultaneously, but I don't. It's entirely possible that Owain is trying to upset me, knowing only too well that my father's chequered history is a bone of contention within the kingdom. Luckily, the scop has taken his place in the centre of the hall, beside the roaring fire, and as I settle in to watch and listen, I notice that it's Owain who now looks unhappy. I wonder why as the words of the scop wash over me.

I think the scop adds something new to his usual repertoire as the evening wears on, but I could be wrong.

# 36

## 931, KING'S WORTHY, ENGLAND

*Owain, king of Strathclyde*

A bead of sweat forms on my lip as I sit and listen to the great scop at work. He uses words to conjure images within his rapt audience's minds, take them to long-ago battles and the times of our ancestors, and have us all believing we, too, are taking part in the story.

He's a wonder and a great man.

He's also King Constantin's pet and his being here makes me uneasy, squashed as I am between the king's brother and his stepmother. The vigour of the youthful Edmund is sobering to my advancing years. I feel as though he knows every thought going through my mind and what I'm thinking even before I do.

I fear Edmund means to trip me with his questions, and I must consider every word I say while at the same time appearing as though my responses are flippant and casually given. As though they're the truth. My head is pounding, and fear makes me regret the multitude of good food, wine and mead that I've consumed.

And then, to top it all, the talented scop approaches the king and begins to recite tales of the Welsh. He speaks of a long-ago mythical king who will one day return and unite our lands, and then, into the thick of it, he launches into his scop song, only a scop song constructed on Constantin's orders. A scop song I've heard before and wish I didn't know. I try not to hear the words, but they crash into my mind.

> *And after peace, commotion everywhere,*
> *Brave, mighty men, in battle tumult.*
> *Swift to attack, stubborn in defence.*
> *Warriors will scatter the interlopers as far as Cait*
> *The Welsh and the men of Dublin, the Scots and the Norsemen,*
> *Those of Cornwall and Strathclyde will reconcile as one.*
> *Kings and nobles will subdue the interlopers, drive them into exile*
> *Bring an end to the dominion, and make them food for the wild beasts.*
> *There will be no return for the tribes of the Saxons.*

I gasp with shock at the arrogant accounting, looking around frantically to see if the great English king is aware of the huge dishonour being shown to him here. He appears oblivious, thinking it no more than an extension of the tales of that same mythical king the scop first mentioned. He doesn't know that this is King Constantin's attempt to undermine him. It is Constantin's call to arms for all of the people of this island who don't think of themselves as English. I catch sight of Constantin's son, sitting with a number of the king's ealdormen, and I see his good humour waver. Does he know of the scop song? Does he suspect his father's involvement? I've not had time to speak to him yet. I also had no instructions to inform him of Constantin's plan.

Neither did I know the scop would be here. Constantin sent instructions that I was to meet with the kings of the Welsh and inform them of the scop's actions. I wasn't to say that Constantin had anything to do with the scop song but to let them know that there was a subversive working to undermine the vision of Athelstan's united island. I was only to mention a few words, drop a few hints of the tales I'd heard, and see how they reacted. Nothing more. But Constantin, or his scop, or both, have placed me in an unenviable situation. I know this scop song, I've learnt it almost word for word, and yes, I approve of it. But not here, not before the bloody English king.

I notice that Idwal and Morgan ap Owain cast barely veiled looks of disbelief my way, amazed at the scop's brazenness. I wonder if they think I should speak out, decry the man and what he's doing. But I can't. King Constantin has played me for a fool, but I'll not undermine him and put an end to his schemes. After all, his ploys keep him away from my court and allow me to rule as I wish. King Athelstan is a blessing to me.

When the scop has finished the final verses of his tale, he swiftly moves to another scop song of our ancient kings, and I feel my frantically beating heart start to slow a little. At my side, Edmund has a fixed expression on his face, almost as though he's trying to look as though he listens to the words, even though he doesn't. Or, it could be that he's deciphered the meaning behind the tale.

'I've not heard that particular one before,' he murmurs when the applause has died away.

'I think it's an ancient version of the story. Perhaps that's why it sounds so strange to your ears.'

'You might be right. These scops seem to have an unlimited store of stories. It's always good to hear something new, though.'

I laugh a little nervously and agree with Edmund. And then, and only then, do I risk a glance at Athelstan's face. He looks intrigued and not a little confused. At his side, Hywel's eagerly talking to him, no doubt of his much-mentioned travels, but Athelstan has his eyes firmly fixed on the scop.

I shudder with fear. This has been too bold a move on behalf of Constantin.

The eyes of Idwal and Morgan ap Owain also bore into my body, and I know I'll need to offer them some explanation. Only I don't know what to say. I'm not known for my ability to think quickly. I like to take my time to consider the options, knowing that when I've made a decision, that will be the decision I stick with. This attempt to decipher Constantin's moves when I don't know what they are is making my head pound in time with my heart.

I reach for my drink, noticing that my hand shakes a little. Cold fluid splashes equally into my mouth and down the front of my tunic. Edmund's face turns even more quizzical, and I desperately try to think of some way to have his attention diverted away from me.

I could do with some air, perhaps a visit to relieve myself, anything to get out of the suddenly too hot room and from under the gaze of everyone there.

Abruptly, I stand, and so too does Edmund, a frown of worry on his forehead.

'I need a little air, a little time to myself,' I offer, and he smiles and waves his hand to show he agrees. My steps are as unsteady as my hand, but with the scop gone from his place, I walk as nonchalantly as I can from the hall. Edmund remains in his seat with one of my servants escorting me.

The outside air is cool and damp on my sweat-stained face. My servant looks at me in surprise when I make no move to visit the shithouse.

'I just feel a little ill,' I say to the man, and he nods in understanding. He's my servant, a man I've known and trusted nearly all my life. Only, he doesn't know about the poem and the scop. Both of these developments have been kept from him, more to protect him than me, for I'd much prefer to have someone with whom to share my worries.

From inside the palace, the level of conversation picks up as they all take the opportunity to move around and converse with others now that the more formal meal and entertainment are over. I'm pleased. It'll be far easier to make an early departure from the feast now and spend some time considering all that has passed here.

Only then Idwal approaches me, accompanied by Morgan ap Owain, and I realise that they've come to seek me out. Abruptly, I tell my servant to return inside, that I'll be well for a few moments while I converse with Morgan and Idwal.

They both mark the man's passing and then hedge me in, one in front and one behind. It's Idwal who does the talking.

'Was that it?' he hisses, his words twisting as anger seethes through his barely open mouth.

'Was what it?' I hiss back, trying to play the innocent even though I know it won't work.

'The scop, did he happen to add the subversive song you mentioned into his set pieces?'

'I don't know,' I try again, desperate to avoid a confrontation.

'I think you do,' Morgan ap Owain says from behind, his voice a bored growl of annoyance.

'I've only heard rumours and snippets,' I say, pleading in my voice.

'I don't believe you,' Idwal says, his words getting angrier. 'And neither does Morgan. So, tell me, and Morgan, why you'd go to all the trouble of discussing your secret little song and then have it presented before the bloody English king before we've taken the time to consider the wisdom of such an act.'

I know it's useless to continue to argue, but I have little choice.

'Which song do you mean? I thought I recognised them all.'

'Don't be such an arse,' Morgan barks in my ear. 'Although if I must make it clearer to you, the song where the peoples of our land are listed one by one and the downfall of the English king is discussed.'

'I don't think I heard that one,' I mutter, looking at the ground to ignore the fierce glow in Idwal's eyes.

'Fine,' he responds, anger making his words spit from his mouth, 'have it your way and deny all knowledge, but I suggest you tell Constantin that we're not happy at being played for fools.'

And with that, they both turn away, their annoyance evident in their sharp steps and straight backs.

Damn bloody Constantin. Why have me speak to them about it if he was just going to flaunt it in their faces? It makes no sense to me, and now I'm angry that I'm being used as a blunt tool in his power games, and I'm helpless to act. Damn them all. I can't wait to get home and never visit with the English king again, and if possible, never see Constantin again either.

So resolved, I turn and make my way back inside. It's the turn of the man from the lands of the Norwegian king now, he's a poet in the true tradition of the Norse, and I know that when he speaks, I'll be able to relax and listen to his rich voice, even though I won't understand the words. He's visited my court before, and I like him, for all that he's a funny rat of a man with no discernible Norse heritage in his bearing. His hair is dark black, his eyes a hooded grey, and he has no muscles apart from those that work his jaw. I doubt he truly is a Norse man, but no one else has ever commented, and I've long kept my thoughts to myself.

Today he has a new tale to tell, and for once, and despite my anger and upset with earlier events, I find myself drawn to the man's words, my head leaning in my hands as I rest my elbows on the table. No one moves; few dare breathe as he tells of men and women going to start a new life in a new land far to the north of here. Again, I've heard tales and rumours of this 'Iceland', but I've never been entirely sure that they were true. The way the poet speaks and the story he recounts makes me believe, finally, that men and women have merely taken all that they can carry in their wooden ships and gone to start a new life in a new world.

I envy them for their bloody freedom.

The next day, I'm in the stables readying my horse for the hunt which King Athelstan has organised for that day, when I hear someone approach behind.

'My lord king.' I turn, startled to be addressed by a man who looks suspiciously like King Athelstan of the English, but, most assuredly, is not. 'I'm Edwin, the stepbrother of the king,' Edwin sways alarmingly, clearly having partaken of too much wine even at this time of the morning.

'My lord?' I know the phrase is a question, but I'm unsure how to address the king's stepbrother. All know that their relationship is difficult and strained.

'Yes, I am a lord, thank you,' Edwin drawls. Somehow, he's managed to catch me unawares, and more importantly, alone, in the stables at King's Worthy. I would sooner have nothing to do with Edwin. I've not been warned against him, but I've detected that he's no ally in the English court.

'A little bird tells me that we have you to thank for last night's rousing tale from the scop.' Immediately, I feel a bead of sweat trickle down my back. I thought no one had noticed the words other than the Welsh kings. Perhaps that's not the case after all. I wonder who the 'little bird' was. It could have been Idwal or Morgan, or even Constantin's son, Alpin.

'My, my lord,' I stutter and then pull myself together. I'm a king, and he's not. 'I don't know what you're talking about,' I offer belligerently. 'I don't know the scop.'

Edwin's eyes gleam at my words, and he suddenly seems very alert.

'Perhaps, my lord King Owain. All the same, I would let you know that I understood the words. Perhaps, this man, whom you don't know, could add another verse to his song. Something about the true Saxons rising up against the pretensions of a man who thinks to be the king of the English? Maybe?' Edwin's words are suddenly sharp, and I realise his veneer of inebriation might just be that.

'Well, if I had anything to do with it, perhaps I could have helped you. But I didn't, and so I can't.' I turn to move aside, to be away from Edwin and his smirking scorn.

'Then perhaps I should inform my lord king, my brother, of the intent behind those words. I'm sure he'd be keen to know that King Constantin of the Scots and King Owain of Strathclyde have set a scop to sow discord amongst the Welsh kingdoms.'

Now I pause, turning to glower at the English bastard. How has he, of everyone here, worked out Constantin's plot? All that I've heard of Edwin paints him as little more than a fool and not one with even half a thought in his head. I'd heard that Edwin was to leave the king's court, but he was at the feast last night, and now he's here and means to cause me trouble, and not just his brother, the king.

'I don't believe there's any need to do that,' I capitulate. 'Not, of course, that King Constantin had anything to do with the words of the scop, but I'm sure I can inform him of your... request, shall we call it?' I'm thinking quickly. I doubt that King Constantin wants to be an ally of Edwin, but neither will he wish his plan to fall away to nothing quite so soon.

'Then if you could do that and send word of it, I can keep my counsel, for now,' Edwin smirks, and I watch him walk away, loathing everything about him and the bloody English king, as well as sodding Constantin. I'd like to see him at King Athelstan's court, handling the slimy filth that is Edwin.

'My lord king.' As though summoned by thinking about him, King Athelstan strides into the stable, dressed for the hunt, and I incline my head to him.

'Apologies, my lord king. I'm ready now,' I inform him, leading my horse clear of the wooden structure. I peer around, convinced that the king will see Edwin skulking in the shadows, but Edwin is nowhere to be seen. How he's managed that, I've no idea, but I must get word to Constantin that his plan may fail before it's truly begun if he doesn't buy Edwin's collusion by adding more words to the poem.

## 37

### 932, THE KINGDOM OF THE SCOTS

*Constantin, king of the Scots*

I hoped to never see this man again, but I've been forced to have the scop brought before me. He does so fearfully, barely standing upright now that he's dismounted, and yet I don't wish to berate him. Perhaps, I consider, arranging to meet him in such a strange location, windswept and far from any habitation, was bound to make him wary.

'My lord king.' The scop bows, his wild hair almost horizontal with the force of the wind. It's bloody cold. I admit that as I wrap my cloak around my body.

'My good man.' I find a smile on my face and beckon him closer. 'You do good work on my behalf,' I offer, trying to put him at ease.

'I'm glad you're pleased, my lord king.' The fear doesn't leave his face. In fact, his eyes are wild. Perhaps, I shouldn't have had Aed, one of my sons, hunt down the man when he was alone and vulnerable, and bring him here under armed guard. But it's too late for such second thoughts now.

'I'm most pleased, yes, but I'd like you to do something else for me, add a few little extras to your scop song. Let's say, something more about the English kingdom fracturing, perhaps something about the old kingdoms reasserting themselves, Mercia and Wessex, with someone to lead each of those kingdoms.' The man's lips slowly widen into a grin, and he nods along.

'Yes, my lord king. Yes. Yes. A little extra, just to make sure the point is entirely understood about the English king.'

'Indeed. It would help me and my fellow Scots no end, as well as the Welsh, of course.'

And now a sly smile replaces his one of understanding, but I speak first.

'More coin, to recompense you for the additional travel and danger, my good man.' Aed hovers in the near distance, his men milling around, ready to return the poet from wherever they found him. Ildulb, though, is at my side, a hand on his weapons belt, but from inside his cloak, he pulls forth a bag bulging with coin, a collection of Athelstan's currency and also some of Hywel's, with a sprinkling of some more exotic specimens, brought in by the traders and the Norse.

My scop takes the bag, almost stumbling with the weight of it, and bows once more, licking his lips.

'And I'm to continue, as I do, spreading the scop song wherever I go?'

'Yes, don't stop. The many Welsh kingdoms and even the lands of the Five Boroughs will be keen to hear what you have to say. And, of course, you must never mention my involvement in any of this.' I keep smiling, but should I find it necessary in the future, I'll have no compunction about having him silenced.

He nods his head frantically, his knuckles white, where he holds the sack of coins too tightly.

'You have my silence, other than when I must speak.' The scop bows once more, and I find a smile playing on my lips. It's taken me some time to organise this meeting. Occasionally, I've feared that Edwin, Athelstan's stepbrother, might just inform his brother of his suspicions. No matter how many times I convinced myself that he wouldn't, the anxiety remained. Now that I've met the scop, I can be reassured that Edwin has got what he demanded from Owain when they met in England. Provided he's as patient as I am, all will be well.

If the Welsh kingdoms rise up against their kings' closeness to the English king, then that will serve my purpose, but it'll be even more satisfying if Athelstan loses more than just his imperium over the Welsh. Should he lose his kingship as well, then all the coin I've spent on these words will have been well worth it.

The scop hastily leaves my side, the coins clinking with his steps. Ildulb and I watch as Aed assists the man in mounting up and then heading south, back towards the borderlands once more. Only when the sound of the horses' hooves has faded away does he speak.

'Do you truly think it's worth the cost?' Ildulb questions. It's far from the first time we've had this discussion. He would sooner I spent the coin having Alpin returned to the kingdom of the Scots, but Alpin, now that he's at the English king's court, is important to me for what he sees on a day-to-day basis. He will know, before I do, what effect the scop song is having on Athelstan's kingship.

'It's cheaper than riding to war to reassert the independence of the kingdom of the Scots, and likely to be just as effective. Words, Ildulb, are important. King Athelstan knows that only too well. Why else has he named himself the king of the English? He could be the king of the Saxons, but no, such a title would remind everyone of Mercia and Wessex, Northumbria and Kent. By naming himself as English he gives everyone a new identity, a new way of being united. It's that, as much as anything else, that must be undermined. And if those words flow from the mouth of a seemingly innocuous scop, then all the better.'

I shiver into my cloak, as Ildulb nods. I think he understands my intentions. It's not as though he doesn't comprehend that's what's happened in the kingdom of the Scots. We were once a collection of smaller kingdoms, but now, united, we are stronger.

'A pity we can't use words to rid ourselves of bloody Mael Coluim,' Ildulb mutters darkly, calling for our horses to be brought. It's bloody cold, and the threat of rain from the low-hanging cloud is impossible to ignore. Ildulb helps me mount and, huddled inside our cloaks, we ride for home. I encourage my horse to ride faster and faster, grinning with delight, despite the drumming rain, while Ildulb and his son attempt to catch me. It's good to know that, despite everything, I can still beat my son at some things.

## 38

### AUGUST 932, KENT, ENGLAND

*Hywel, king of the South Welsh*

I greet Athelstan warmly, as normal. I never tire of spending time with him and visiting his court. I'd like it if he visited mine, but I know that would give the wrong impression. King Athelstan is the master over every kingdom on this island. As such, I must come to his court and bow before him, so that all can see I'm obedient to his wishes.

I'm accompanied by my cousin Idwal, Morgan ap Owain and Gwriad. Between us, we represent almost every tribe from the Welsh lands. Athelstan has accomplished a real accord with us. We all smile and laugh and pay our tithes gladly. I'm amazed and awed both. I honestly didn't think that an outsider could unite us, and yet, he has. Not since my grandfather's day have our people been so unified in thoughts and deeds. I fear it'll not last. There are rumours and rumblings that not everyone is as happy as we kings believe.

My sons and men bring me details of the whispers they hear, and I, too, put them to King Athelstan, as I should as his subordinate, but they worry me. The rumours speak of a united land of all the Welsh, and also of an England in tatters, with its English ruler dead, and a resurgence of the Saxon kingdoms of Wessex, Mercia, the kingdom of the East Angles and even Northumbria. I think the story is nothing more than a tale to tell children before they sleep, but many are listening and planning. Our people have long thought that the English were the interlopers, that they stole our lands and pushed us to the inhospitable places behind the current border when they first invaded hundreds of years ago, where the hills are good for little but sheep and the farming land sparse and difficult to manage.

As I watch Athelstan and his brother, I think the English are capable of anything, but I have concerns about these rumours. Once more, I believe that it's a tale for children, not one for adults. And yet, I glimpse the smirking expression on the face of a man who strongly resembles King Athelstan, and I know it's Edwin, his useless brother. Edwin is a man keen to make mischief for the king.

For now, I push my fears aside. The king won't want to see my glum face or hear my concerns. We've come together to celebrate and feast, for the summer has been good, the harvests huge, and Constantin of the Scots and Owain of Strathclyde have been quiet on their borders. If this is what peace can be like, then I'll gladly embrace Athelstan and offer him my thanks. I want my people to thrive, and my land to flourish, and peace is needed for that. I want to be remembered with the same affection that my grandfather's name occasions. I want to be as great as Rhodri. I want my people to have law and order and coin.

The coin is what currently drives me, and Athelstan has informed me that I can make use of his moneyers and my precious metals to make coins for my people. This trip is to watch the work in progress, see how the gifted moneyers strike the coins that people use to live their lives. With a coinage system, the people of Deheubarth will rise in prosperity, be as powerful as the English, and I, well, I'll have my image struck on the coin, and then I'll be remembered for eternity.

The thought brings a smile to my face. Away from my lands and worries, this is a time to relax a little, enjoy being with other men as powerful as I and who, one day, will die, and then I can have their land as well.

The future is bright and full of possibilities. If these bloody rumours about the English and the Welsh would just vanish, my life would be much simpler, my future much easier to determine, but, as always, I trust in my God, and I know that as I do his work, he too does mine. And yet, again, I catch sight of Edwin, lounging in the king's hall. I believed he'd been sent from King Athelstan's presence, restricted to the book land he holds, and unable to do more than that. And yet Edwin is no longer as isolated as he once was. There are men sitting with him, their wives as well, and I don't miss that King Athelstan, and his stepmother, Lady Eadgifu, occasionally share a concerned look and that every time laughter erupts from the collection of adherents, they look to see what's happening. Edwin has, somehow, won his way back into the king's favour, even if Athelstan is uneasy about it.

I believed King Athelstan was assured in his position. I understood that he'd won over all the ealdormen and Danish jarls to his side. But what if he hasn't? There's been no war since Athelstan became king, not really. Affairs in York following Lord Sihtric's death were really more of a skirmish when King Athelstan faced Lord Gothfrith, and since then, no one has been forced to defend their kingdom or their home. Without such war, how will men be rewarded? How will they earn wealth and advancement?

And Edwin concerns me. He seems altogether too confident for a man who has no chance of wearing the crown of the king of the English.

I consider the rumours I've heard all over again. When they speak of the Saxon kingdoms, as opposed to the English kingdom, is this concerned with Edwin, and not Athelstan? Does Edwin, despite every evidence to the contrary, think himself capable of making Athelstan king only of the Mercians?

I shake my head, trying to dismiss my growing sense of unease. I must think that King Athelstan is aware of these problems, that he thinks them unimportant and no real threat, for King Athelstan is my ally, and without him, and no matter events in Dublin Norse, my kingdom would soon become vulnerable should he no longer be the king of the English.

## 39

## 932, WINCHESTER, ENGLAND

*Eadgifu, the lady of Wessex*

'My lord king.' I curtsey deeply before him, head lowered.

'There's no need to do that when we're alone,' King Athelstan repeats once more, a faint smile on his lips but a complaint in his voice.

I stand and meet his eyes, seeing before me so much of his father. I never loved King Edward. I never had any reason to. But perhaps if I'd been wed to the son and not the father, that would have been different.

'Have you also come to speak to me about rumours and whispers?' he asks, leaning back in his chair.

'I have, yes, but not in relation to those outside England's boundaries.'

Athelstan sighs heavily and looks away. 'Edwin,' he announces, and it's not even a question.

'Edwin,' I confirm, settling myself in the chair in front of the desk he has in his small space, from where he rules much of England while at Winchester.

'I try to consider how I would behave, had our positions been reversed, but I just don't see that I would have undermined his kingship and put the lives of so many people at stake.'

I nod. I know that Athelstan is too magnanimous in his dealings with his brother. I can't see that Edward would have allowed all that Edwin does to go unpunished, but Athelstan is not his father. He's made that clear on many previous occasions.

'He was banished from court for over a year,' Athelstan comments. 'And then he swore to stop drinking and become a part of this family once more.'

'It's made no difference, despite his promises to stop drinking and whoring, I don't believe that he's done either of those things,' I retort. I'm prepared to have this argument with Athelstan. Something must be done to curb Edwin. 'He still has those who support him.'

'But Bishop Frithestan of Winchester is dead. I understood he was his main supporter.'

'He was, but now Edwin has others, and not many of them are actually English. And, Athelstan, you must know that some would happily see you fail, and those who would see it aren't English.'

Now he fixes me with his deep eyes, assessing my words.

'He makes alliances with what, the Scots? The men of Strathclyde?'

'The Welsh?' I conclude.

'King Hywel would tell me.' Athelstan counters, assured of that man's allegiance.

'King Hywel does not know. Hywel is your firm ally. None would deny that.'

'But Edwin's watched?'

'He is, yes, but there are always opportunities for him to cause trouble.'

'What would you have me do?' Athelstan stands and paces in the small space behind his desk. This is most unlike him. Athelstan is a man of reasoned decisions. This problem of his brother is too big for him to solve alone.

'He must be married off to someone in Frankia, perhaps West Frankia, where war will be most likely to claim his life.'

Athelstan rounds on me. 'You can't mean that?' he demands, and yet

I detect something else in his voice. Perhaps a wistfulness that it could all be so simple.

'Edwin means to undermine your kingship. He means to fracture this kingdom that your grandfather, your father, your aunt and uncle and you have worked so hard to unite. Men and women have lost their lives in doing so. You must weigh up one life against so many others.' I don't speak angrily but rather frankly. The problem of Edwin is an emotional one for Athelstan. He hopes, time and time again, that Edwin will conform, that he'll become the brother he should be, just as my sons are becoming. But Edwin is a lost cause, and Athelstan must understand that.

'No one wants him,' Athelstan finally admits, his hands tightly gripping the back of his chair. 'My cousin, Count Adelolf of Flanders, has tried to find him a wife, as has Count Hugh, but it's come to nothing. Edwin is known as a drunkard throughout East and West Frankia. And all know that he has no true standing at my court other than as the king's brother.'

'Then perhaps an alliance with King Harald.'

'What, you would have me send him to Denmark?' Athelstan startles at the statement.

'Better perhaps if it were to this Iceland,' I counter. Edwin needs to be far distant from England, Athelstan, and the future I foresee for my sons.

'I'll have the guard around him tightened and have him sent back to his estates,' Athelstan murmurs after a silence has fallen between us. Perhaps he thinks there's no merit to sending him to Iceland. I do have a great deal of sympathy for Athelstan. In the matter of all of his sisters, he's done well. It's unfortunate that Queen Dowager Eadgifu of West Frankia married a man who couldn't hold his kingdom against his mighty subjects, but Eadgyth and Eadhild have fared much better in their marriages, as has Ælfgifu, who has found a husband and married, it's said, for love. She no longer lives at the court of the East Frankish king. And, of course, my daughter, and three of her sisters are either nuns or live inside a nunnery. My sons adore their stepbrother. Edmund and Eadred are both too young to consider rising up against Athelstan's kingship, but they wouldn't do it. There's no need. I wouldn't allow it. And so, Athelstan is left with the problem of Edwin, and Edwin is a huge problem. If he ever gets himself in the right position, he could become an obstacle for Athelstan. While most now support Athelstan within England, there are many who don't outside it. And Edwin is an easy target – the disgruntled brother of the king.

I stand. I've said what I came to say.

'Thank you,' Athelstan offers, surprising me.

'You would thank me for bringing such problems to you?'

'I would thank you for not being afraid to speak your mind to me. All kings must have people who can be honest, as well as sycophantic.'

'And all kings must sometimes make decisions that go against everything they believe,' I counter, and leave before he can deny those words. There's a reckoning coming for Edwin. At the moment, there's only Athelstan who doesn't realise that.

## 40

### 933, WINCHESTER, ENGLAND

*Athelstan, king of the English*

'Brother.' I eye Edwin easily. He does seem to have made some effort to sober up since our previous meeting. He doesn't sway as much as in the past. And he looks well. There's colour to his cheeks, and his eyes are bright and alert. Perhaps Lady Eadgifu was wrong last year. Maybe my brother has stopped drinking, as he promised.

Together, away from the prying eyes of the men and women of the witan, I welcome him back. But not quite enough that I move to embrace him. Not yet. I'll see how far his remorse takes him. He played me for a fool last year, only to beg to return to the royal court, and renew his attempts at plotting against me. This time, I hope to see him entirely changed.

'My lord king.' Edwin bows his head before me, and I see the shimmer of candlelight on his blond hair. It is, I confess, starting to thin on the crown of his head. Edwin names me as his king willingly. That might be the first time that I've ever known him to do so. Usually, he insists on naming me his brother.

'Sit. Wine? Water?' I ask, gesturing to the jugs before me.

'Water,' Edwin replies, without so much as a thought, although he doesn't sit. Perhaps, after all, he is entirely changed, as he seems to be. My spies in his household have told me differing accounts. I hope he is. I've been warned, repeatedly, of Edwin's attempts to destabilise my rule. I've tried my best to ignore them and think the best of him. But, I'm well aware that my stepbrother is my weakness. I seek to find something in him that others don't. I was beginning to fear it didn't exist, but his request for water gives me hope.

'It is good to see you,' and I find I mean those words. Edmund and Eadred are also good company, but Edwin is closer in age to me. I think we would share much in common if Edwin just allowed it.

'It is, yes, I've learned much from my second time away,' Edwin offers. I stay standing as he does. I don't wish to sit while he stands. And now I hover awkwardly, the seat of my chair pressing into my legs.

Edwin takes the goblet of water from me, but he doesn't drink from it, preferring instead to place it precariously on the side of my cluttered worktable. There are charters needing my attention, and also an open text recounting the life's work of Saint Cuthbert of Lindisfarne. Hastily, I spring forwards, keen to move the drinking goblet before the water can damage the charters or the sacred written text should it topple over. Inwardly, I curse. I had hoped that Edwin knew the value of such works, but perhaps I should seek no more than his sobriety and apology at this initial meeting.

Hands on the thick book, the cover decorated with priceless jewels, the text flashing green and golden beneath the light of the candles, I detect Edwin coming closer to me. From my peripheral vision, I sense a change in him. He's suddenly too alert, and I turn, keeping the book in my hand as I do so.

The shimmer of a bladed edge absorbs my attention, the smirk on Edwin's face assuring me that he isn't changed at all. Indeed, he means to kill me. The damn bastard.

'Don't,' I manage to utter, only the blade is closer, closer, and I have nothing but the holy book recounting the story of Saint Cuthbert to protect myself with. And I use it.

The book is thick, bound in leather and jewels, and I manage to insert it between me and Edwin, knocking his arm aside. Although, I realise quickly, he still retains his hold on the seax.

'You bastard,' Edwin rages, and I suddenly appreciate that the brightness in his eyes isn't because he's become a better man. He's driven to it by rage and fury, directed only at me.

Quickly, I reach out, using the book as a shield, wishing I had a seax to hand, as Edwin lunges towards me, the knife too close, too bright, until I manage to knock it aside, but only by opening a cut along my right arm. The seax clatters to the wooden floor, turning end over end until it stops, the blade within easy reach of Edwin and his grasping foot.

'Don't,' I urge once more, wincing at the sharpness of the bite of metal into my skin. At that moment, I can't recall the last time I took such a wound. But it's not my first wound, and it certainly won't be my last.

'You need to die,' Edwin growls, spittle flying from his mouth as he bends, but I finally recover my senses, using my foot to kick him over so that he falls sideways onto his back, hand groping for the blade.

'Guards,' I manage to lift my voice loud enough to shout. It's a strange cry, one not heard in my hall before. 'Guards,' I bellow once more, straddling Edwin and gripping his right hand so that he can't reach for the seax. Beneath me, his build is slim, and he lacks the muscles in his thighs to surge upwards and dislodge me, and it doesn't matter anyway because while the cry might never have come before, I can hear my warriors coming, thundering steps over the wooden floorboards.

'You bastard.' Edwin spits into my face once more, his chest heaving as heavily as mine. The door opens, Ealdorman Guthrum standing there, his seax to hand, or at least someone's seax, for he should not be wearing one in my presence. The shocked eyes of three of my guards peer inside as well.

'I'll deal with him,' Ealdorman Guthrum growls, standing above us both, the seax already at Edwin's throat so quickly that I only realise it's there when Edwin stills suddenly.

'Do it,' Edwin urges, but I shake my head.

'No. It must be done correctly,' I urge my ealdorman.

'Must it?' the ealdorman questions quickly, menacingly.

'Yes. It must.' My three warriors have hold of Edwin's hands and feet, ensuring he can't escape, and I stand, trying not to shake, thinking that now, I will have to offer my thanks to the sainted Cuthbert for saving my life. Perhaps a miracle, after all.

'Get him out of my sight. But he's not to be injured,' I call to my warriors, but the warning is too late as Ealdorman Guthrum punches him so hard Edwin's eyes roll in his head.

'Apologies, my lord king.' Ealdorman Guthrum bows to me, but it lacks all sincerity. I shake my head and then, with Edwin gone from my sight, reach over and grip his arm tightly.

'Thank you, my friend,' I offer.

'I'm only sorry it came to this,' is the ealdorman's response. I can't help but think he's right. I should never have let it come to this. I was warned, time and time again. Edwin is my weakness, and others must see it as well. I will have to make a difficult decision, but it is time to face my weakness. Edwin doesn't deserve the title of my brother.

## 41

### 933, WINCHESTER, ENGLAND

*Prince Edmund, ætheling of the English*

A stunned hush fills the king's hall. Edwin wobbles from side to side, so drunk that he can't even sit straight, let alone walk. I don't know how he's found mead and ale to drink. I heard my brother command that Edwin be kept in strict confinement.

My brother, King Athelstan, sits regally on the raised dais, giving the appearance that Edwin hasn't upset him at all. Unlike the rest of us. The whispered conversations taking place are manifest and shocked. Beside me, my mother's eyes are focused on Edwin, not Athelstan, and I feel as though my chest is too tight to breathe deeply. Everyone in that hall watches Edwin while Ealdorman Ælfstan, and his brother, Athelstan, newly named as the ealdorman of the East Angles, stand, ready to intervene if needed. Ealdorman Guthrum is also on his feet, his hand resting where his weapons belt nestles around his waist.

The rumours of Edwin's attempts to undermine his stepbrother by calling on the neighbouring kings to support him in overthrowing Athelstan are well known. There's talk that he had an agreement with

Constantin of the Scots to let him become king of Wessex should Athelstan die. Of what would happen to Mercia, the kingdom of the East Angles, the Danish Five Boroughs, and the kingdom of York, there was no certainty, but I can well imagine Constantin of the Scots claiming them as his own to rule.

But, despite those rumours, I didn't think Edwin capable of trying to murder his brother so that he could be king in his place. But the proof is incontrovertible. I can hardly think of it, but Edwin's intention was to make amends to his stepbrother and, in that moment of time between them, slip a blade through Athelstan's neck. Now, Athelstan sits, regal, with little to show for the attack but a cut on his right arm. When Edwin launched his attack, in the king's private room, with no one around to protect him but himself, Athelstan was alert enough to stop it.

King Athelstan has assured me that he wouldn't have been able to do it without the aid of Saint Cuthbert. I would dismiss his words as exaggeration, but I saw the book discarded on the table. I saw the damage to its cover. No one reading the book would have been able to do such damage.

Edwin's so drunk that he can barely speak, and still, he tries to. Whoever has disobeyed the king and given Edwin drink will face his wrath, I'm sure of it.

'My lord King Athelstan,' Edwin slurs, attempting to bend his knee. Instead, he falls sideways onto the wooden floorboards with a heavy crash before scrambling to right himself. The noise is too similar to rats in the harvest barns.

'Keep your thoughts from your face,' my mother whispers urgently to me and my brother, and I try to do as she says. I know that while most watch Edwin, there will be some with their keen gaze on me.

'My dear brother, Edwin,' Athelstan replies, his tone severe. He won't be changed from his decision, and Edwin surely knows it and yet is prepared to make even more of a spectacle of himself.

'I've come to make amends for my hasty words and actions,' Edwin slurs, oblivious to the king's simmering anger. Perhaps someone should step forward and inform Edwin that he has no hope of turning the king aside, but none are brave enough to stand between the king and his pathetic wreck of a stepbrother. And every time I try to, my mother's hand is firm on my arm, warning me and stopping me. I'm grateful she's here. I don't wish to do anything I'll regret at a later date. Some might dismiss it as a childhood mistake, but I know that the men and women of this court have long memories.

'Your words will have no impact on my judgement, but you're welcome to utter them all the same. An apology would be a good start,' Athelstan announces, forced, despite his better wishes, to speak to Edwin.

Edwin begins to chuckle, a long, evil sound, all of his remorse gone, somehow appearing sober in an instant. He stands tall, the resemblance between the two men impossible to ignore.

'I'll not apologise for failing to do something that should have been done to you at birth,' Edwin snaps, all his drunken stupor fallen away in the face of his intense anger. 'Father was too caught up in the idea of you being his firstborn son to think clearly. I'd not have made the same mistake, and nor would my mother.' The words occasion an intake of breath from everyone there. I can feel the tremor in my mother's hand. As much as I want to, I don't allow my gaze to turn towards Edwin's sisters, the Queen Dowager Eadgifu, and those who've chosen to live as nuns, summoned from Wilton nunnery, to witness Edwin's ultimate fate.

'Our father loved his children equally. He provided for all of us, and I've continued to do the same. He'd not have welcomed us turning on each other.' Athelstan's words are deceptively bland.

'He was blinded by his feelings for you,' Edwin roars.

And now it's Athelstan's turn to laugh mockingly, his angry face terrifying to behold. Athelstan never lets his emotions run away from him, but then, he's never been tested in such a way before.

'Our father had a strange way of showing his feelings towards me. Do you forget that he had me raised in the Mercian lands of our aunt, Lady Æthelflæd? Do you forget that he bequeathed the kingdom to your full brother and not me? Do you forget that it is I he sent into battle to fight his wars against the Norse? Do you forget how he cast aside my mother to make way for yours?'

I've never heard Athelstan speak in this way. Never before has he criticised our father or shown his unhappiness at the way he was sent to war when the rest of my father's children were pampered in the safety of the Wessex heartlands. Even now, my brother, my king, surprises me.

'And you think that was a punishment?' Edwin shouts, his anger as bright as Athelstan's. 'You, he allowed to fight and train and live away from the confines of the bloody royal court. You, he gave as much freedom as he could, and you, he spared from the politics of this bloody snake-infested witan.' A hiss of fury greets those words, and not just from my mother's mouth.

Abruptly, Athelstan shuts his mouth. It's obvious to me that Athelstan's not considered it in such a way before. Such festering rage between the two men. I can hardly call them my brothers at this moment. It's as though I know neither of them. My mother's grip is so tight that I fear she'll leave a bruise. How it must pain her to hear her husband spoken about in such a way. And yet, I find this interaction intriguing. I didn't know my father. I have no memories of him.

'And I, brother king, I was to live my life in your shadow, always. You didn't hear *our* father praise you at each festival and gathering of the ealdormen; you didn't hear how he relished *your* prowess with the sword and *your* understanding of the politics of the Viking kingdom of York and the Boroughs of the Danish. Oh no, you were too busy playing the abandoned child in a more loving home than I've ever known. Just as your mother was replaced, so was mine.' Edwin's finger stabs into his chest to accentuate those words, his words almost a howl.

I feel my mother stiffen beside me, and now it's my turn to hold her arm and stop her from any rash actions. Edwin has always been resentful, but with the herd of children my father sired, it's no surprise. It seems to me that Athelstan and Edwin are more alike than either would like to admit.

'And through all that, everyone knew that you'd be the king one day. You. You might have to share it with your brother, but Mercia would be yours, as our grandfather, King Alfred, determined. Only then my bloody brother died, and you got it all. And you didn't even once think of sharing it out and giving to me what our father denied,' Edwin shrieks like a startled pig.

'You'd done nothing to prepare yourself for kingship. Nothing.' Athelstan's words have lost their searing rage, and yet, the hurt is impossible to deny. Perhaps, I consider, Athelstan should have made this audience with his condemned brother more private. No one needed to witness this, not even Athelstan's greatest allies.

'Because bloody father wouldn't let me,' Edwin screams, angry beyond coherence. His chest heaves, and I hear his laboured breathing in the sudden silence.

When Athelstan speaks, his words are soft, his face bleached of colour. 'Brother, if you think to make me have any sympathy for you, you're an even bigger fool than I thought possible. You can't try to kill me and expect me to forgive you. You have to die.' The words thrum with conviction.

'So, I'm to be punished for our father's sins?' Edwin taunts, his face twisted.

'No, you're to be punished for attempting to attack your anointed king. That we're related makes no difference to me. I'll let you choose the way you die if you prefer that.'

Edwin suddenly slumps to the floor as though dead already, and Athelstan's angular face softens. He stands and walks towards Edwin as men all around reach for their weapons, far less confident of Edwin than Athelstan. The king waves their weapons away with an imperious hand, which only serves to highlight the cut on his arm. Even now, he's far more trusting than anyone else in this room.

Athelstan drops to his knees before Edwin, unheeding his fine clothes as he reaches his arms out to either side and embraces Edwin's limp body. Now we can all see that Edwin is sobbing uncontrollably. His games might have passed the cold winters away from the royal court, but he knows he was wrong to conspire against his king, who happens to be his brother. Edwin tried to kill the king, and he must be punished.

Athelstan whispers something to Edwin, his lips close to Edwin's ears, an exchange too quiet for anyone else to hear. But I watch as Edwin's body regains its substance, he sits up, and then stands with the aid of Athelstan and appears to grow in stature. And then Edwin's eyes sweep the room, taking in all who watch him before resting his gaze on me, my mother's hand firm on my shoulder once more.

It's like looking into my own eyes. They're the same deep ocean blue, crowned by the same thick eyebrows, the same firm chin, although his is covered by a long beard. His mouth is like mine, a pale pink with straight white teeth underneath it. He must be thinking as I do. Our positions could so easily be reversed.

But then Edwin's eyes continue their arc, resting instead on his sister's, the Dowager Queen Eadgifu of the West Franks. Her face shows no sympathy, only disgust for Edwin's current condition and for the dishonour he's brought to the family. Edwin's swaying on his feet, Athelstan supporting him, his movements so much more fluid than Edwin's. But Edwin stands as a king should do, or as the case will be, standing as a would-be king should, one who's only himself to blame for his execution on the order of his brother.

I don't envy Athelstan or Edwin. I'm glad to be so much younger than them that, as of yet, I've little part to play in Athelstan's royal court. But I'm learning all the time. I turn to my brother, Eadred, two years younger than me. His eyes are wild in his still chubby face, and I tug on his arm and smile at him. He grins in return, his eyes so similar to Edwin's, but I know we'll never allow such discord to form between us.

## 42

### LATE 933, BAMBURGH

*King Ealdred of the independent kingdom of Bamburgh*

My breath rattles in my throat, and I turn to cough aside the foulness of my mouth, a bowl held beneath my chin to catch my spit and mucus. I meet the gleaming eyes of my wife, Hild, but she turns away as though she can't bear to look at the ruin I've become. Not that she's one to talk. She looks older than her years, aged by her disappointment. But my son is here, and he holds my hand, sitting beside me as I lie down, covered in every fur imaginable, although I'm still cold, close to the hearth, concern on his face. He's little more than a boy in my eyes. Some might call Ealdwulf a man, but I don't. And yet, he will become one, and soon.

'You must win the support of King Constantin,' I urge my son, not recognising the crackle of my voice. He nods, but I don't believe he understands what I'm saying to him. I've never thought him lacking wit, and yet, I'm not sure he truly perceives my words. I don't believe he thinks I'll actually die, but I know I will. The healers know it as well.

'King Constantin,' I urge him, trying to squeeze his hand to affirm my wish, but my hands are too weak.

'The Scots king,' my son surprises me by saying. 'I'll seek him out, ask for his support,' he confirms.

'But don't give into his demands for land. Don't give him a hide of Bamburgh's kingdom. He'll have to be content with coins and the knowledge that he'll upset Athelstan by assisting you.'

'What of York?' my son whispers. I wince at that. There should be no fear in his voice when he speaks of York. The fact there is assures me that I've not taught him as well as I should have done. I didn't expect to die yet. I should have had years to teach him more and to win him the support of my warriors and nobles.

I consider my wife again. Has she done this to me? Not content with me still being alive, has she stolen my life by some foul means? The healers assure me that's not the case, and yet I have my suspicions all the same. We've not been kind to one another for years. Perhaps, after all, she's won the battle to outlive me.

I should have remarried. I should have taken King Athelstan up on his offer of a sister to wed. If a new wife from the House of Wessex hadn't given me more children, she would at least have ruled with the confidence that her other sisters have exhibited in East and West Frankia. I've been a fool, and I fear my family's hold on Bamburgh might be at an end. King Constantin is my only hope.

'Affairs in York mustn't be allowed to interfere in Bamburgh,' I urge my son forcefully, only to subside into a fit of coughing. Damn this illness. Damn my foolishness in thinking I had time yet to ensure my son would rule after me. When I'm recovered, I realise that my son has left the room, no doubt to ride his horse or drink and play games of chance. I confess I'm disappointed in him.

I turn to the healer, who watches me with more concern on his face than anyone else within my household shows.

'Bring me King Constantin's messenger,' I urge him. He nods and turns aside, only to face me once more.

'You mustn't overtask yourself,' he cautions. 'You can only talk for so long.'

I listen to his footsteps as he walks away and turn my mind to what I need King Constantin to know. He's the only hope for Bamburgh to retain its independence. Perhaps, I consider, he might send one of his sons to assist my son. Maybe, even though it burns, it would be better for Bamburgh to become absorbed into the kingdom of the Scots rather than that of the English. The thought horrifies me, and yet, English or Scots? What would I sooner do for my people?

'My lord king.' The messenger bows before me, his eyes taking in the state of me. I find a smile for my lips.

'Sit beside me. I should sooner not look up,' I advise him.

'Of course, my lord king.' I give him time to sit. His face is pink from the heat of my hall, and his breath is rich with the scent of wine and good food. He would be a handsome man if not for his bent nose.

'I am dying,' I begin, grateful not to cough at the end of the sentence.

'My lord?' he tries to interject. I purse my lips.

'I know it's the truth,' I hastily reply. 'I know it will not be long. The relic that King Athelstan sent me before the peace accord has brought me nothing but misery. I think it's not even King Oswald's holy arm.'

He remains silent, and I remember his name is Denewulf.

'You must journey to King Constantin, tell him of my coming death, and urge him to assist my son in claiming and holding the kingdom, for if he doesn't, King Athelstan will take it for himself. He will think of it as uniting the Saxons under his kingship, but it must not happen.' My voice quivers and a fit of coughing consumes me. I wave aside the ministrations of my healer and focus only on Denewulf. He doesn't move. He doesn't even seem concerned by my feeble body.

'You must stress the urgency of my request,' I finally manage to gasp out. Denewulf nods, and yet he doesn't seem to be imbued with the imperativeness of my demands to him, and then he speaks.

'I came here to tell you of the death of King Athelstan's brother, Edwin. He was drowned in the Narrow Sea, but King Constantin says he was plotting against the English king, and was discovered. He says the English king killed his brother.'

I startle at such news. I believed King Athelstan a man of honour. A man of his God, as he so often said. But it seems he's as mortal as the rest of us, and as like to lash out at those who threaten him. I don't believe that's good for the future of my kingdom.

'Then tell King Constantin that I thank him for sending such news but that my own death will not be long in coming.' He nods but still doesn't stand.

'Tell me, my lord king,' he finally says, my eyes opening as I'd forgotten he was beside me.

'Yes, what is it?' I growl. He should already be riding north.

'Why do you turn to King Constantin, and not to the English king? King Constantin cares nothing for you. He never has.' I narrow my eyes. What does Denewulf know that I don't? Is this a caution or little more than idle curiosity?

'King Constantin has been my ally for many years, as he was my father's ally before that.'

'And that makes him the best choice?' Denewulf shakes his head, preparing to stand. 'You would be better inviting the Norse into Bamburgh than Constantin.' Venom fills his words, and I want to call him back, ask why he says such a thing, but I'm coughing once more, and by the time I recover, I'm too tired to think of politics.

The Norse? Why would Denewulf think the Norse were better than allying with King Constantin? I consider as I fall into an uneasy sleep. Not, I realise, that it truly matters. I'll be dead soon enough, and then King Constantin will either assist my son or he won't. Either way, I will, sadly, be beyond caring.

## 43

### 28 MAY 934, WINCHESTER

*Athelstan, king of the English*

I take a moment, pause for a deep breath, and only then do I turn to meet the eyes of my ealdormen, bishops, the archbishop of Canterbury and those of my household warriors within the great hall. I eye them, sweeping my gaze from left to right, and then I nod, hand reaching for my warrior's belt where my weapons are ready and waiting, for all our battle is far distant from here.

'Welcome,' I begin, infusing my voice with warmth. 'Welcome, and my thanks for arriving so promptly. Tomorrow, we'll leave this place, riding or marching along the Portway to London, and from there, along Watling Street until it meets the Fosse Way while our ship men take the roads of the Norse men, the seaways. Our intention is clear. King Ealdred of Bamburgh is dead, and we'll claim his kingdom, for if we do not, Constantin of the Scots will sink his claws into it. We must hope, as I know we will, that we arrive before our enemy does.' A cheer greets my words, and I nod once more. I wasn't sure, until now, as to how many of my allies would join this venture. I was prepared for many to refuse to continue the English advance beyond the kingdom of York. But luckily, I don't believe, just from a quick glance, that many have opted to stay away. Perhaps, they all seek war booty. Men can become both poorer and richer thanks to war.

'And there are more to join with us at Nottingham. The Mercian ealdormen, and the Welsh kings as well,' I continue. News of King Ealdred's death was only received at Easter time. It's been a rush to gather together the resources I need to ensure two things: that Bamburgh becomes a part of England, and that, finally, King Constantin of the Scots bends the knee to me. His refusal to do so in the past has been a constant cause of discord between us. He's tried various ploys since the treaty at Eamont, eventually sending his son to my court, but now, he's lost one of his allies. And that loss is to be my gain.

I notice that servants walk amongst my warriors, and holy men, offering them ale or wine, whichever they prefer. The number of warriors here far exceeds the number who went north when I went to claim York on the death of Sihtric, but this time, I must travel further and further from my homeland. I know that it's imperative the might of the English king is shown to be so great, so vast, that none dare disobey me. I raise my own wine goblet, noting the flash of the shimmering metal as I do so. I hold my grin of triumph in place. Not only is Ealdred of Bamburgh dead, but so too is Gothfrith of the Dublin Norse, the man who thought he had a claim to York, which I quickly corrected. I don't lament his death. While he lived, it was impossible for the Norse to offer resistance to my control of York. Now that Gothfrith's dead, the power struggle within Dublin and Waterford will be savage between Gothfrith's sons and others who would think to rule there, most notably the displaced sons of Sihtric, my one-time brother by marriage. I can't see any Norse coming to counter my actions against Bamburgh for many years to come.

'To England,' I call, splashing fluid into my mouth as the actions are mirrored in the great hall. I turn and meet the eyes of Lady Eadgifu, and she inclines her head, a touch of colour in her cheeks, while before her Edmund stands proudly, his legs apart, making himself appear taller, wider, more filled with muscles than anyone would expect for a lad of only thirteen winters.

Beside him, Eadred looks mutinous at being left behind. I understand his fury towards me. I'd feel the same had I been overlooked. But Eadred is yet far too young. He is also my only surviving brother other than Edmund, following Edwin's execution for treason, the arrangement of which he determined should be to be cast, oarless, into the Narrow Sea in a boat that wouldn't survive the rolling waves. He is dead, his body washed up in Flanders. My cousin there saw to his burial. If something should befall me, or Edmund, on our journey north, then Eadred must be here to claim the kingship, continue the House of Wessex and ensure all that I've accomplished doesn't lay waste upon my death. That is imperative.

I also meet the eye of the Dowager Queen Eadgifu of the West Franks. She stands almost as proudly as her stepmother, young Louis and Eadred together, bemoaning their fate at being left behind. I incline my head towards her, a sign of the growing respect and accord between us. It's been a long time in coming. The death of Edwin last year has made it much easier to be friendly toward one another.

'To England,' another roars and I notice that it's Ealdorman Guthrum. He's keen to ride to war. I think, over the last few years, the continued peace has settled uneasily around him. Ealdorman Guthrum has lived for most of his life making war on our Norse enemies. The continued peace has, strangely, not appealed to him.

Not that I foresee that continuing. I know full well that Constantin of the Scots will think to assume control of Bamburgh. I can't allow that to happen. If need be, I'll ride roughshod through his kingdom and force him to his knees. It's about time he was subservient. It's about time Constantin realised that when he agreed to the peace accord of Eamont it was no empty promise, as he gave to my aunt and father. No, Eamont was meant to end all war, and it would have worked, if not for Constantin and his rampant ambitions.

## 44

### JUNE 934, HEREFORD, THE KINGDOM OF ENGLAND

*Hywel, king of the South Welsh*

I settle on my horse and wait for the arrival of the other kings, summoned by King Athelstan to join him on his foray north.

At my side, my son, Owain ap Hywel, is uneasy. He shouldn't be here. I ordered him to remain at St David's, but he's persisted in following me, even over the border with the English, and now he scowls into the brightness of the day. I'm tired of his arguments, and yet he persists, all the same.

He demands I don't ride to war with the English king. I inform him that I must. It's my duty as one of Athelstan's sworn allies. And anyway, as I tell him, I can't imagine that there'll be much fighting. King Constantin of the Scots will run over his border as soon as he sees the size of the English king's force. Constantin can't lay claim to half as many allies as Athelstan, and half of them will secretly be hoping for his death, and I don't just mean the allies of Mael Coluim. A long life, such as Constantin has enjoyed, is bound to bring a long list of enemies.

'I'll go in your place,' Owain ap Hywel informs me. I smile, head turned away so that he can't see it. My son is a great warrior, but he's not the king of the South Welsh, and it's the king of the South Welsh who must ride at Athelstan's side.

'You'll rule in my place alongside your brothers, and I'll return shortly. I won't be gone for long.'

Owain's face is still mutinous. He reminds me of when I found him fighting his brothers when he was a boy, with a sharpened blade to hand, not a blunt one. Then, it was as though I acted to purposefully embarrass him and not for his safety. It seems little has changed in the intervening two decades.

'Morgan ap Owain and Idwal will be here soon,' I inform my son. Morgan is the son of Owain who was so reluctant to ally with Athelstan seven years ago. While Morgan eventually renewed the alliance on becoming king of Gwent, I'm not sure he's any keener to be one of Athelstan's allies. He shares much with his father.

'Why should that concern me?' my son complains, fury in his eyes.

'I would sooner they didn't witness our family disagreement,' I inform him. And that's true, but equally, I don't want my son to be known to Morgan ap Owain and Idwal. They've never met, as far as I know, and I don't want them to meet now. It's better if my sons, and Idwal's sons, remain as strangers to one another. It will make it easier for my son to help me when I do move against Idwal. It will make it possible for my son to infiltrate Idwal's kingdom, when the time comes to forward my claim to Gwynedd.

My son sighs heavily and summons his guard to him.

'We ride for home,' he informs them, and I hear the gasps of unhappiness. Perhaps, after all, it was merely that these men wished to fight. Maybe they've grown weary from having no true enemy. I eye them and my son, and then I decide.

'I believe there will be problems, soon, from the Dublin Norse. With Gothfrith's death, there are many who'll look to make a name for themselves now, and I need you to be alert. Watch the waterways. Ensure all ships are checked at the harbours and that we have boats on hand should war erupt from the isle of the Manx. I'll not allow the Norse to attack our coastlines again.' Owain nods, a faint gleam in his eye, and then he leans towards me and grips my arm.

'Be safe, father,' he whispers. 'There's much that my brothers and I can't do, not yet. We need you, or bloody Idwal will come marching into Deheubarth, claiming it as his right.'

'Idwal isn't to be feared,' I assure my son, startled to hear the anxiety in his voice. 'Idwal is a pig-headed fool, and one day, he'll overreach himself, perhaps by allying with the wrong people. But I assure you, I'll return and soon. If I can travel all the way to Rome and back without mishap, then I can take a little journey north.'

I think this reassures my son, for he turns to face home, a more relaxed expression on his face as he follows the earlier path in reverse.

'I'll see you soon,' he calls to me, hurrying his horse to retrace the steps taken only that morning. In the distance, I can hear the clatter of hooves, and realise that Owain has left only just in time.

I turn and peer into the distance, considering who comes this way next. I imagine it'll be Idwal, for Morgan ap Owain has the least distance to travel and, as such, will have left latest. Idwal will have been on the road for a number of days already.

And indeed, from my position outside Hereford's walls, I sight the advance of Idwal and his warriors. Banners fly above the heads of Idwal's Welsh warriors, and I take a quick count, although my scout has already informed me that Idwal brings just over two hundred men to the English king's war. It's not a huge amount and not a small amount. I have three hundred men at my command. Morgan ap Owain, I imagine, will have fewer than Idwal. If he ever arrives.

While the men find places to take their ease, water their horses, and relieve themselves, Idwal directs his horse, a chestnut animal, gleaming with good health, towards me. Mounted, there's little difference between us other than the colour of our tunics and the grey beginning to thread its way through my hair.

'Hywel, well met,' Idwal calls to me, his voice warm with the welcome and not a little amusement. I consider what's happened to make him so cheerful. I've not seen him for two years. I notice, with some delight, the pattern of creases around his eyes. I'm not the only one who's getting old.

'Cousin Idwal, it's good to see you,' I reply. And it is. It means that Idwal is prepared to honour his alliance with Athelstan. It also means that my son's fears are less likely to come true. If Idwal is with the English king, it's just about impossible for him to attack my kingdom.

'And so, it seems, we're to ride to war,' Idwal smirks. 'Bloody Lord Ealdred, who styled himself king. He was bugger all use when he was alive, and now he's dead, he's even more useless.' Idwal's words are rich with derision. He never liked King Ealdred, even though he never met him. I can't say that I truly thought about King Ealdred. It's unfortunate that he's dead, but all men must die.

'He did hold out against Constantin and the Norse,' I feel compelled to point out, although I'm not defending King Ealdred. He really didn't accomplish a great deal in his life.

'He had a fortress inside which he could hide. I think we could all hold out against Constantin and the Norse if we had such walls and the natural defence of rocks and the sea.' Idwal is not to be dissuaded, and I realise I don't really want to defend Ealdred anyway.

'I hear we're going to be praying as well on our journey north,' Idwal resumes, his words mocking. Idwal's faith is lacking in comparison to mine and Athelstan's.

'Yes, the shrine of Saint Cuthbert, as I understand it.'

'And what do you think the king means to do with the lands on the west of this island? They call it Amounderness, don't they? I hear he's purchased the lot from one of Olaf Gothfrithson's enemies.'

I shake my head. I'm always amazed by how much Idwal knows about affairs that shouldn't concern him.

'I have no idea, but I'm sure King Athelstan will put it to good use.'

'I hear he means to gift it to the new archbishop of York, Wulfstan?' Again, Idwal knows a great deal. I consider whether he spends any of his time ruling Gwynedd or if he merely sits on his throne and beckons informants to whisper in his ears.

'I'm sure King Athelstan is merely enforcing his claim to York and building alliances with his actions,' I respond evenly. I know full well where this argument is going, and I'm also aware that Idwal misses the true meaning of Athelstan's intentions. During the reign of my father, a man was made king of Northumbria, and it was done with the connivance of the community at Chester Le Street who had possession of St Cuthbert's relics, as they still do.

'He tithes me and my people, and yet he gifts land to the bloody archbishopric,' Idwal exclaims, all mock anger.

'You know he's very devout,' I caution him, eyebrows high.

'I know he could do much better than give it to a bloody archbishop. How will the archbishop protect the people of those lands? Will he fight off the Norse who want it with words and prayers?'

I chuckle then. Idwal does make a fine point, and as with King Ealdred, I'm not here to defend Athelstan. I don't know how his mind works. I don't know all of his intentions. I was summoned to bring a war band and be prepared to meet my fellow Welsh kings at Hereford, and the majority of the English force at Nottingham. While I know about that which Idwal speaks, I've not asked too many questions of King Athelstan's messenger. I'll see Athelstan soon enough and speak with him directly.

Luckily, I'm saved from answering by the arrival of Morgan ap Owain. He rides a high-stepping mount while many of his men have animals that are clearly less keen on what's about to happen.

'My lord King Hywel, my lord King Idwal, what a fine day this is to ride to war.' Morgan's eyes alight with mischief and delight. I hope King Athelstan knows what he's doing by having all of his allies in one place at the same time. I really bloody do.

## 45

### 6 JUNE 934, NOTTINGHAM, ENGLAND

*Athelstan, cousin to the king, now the ealdorman of the East Angles*

'My lord king, the Welsh kings will be here before nightfall.' I bow before the king as he stands, overseeing the arrangements for the next part of this journey.

So far, we've travelled from Winchester along the Portway to London, and from there, along Watling Street until it met the Fosse Way and then to Nottingham. At Nottingham, we've paused, waiting for the remainder of the men to arrive.

Young Edmund stands to the side of Athelstan, eyes wide as he takes in everything happening around him. I'm not surprised. This is a huge military endeavour, and it's not yet complete. At Nottingham, the Welsh kings will join us. At York, yet more will meet the king's northern advances, while along the coastline, the king's fleet will merge with us at York as well.

The smell of horseshit, horse piss, and badly cooked pottage is rife in the air. Men and women, but mostly men, call one to another. Arguments have been settled with bloody fists amongst the fighting men and even by the king's order when that proved ineffectual.

I'm reminded of the battles I fought in and witnessed. When no older than Edmund is now, I rode beside my father, one of Mercia's ealdormen, and under the command of Lady Æthelflæd of the Mercians. A lot has changed since then, but the business of war isn't one of them.

'Good. We'll be assembled and ready to depart on time,' King Athelstan informs me, turning to survey the sight that surrounds us. Nottingham, once one of the Danish Five Boroughs, was returned to Mercian hands only during the reign of Athelstan's aunt. The voices that ripple from behind its walls are a mixture of English and Norse, and here the Danish jarls will join with Athelstan and proceed north alongside what feels like every mounted warrior in England. And any who own a sword, seax or war axe as well.

A formal feast has been arranged for tonight to take place outside Nottingham's walls and with the same pomp and ceremony that occurred at the treaty of Eamont. I'll stand at the side of the king, alongside my brother, Ealdorman Ælfstan. My two younger brothers are here as well, Eadric and Æthelwald. They're as keen to make a name for themselves fighting for England as any other man called upon to fight for their king.

'Cousin Athelstan, or should I say Ealdorman Athelstan?' My king calls me closer to his side, the rest of his men dismissed to obey his commands, whatever they might be. 'Tell me, how fares my cousin, Lady Ælfwynn?'

I smile at his question. He never forgets how much he owes my wife.

'She's well. Not long until the birth of our fourth child.' I smile at that. Our sons are good boys. There will soon be four children. The first three have been sons. I consider if this fourth one will also be a boy, and then I'll be the father of four sons, just as I'm one of four sons.

'Good, then you can concentrate on our current endeavour without too much worry?' King Athelstan persists, eyebrows raised. He doesn't mean it as a complaint. I think he hopes for reassurance as well.

'Yes, my lord king. I've been informed that she's done this many times before, and I'm to think nothing of it. She assures me all will be well, and I'm minded not to argue with her.'

King Athelstan chuckles at my wry words. 'She's a fine woman, and I'm pleased she keeps you in your place.' He continues to laugh, pulling me closer to him so that none can hear our conversation. 'Tell me, how are the Danish jarls? You and your brother have most to do with them, sharing land and borders as you do in Mercia and East Anglia.' When the Five Boroughs returned to the control of Mercia and then England when Athelstan became its king, the Danish were not ejected. Instead, the jarls, as they term an ealdorman, remained in place, provided they swore a commendatory oath to King Athelstan.

'They're good men, mostly. The rules of law here, for both those who are English and those who are Danes, are sometimes resented and sometimes not. Overall, men and women are content with things the way they are. Your coinage has been accepted by all. There are few who think to deal in hack silver these days.'

'Thank you,' King Athelstan confirms, holding my gaze. 'It pleases me to hear that. I've high hopes that this expedition will finally reunite the lands of all the Saxons into a complete whole. The kingdom of Bamburgh has long been a bastion in the far north, ruled by worthy Saxons, and I'm sure the people will welcome being reunited with their southern neighbours.'

'And what of King Constantin?' I probe.

'We'll attack the kingdom of the Scots, if that's the only way forward,' King Athelstan confirms. 'You'll fight for me, as you did outside York. Once more, you'll win glory on the battlefield, and I'll be forced to reward you for what you achieve.'

'You mean as Lady Ælfwynn demands?' I murmur, and King Athelstan grins once more.

'Yes, as your good lady wife, and my dear cousin, demands. Now come. We'll prepare to meet the Welsh kings and see which one of them has brought the best warriors. The Welsh, as you know, are feisty fighters. I'm pleased to know they'll be my allies and not my enemies. On this occasion.'

Together we stride towards the extremities of the camp, where men are preparing to welcome the latest additions to Athelstan's expedition north. Already, areas have been marked out for the horses and men to make camp for the night.

My brothers join me and the king, and together, with Athelstan's household warriors in close proximity, we listen to the distant echo of horses as they draw nearer. Sound swells as the banners of the Welsh kings come into focus. I smirk to see Idwal leading the other kings. Idwal never likes to be last to do anything any more, not after the terms imposed on him by King Athelstan at Hereford. He scans the area around him, and a slither of unease shivers down my spine. Idwal has the look of a man come to see what he can take for himself. Perhaps King Athelstan should have been warier of meeting here. Maybe it would have been more sensible to summon the Welsh kings to Eamont.

'My lord king.' Idwal is off his horse and on his knee before I can continue my thoughts. I hear my brother suppress a chuckle of amusement that, luckily, only seems to be audible to my hearing.

'King Idwal, you and your warriors are welcomed to Nottingham. I'm pleased to see you so well provisioned.' King Athelstan raises his voice so that as many as possible can hear. The bishops and archbishops have also hastened to join the king. There are, I imagine, almost as many men standing respectfully behind Athelstan as there are before him. Idwal's force isn't inconsiderable. It's just that Athelstan has many, many men joining him on his expedition north.

'We look forward to riding north with you, my lord king. I welcome the opportunity to see so much more of your kingdom.' If Idwal didn't speak with a smile on his face, I'd think there was a threat there. But Athelstan is too used to these Welsh kings.

'Well, you've seen the extent of my kingdom to the south, so why not the north as well?' Athelstan rejoins, gesturing for wine to be brought for Idwal and the men who flank him, one of which I know is his brother, Elisedd.

'Indeed, my lord king. And we continue north tomorrow?' Idwal queries, turning to survey the huge camping ground, where warriors, horses, servants and the inhabitants of Nottingham dash hither and thither, keen to complete tasks.

'We do, yes. A feast this evening. And then tomorrow, northwards. I see your men have been shown where to sleep for the night. Luckily, the weather is warm. I don't believe it'll rain, at least, not until we reach the borderlands of the York kingdom.'

'My lord king,' Idwal offers, wiping a swill of red wine from his lips. 'You should come to my kingdom if you wish to see real rain. There, it rains so hard you can't see your hand in front of your face.' His brother laughs at those words, and I offer a chuckle as well. Funny how we're talking about the weather when, really, it should be about our offensive.

'Here comes Hywel and Morgan ap Owain,' Edmund interjects. I startle. I'd not realised Edmund had joined us. I smile to see him, dressed as though we're about to attack our enemies, as opposed to meet our allies. But then, Edmund needs to make himself a reputation to rival that of his brother. He lacks Athelstan's confidence, and I feel some sympathy for him. It's not easy to live up to the expectations of your own family, and that must be even more difficult when your family is the ruling House of Wessex.

## 46

### 6 JUNE 934, NOTTINGHAM

*Hywel, king of the South Welsh*

The feast is a fine one, taken outdoors, on tables and stools set up by the English king's servants, as the evening slowly descends towards darkness.

We've been filled with fine wine and good food. Not fine food. That would be impossible when there are so many mouths to feed. Still, I can't see that anyone will complain. Better to eat food that doesn't block one's innards when embarking on a journey such as this one.

I'm sat between two of the Danish jarls, Scule and Inhwaer. I've met both men before, at Athelstan's court two years ago. They're what I would think of as typically Norse. While Scule is entirely bald, Inhwaer wears his hair in tight braids, and both have full beards and moustaches that cover much of their faces. They both smile and joke. For them, this journey north is nothing to fear.

'What do you know of King Constantin?' Scule asks me carefully. His Danish accent mangles some of the words, but I know what he means well enough. It's strange that his birth language was Danish and mine Welsh and that we must converse in English to understand one another.

'King Constantin is a stubborn old git,' I offer, a smirk on my lips. 'He doesn't wish to truly give his allegiance to Athelstan. He thought to add his name to the treaty at Eamont and never be called upon to do anything about it.' I'm not saying anything that these men don't know. But neither of them has met the king of the Scots. I'm unsurprised that they have questions about him.

'They say his son, Ildulb, is a lethal warrior.'

'And his heir, Mael Coluim, doesn't know the pointy end of a sword from its hilt.' Inhwaer laughs uproariously as he speaks. Both men have been drinking since long before I arrived, trying not to choke on the dust of bloody Idwal's warriors. I should have made sure that I led him from our night's rest and not allowed him the time to get ahead.

'I've not met Mael Coluim. Only Constantin.' I can't offer them more information, and although it does amuse me to hear him spoken about in such a way, I would sooner be speaking with King Athelstan and not the two Danish jarls. But King Athelstan is speaking to his archbishops. I almost pity him being hemmed in by both men. But I imagine there is truth to what Idwal told me about the king of the English trying to ensure he has the support of the archbishop of York as he ventures to Bamburgh. Archbishop Wulfstan is no doubt happy with the current status quo. I can't imagine he wants to upset that. But, well, King Athelstan has a mighty gift for him: the lands of Amounderness, once held by the Norse descendants of the men of the Great Heathen Army. And now, Athelstan's to gift as he needs to win the support he requires. And St Cuthbert's intervention when Edwin tried to kill his brother surely reveals that Athelstan is the saint's acknowledged successor in the far northern kingdom of Bamburgh.

I listen to the conversation between the two drunk men.

'I tell you, the scop had this tale of war and uprising to share with us. It was so stirring, my warriors cheered when he finished speaking. I almost thought he wanted to incite war between the Five Boroughs and King Athelstan, but my wife told me that the poet spoke of the Welsh and not the Norse.' Scule shrugs as he finishes speaking, while Inhwaer glowers at him, with all the focus of a man deep in his cups.

'I think I've heard it as well,' he slurs, his words coming out conjoined, so that it's hard to make sense of them. 'He was a tall fellow, long and straggling grey hair. He walked with a slight limp.' Inhwaer seems to recall the man very well.

'That's the fellow. He recited Beowulf and the Gododdin, and then he started on this other thing. I wish I could remember the words. I know that King Athelstan thinks highly of him. That was why I welcomed him into my hall.' Scule looks pleased that Inhwaer knows about whom he speaks.

'Well, if what my wife said was true, King Athelstan won't welcome the toerag into his hall again. Not unless he'd welcome war with the Welsh once more.' And then I feel the heat of both men's gaze, and I'm grateful when King Athelstan stands to address those within earshot. The number of men is so vast the feast stretches over at least a hide, and only the kings, ealdormen, jarls and holy men are actually close enough to hear anything.

'Welcome, one and all.' King Athelstan once more stands as a warrior before his host. His weapons belt remains prominent around his waist, although he's removed his byrnie. Neither, I notice, does he wear his crown or helm, but everyone there knows him as the king.

'I'm grateful to see so many of you here, today, united as one to ensure the Scots king stays firmly in his kingdom.' A murmur of approval echoes through the collection of men. 'This island has long been divided, Saxon against Norse, Norse against Welsh, and even Wessex warrior against Mercian warrior. This endeavour, this journey to the northern reaches of my kingdom, will ensure that peace will ring throughout this island for many long years to come. United, in one accord, we can drive back all those who think to fracture the peace of Britain.' Athelstan pauses, a determined expression on his face. In the fading daylight, he's illuminated by a handful of candles and little more. He does, I confess, look warlike and magnificent. With the number of warriors who ride at his side or behind him, I can't see that he won't be victorious in his determination to take back Bamburgh and ensuring

King Constantin of the Scots never crosses the border between the two kingdoms again.

Looking out across the mass of men and war equipment, hearing the nicker of horses, and smelling the remnants of meals that have been prepared for thousands of hungry bellies, I can only see that England, Athelstan's construct of the united Saxon people, will endure.

I genuinely don't see how it can fail. Equally, it fills me with firm resolve. This is what I want. I need to rebuild the kingdom that my grandfather built, of a united Wales from the Welsh kingdoms. And, because I know that it existed once, I also know that I can't build it only around myself. I must put in place the mechanisms needed for the kingship of Wales to survive beyond my life. I'll accomplish all that Athelstan has for the English, the men and women who once thought of themselves as Saxons, and I will go one better. I'll ensure that it endures. But first, first, I must ride to the northern reaches of Bamburgh and fight beside my overlord, Athelstan of the English. If my cousin, Idwal, should fall in battle, or even Morgan ap Owain, then that will allow me the perfect opportunity to claim their kingdoms as well.

I only hope that King Constantin of the Scots can mount an effective force against King Athelstan, or I fear, there'll be no real war, and I'll have to return to St David's and be patient once more.

## 47

### 934, CHESTER-LE-STREET, ENGLAND

*Prince Edmund, ætheling of the English*

I turn and glance behind me. I almost can't comprehend the line of men, horses and carts stretching out into the far distance. If I didn't know better, I'd think the stragglers were still at York, and not heading northwards along Dere Street to Chester-le-Street.

'Edmund.' My brother beckons me to his side, and I spur my fine mount onwards, keen to ride beside him. He smiles as he greets me. Athelstan is in jubilant mood. 'Not long now, and we'll stop for the night,' he informs me, eyes peering into the brightness of the day, as though the place he seeks might be obscured by the brightness of the sun.

'And what's here?' I find myself asking. So far, I've known about the places that we've stopped in, but Chester-le-Street, in the kingdom of Bamburgh, eludes me.

'It's the burial place of the holy Cuthbert,' my brother informs me, eyes gleaming with excitement.

'The saint?' I find myself grumbling, and he chuckles. My brother likes to talk about saints.

'I appreciate collecting saints' relics isn't for everyone,' he confirms. 'But they're a powerful weapon against your enemy. Our aunt knew that well. And, of course, Saint Cuthbert saved my life not that long ago.'

I nod, biting my lower lip, wishing I hadn't reminded Athelstan of Edwin's attack on him, or myself of Edwin's execution. He drowned in a ship with no oars, far out in the Narrow Sea. It was Edwin's choice to determine the means of his execution. I believe there must have been quicker ways for him to die than marooned in the middle of the Narrow Sea. His body is buried at Saint Bertin in West Frankia by one of our cousins, the Count of Flanders, or perhaps his brother, the Count of Bolougne. I can't keep the two of them straight in my mind.

Still, I'm keen to make my name as a warrior, not to take to my knees and pray for a man who's been dead for centuries, even if Athelstan does hold Saint Cuthbert in high regard for saving him from Edwin's blade.

Athelstan reaches over and grips my forearm. 'Edmund, listen, and I'll explain. It isn't all about praying, I assure you. Our religion is a justification for our kingship. Being anointed, and made as one with our God, ensures that the people we rule over see us as somehow different, perhaps less worldly. I'm not alone in taking advantage of being seen as devout. Our grandfather was a firm believer in our Lord God, but equally, he understood that a thriving religion was a benefit to him. My scribes, my bishops, even my archbishops, are men trained in the way of God, and their education assists me in ruling such a vast kingdom.'

'So, it's not all about incorrupt bodies and bits of thorn,' I offer, trying to understand, for all I find it next to impossible.

'No,' my brother laughs gently. 'It's not all about digging up the dead and gazing at their unchanged faces despite being dead for many long years. But, some of it is. We become holier by associating with people revered as holy, and whom others seek out for assistance through miracles. Many of these miracles are natural. Some, even I admit, are fantastical, or downright tedious. But the holy men, and women, understand the power of such belief. And, as a king, and as an ætheling, you would do well to learn the value of such devotion. And, on occasion, it might even save your life.'

'And so, we go to pray at Saint Cuthbert's tomb?' I query. I don't want to talk about those who've long been dead. I want to discuss our tactics against King Constantin. I want to be reassured that I'll blood my seax and sword.

'We do, yes, and while we're visiting, I'll offer gifts to the monks, and in years to come, those gifts will reassure my English subjects that their king isn't a distant entity far to the south. They'll know that I've visited here and prayed where they might pray.'

I sigh. It all sounds tedious, and once more, my brother chuckles. But there's nothing malicious in his laughter.

'My aunt, as you know, had the relics of Saint Oswald, a Northumbrian saint, moved from Bardney to Gloucester. She had those remains brought into Mercia from an area that was still very much under threat from the Norse. In doing so, she made a pact with the people of Northumbria. She adopted their saint and showed herself to be just like them. In returning one part of the saint to Bamburgh, I also showed myself to be a benign force, and a benevolent one. And by associating with Saint Cuthbert, a man revered by those who look to Bamburgh, I do the same.'

'But who really cares?' I sigh, and now Athelstan's eyes narrow slightly. But he holds his tongue and summons another to our side.

'Cousin Athelstan, my young brother would like to know more about Saint Oswald's relics,' he informs the other man, riding high on his chestnut-hued mount.

'Would he now?' Ealdorman Athelstan inclines his head respectfully, and falls silent, so that the sound of so many horses and carts on the move resounds in my ears. I shake my head. My brother talks of saints and bones, and yet he's at the fore of a vast force. Behind him stretch all of his ealdormen, his archbishops, bishops, the Welsh kings and all his household warriors. I can't put a number to the size of his force. It thrills me to appreciate just how powerful my brother is, and yet he wishes to speak to me of holy bones.

'Well, Prince Edmund, let me assure you, the translation of Saint

Oswald's bones was a powerful tool in Lady Æthelflæd's attempts to drive back the Norse and to conquer the Five Boroughs. Saint Oswald is a Northumbrian saint, and yet a Mercian lord and lady claimed him, and gained control of his reputation and legend. In doing so, Lady Æthelflæd showed the might of Mercia. And that is what King Athelstan will accomplish in coming to Chester-le-Street, to lay his gifts at the tomb of Saint Cuthbert, another saint of the north.'

I nod, biting my lip, a flicker of understanding trying to make itself heard. 'So, you claim the saints as your own, and the people associate that saint with the House of Wessex, and not just with their own kingdoms?' I speak slowly, still trying to determine if my interpretation is correct.

'Just about yes,' Ealdorman Athelstan confirms, a smile playing at the edges of his lips. Even I think Ealdorman Athelstan a handsome man. I can see why my cousin married him. One day, I'll be as tall as Ealdorman Athelstan, who overtops my brother. I might even have his warrior's build and stance. He's another who's forged a reputation fighting for Mercia. He's a warrior, as I wish to be.

'And, of course, it always helps to have the assistance of all the saints when riding to war,' my brother muses. He watches me carefully. 'Your mother will be praying for your safe return to Winchester. I'm sure she'd welcome you making an entreaty to the saint for your safe return and a victory for England.'

I'm beginning to realise that there's a lot more to this stop on the journey north than I thought there would be.

'And King Hywel shares your fascination with the sainted dead?' I query.

'As does King Constantin of the Scots,' my brother assures me, as though that in and of itself makes what we're going to do worthy of undertaking.

'Then, I'll bend my head and offer my words, and let us hope that Saint Cuthbert offers his benediction for those who mean to attack Bamburgh as opposed to defending it.'

As I speak, both men nod solemnly, and then Ealdorman Athelstan offers me a wry smile.

'You're learning very quickly, my lord.' He inclines his head once more as he speaks. 'You're blessed to have such as King Athelstan to learn from. Heed his lessons well, my lord.' And with that, Ealdorman Athelstan steers his horse away from my brother's side, and I notice a surprised smile sitting on my brother's lips. It seems that even kings sometimes need to hear some reassurance. I realise that, too, is a valuable lesson to be taught.

## 48

## 934, BAMBURGH, NORTHERN ENGLAND

*Cousin Athelstan of the English, now ealdorman of the East Angles*

I eye the building before me. I've heard a great deal about the fortress at Bamburgh. I'm not disappointed by it. It is indeed truly formidable with waves crashing against the steep sides of the embankment upon which it sits. The day is bright, the sea a welcome sight. As is the submission of the men and women who've poured from inside Bamburgh to bow before King Athelstan.

Reports of warriors further north have trickled back to us. Constantin has sent men into the kingdom of Bamburgh, but not many of them. There'll be no battle here.

'My lord Athelstan.' A messenger bows before me as I prepare to dismount. 'My lord king requests your presence.' Hastily, I dismount, and stride to where King Athelstan, and his brother, are standing before those submitting to his rule.

'My lord king?' I question, trying to determine why he needs me here. I need to ensure my men have somewhere to sleep for the night and also food to eat. I don't see that I'm truly needed to be with the king now.

'Ealdorman Athelstan' The king has become majestic in this place. All traces of our familiarity have bled away, and now he stands, regal and composed, Edmund at his side, trying to mirror his actions. I note the way he tries not to fidget and feel some sympathy for him. Edmund wants to become a warrior. All this politicking is painful for him. 'I would ask you to take command of Lady Hild, King Ealdred's wife.' I startle as the king points her out to me. She's dressed little better than one of the servants. In fact, I thought she was one of the servants.

'Very well, my lord king,' I reply quickly, trying to cover my surprise. And then the king beckons me closer.

'I've heard rumours that she's not of sound mind,' King Athelstan informs me quietly. 'I'd not believed them to be true, but alas, it seems that is the case. I think we should find her somewhere warm and safe and some reliable women to tend to her needs.'

'Of course, I understand,' I reply immediately, trying to decide whom that might be. Maybe, I should have her taken to my ealdordom of the East Angles. Perhaps, there, my wife might take pity on her and ensure she's tended to as a woman of her status should be. But that's not possible here, with a war host on the march.

'Archbishop Wulfstan might be able to aid you,' the king further offers. 'He should know of nunneries close by.'

'Very well, my lord king.' But it still doesn't solve the problem of how I'll get her away from her servants without humiliating her further.

'I'll help,' Prince Edmund offers, and he walks forward, and I'm aware of King Athelstan's warriors with hands on their weapons. A soft huff of annoyance from the king is the only sign of his unease. 'Come, my lady.' Edmund takes to his knees before her. All of the inhabitants of Bamburgh, and even those living in the nearby settlement, are on their knees before the king. They determined on submission as opposed to any form of resistance. I doubt that King Constantin will do the same.

Wild eyes, in a face streaked with filth and grief, meet Edmund's.

'My name's Edmund,' he offers. His words ripple and seem to intensify as they undulate in the wind. 'I'll take you to safety.' Edmund encourages her to stand, which she does unsteadily. There was once talk that King Ealdred needed a new wife. I can see now why those rumours started. I can smell her stink from here. I could be kind and say that grief has made a ruin of her, but I don't believe she's bathed since long before her husband's death.

Easily, almost as though she's a trusting child and not the lady of a formidable fortress, a bastion between the kingdom of the Scots and the English of York, Lady Hild stands and allows Edmund to lead her away. Belatedly, I hasten to follow the pair of them, while behind me, King Athelstan speaks to the people of Bamburgh, who will understand his words.

I want to stand and listen, see what the king offers these people, but I know well enough. They'll all keep their lives, provided they give up Lord Ealdwulf, the son of Lord Ealdred and his wife. He's not claimed Bamburgh for himself, but like his father, it's feared that he's called on King Constantin to assist him in keeping hold of Bamburgh.

Instead, I hasten to follow Prince Edmund, where he leads Lady Hild towards one of only two canvas tents erected so far. I don't think he wants the lady in his own tent, but I can't fault his kindness.

'My lord Edmund,' I call to him, and he turns, startled. 'I think we should go towards my own encampment,' I urge him, pointing to where I can see a canvas surging upwards, the ropes being tightened to keep it upright.

'I'll come with you.' He's quick to agree, and together we take the woman towards where I hope there'll soon be a fire and warm food. All the time, I try not to smell her clothes or to think of what there might be beneath the matt of grey hair that sits tangled around her face. I've not seen her face yet. I consider whether she's pretty or if the years sit heavily on her. Her son is a man grown, so she must be much older than I am.

'My son,' she startles me by saying when she has a bowl of warm pottage in her hand and one of my servants is gently trying to untangle her hair, something which Lady Hild seems to be unaware of. 'My son,' she repeats, her eyes unfocused, and I think she'll say nothing more, but then she does. 'He's gone north, to King Constantin. He says he'll return with a war host,' and then she lapses into silence, and I consider whether she meant to tell us this or if this merely slipped from her tongue by mistake. All the same, Edmund is quickly on his feet, and I know he runs to inform his brother that those fears of Constantin's intentions are correct.

The objective was to be war anyway, but now that we know where the heir of Bamburgh is, it'll be impossible to avert. Prince Edmund will get his chance to make a name for himself. I imagine he'll welcome that. It'll be far more exciting than praying before a box of bones.

## 49

## 934, DUNNOTTAR, THE KINGDOM OF THE SCOTS

*Constantin, king of the Scots*

My palace is in chaos. Messenger after messenger rushes in, most contradicting each other so that none truly know what's happening.

The only certainty is that King Athelstan of the bloody English is coming to the north of his kingdom. What else he might do, I'm yet unsure. I don't know whether to be outraged or incredulous. I could never have imagined that an English king would concern himself with events so far from the heart of his kingdom. In all honesty, I'd relied on him not doing so when King Ealdred sent me an urgent message that he was ill and close to death. Ealdred begged me to intervene for his son, Ealdwulf, and ensure he was able to succeed him, as he lacked the support of the men and women of the kingdom. I dithered and did little about it, the winter weather making it seem that I had all the time in the world to make a decision about what I'd do, and then, when summer came, Bamburgh was there for me to take. But still, I delayed. Whom should I send south? Should it be my son, or my heir, Mael Coluim? Should I support Ealdwulf or not? And now, it doesn't really matter.

Ealdred's son, Ealdwulf, is here, at my court, awaiting my decision still, or perhaps, as now seems probable, running away from Athelstan, for the English king is said to be at Bamburgh already. Ealdwulf arrived as soon as the weather made it possible to travel. He's lingered ever since, enjoying my hospitality and not seeming to mind that I've constantly delayed my decision with regard to the kingdom of Bamburgh.

King Athelstan's objective, my messengers inform me, is to come into my kingdom and punish me for daring to interfere in the matter of the final, independent Saxon kingdom. But I've done nothing. Yet. King Ealdred's son lacks the support his father had. He came scampering over the border to my kingdom even more quickly than Ealdred ever did. Now I glower at him. I can't help thinking that much of this is his fault. He should have been stronger. He should have been able to hold Bamburgh against the might of the English. Damn him for involving me in what must surely be a war against the bloody English king.

I thought King Athelstan might send the men of York north, perhaps under the command of the archbishop. That he might suggest a marriage alliance between either one of my sons, perhaps Alpin, still trapped at his court, and one of his sisters, or even between Ealdwulf of Bamburgh and one of his sisters. I'm sure Athelstan still has a few spare sisters he could marry to ensure peaceful relations continue between our kingdoms. But no. Athelstan has entirely overreacted to my perceived interference, gathering together the war bands of his ealdormen, the Danish jarls of the Five Boroughs, and even the Welsh kings who lick his boots to stop him from overrunning their kingdoms. And now they mean to make war on my kingdom. And for what? I haven't even sent men south. Well, I confess, that's not quite true. Some of my warriors are at Bamburgh, just to keep my interest there evident, but not enough to hold it against such a vast force which, my messenger informs me, Athelstan commands.

'You must raise a bigger war band to protect Bamburgh,' Mael Coluim demands, his face flushed with anger, which masks his fear that he might be about to lose his kingdom before he's even got his greasy hands on it.

'I have every intention of raising my warriors to form a bigger war band,' I growl, stressing the 'my'. Mael Coluim's not offered to raise his men. The pompous arse. In fact, he hasn't actually asked to be sent south. If I wasn't so sure that he meant to undermine me, I'd have commanded him to Bamburgh, and then he could have faced Athelstan's army. I might not have minded losing any chance of controlling Bamburgh provided Mael Coluim was killed in the fighting.

'And I'll raise mine as well,' Ildulb announces, glaring at Mael Coluim. There's no love lost between my eldest son and my heir, and there never will be. They both hope the other will drop dead before them, but while Mael Coluim wishes for my death as well, my son actively labours to keep me alive. He doesn't want to lose his position of power within the royal court.

I nod in thanks to him and stand abruptly for once, my aches and pains leaving me in the face of this crisis. It's warm in my hall, and I feel the need for some fresh air.

The men who support my kingship watch me with eyes that show fear, horror and anger. Not one of them has advised me to hold myself true to the alliance with the English. They've all been busily voicing their belief that I was right to keep myself at arm's length from the treaty forged at Eamont, and that the death of King Ealdred was a welcome opportunity at Bamburgh. That was until now. Now I know that their memories will be short and their comments vocal and widespread. I doubt many of them will offer to send their warriors to assist me.

'Do we know where they are?' I demand from no one in particular. Still, I glower at Ealdwulf. Of everyone here, he shows the least concern. But then, they say his mother is not of sound mind. Perhaps he isn't, either? Equally, he's gained nothing yet, and so has nothing to lose. Damn him.

'Yes, we do know where they are,' Ildulb replies. He's working hard to make some order out of the constant messages we're receiving from men who've rushed here with the dread news, including Denewulf. Every time I meet him, I'm forced to face afresh the knowledge that I hit him on that long-ago day. I know he hasn't forgotten it. Perhaps I should have made further amends to him or stopped using him as one of my messengers. I would hold out half a hope that he's fabricated his dire warnings of the coming war, but he's not the only one of my messengers to bring them to me.

'He's heading north from Bamburgh, along Dere Street. Well, the land army is there. We don't know where the ship army is.' This is another part of Athelstan's plan that astounds me. Why has he summoned as many of his men as possible? Was there truly a need for a ship, as well as a land army? Did he need the Welsh kings as well as the Danish jarls of the Five Boroughs? Would the warriors of York not have been enough? The fact that he brings his ships as well as his mounted warriors assures me that he intends to use his ship army to navigate over the rivers that might have protected us from him, the Forth and the Tay, should he make it into my kingdom. As such, he must be stopped.

The most important thing is to keep Athelstan from my lands, and if that's not possible, then I must mount a defensive attack, although where I'm unsure, perhaps here, at Dunnottar. This is a fine defensive structure. We should be able to keep Athelstan's army from infiltrating us. Although, well, I became king on the death of Mael Coluim's father, and he met his death at Dunnottar. Perhaps, then, I won't invite Athelstan and his warriors here.

'Ildulb, collect your war band and head towards the border between Bamburgh and the kingdom of the Scots, towards Dere Street. Take messengers with you and fast horses so that you can keep us appraised of Athelstan's actions.' Ildulb doesn't even falter in his current task as I speak. Instead, he hands the scraps of parchment he's reading to my next son, Aed, and strides confidently from my hall. He's a man of action, never happier than when hunting, riding or fighting. 'Take Ealdwulf with you,' I add just before he's out of sight. This should be Ealdwulf's fight, not mine, and so he can bloody well join in with the attempts to stop Athelstan. 'But, don't hand him over as any sort of hostage,' I caution, looking from Ealdwulf's shocked face to my son's equally baffled one.

I need Ealdwulf for when I defeat Athelstan and renew my claim on Bamburgh. I turn aside from the lad's startled look and fearful gaze, as he struggles to get to his feet. Suddenly, I consider whether he's ever fought in a battle before. Surely, he must have done, living in the kingdom of Bamburgh, and yet, perhaps he hasn't. I dismiss him from my thoughts. I don't want him to die, but perhaps if he does, this war with Athelstan will be over quickly. Or maybe not. I still want Bamburgh for myself.

There was a time when the ancient kingdom of Northumbria extended far into lands I now control. I should love to bring into effect the opposite of that. Then bloody Athelstan would be put in his place.

I don't miss that Ildulb's son, Amlaib, hastens to follow his father. The boy is too young to fight, and yet Ildulb is a firm believer that his sons should be able to battle as well as he can. He'll take the boy with him. I know he will. I sigh softly. I don't believe it's a good idea, but I can hardly berate my son for that. He'll keep his son safe or die trying, I'm sure of it.

Mael Coluim watches me with narrowed eyes. I meet his gaze evenly. He thinks that I can't order him to join the offensive, as I would my son, but he's incorrect. I can, and I will.

'Mael, collect your war band and take them to the borderlands with Strathclyde. Meet with Owain if you can and ensure that Athelstan doesn't sneak into our lands that way.' I use the word 'our' on purpose, reminding him of his obligations and aspirations. He draws a breath as if he's going to speak, but then thinks better of it, bowing to me before walking away, not quite with the sharp snap that Ildulb had. I'm just pleased he's gone without too much of a fight. I regret the opportunity of amassing his warriors that I've given to him, but I need him to hold off Athelstan. And I'll just have to hope that Mael Coluim does nothing further to undermine my kingship.

The other men in my hall are nodding or shaking their heads, depending on whether they agree with me or not. My other sons are talking amongst themselves, discussing tactics and trying to decide who should go where. No one addresses me directly. In this moment of crisis, they all know it's vital that only one man makes choices and decisions. But I need time to think, for there'll be no second-guessing. Even Mael will know that. It's after Athelstan has gone home that I'll worry about Mael's actions with his warriors, not during Athelstan's attack.

'Aed, you must collect your warriors and head toward the coast. Gather as many ships as you can and fill them with your men. If you see Athelstan's ship army, engage them or watch them and inform me of where they are. Count them, see how well they're armed, and keep me appraised of what you think they're going to do next.' Aed, like his brother before, leaves my palace quickly. He has a job to do, and he'll do it well.

Next, I call Denewulf to me. He bows low, his forehead almost scraping the floor.

'I have a task for you,' I inform him. He arches one eyebrow, which only serves to highlight the fact his nose is no longer straight.

'My lord king,' he murmurs, and I smirk. This task isn't an easy one, and it'll be bloody dangerous. But while I have only my sons and my heir to support me in trying to drive back Athelstan from my borders, there's another force who might well support me, a force to the north of my kingdom. And they hate the English as much as I do.

'Come closer,' I urge Denewulf. 'And listen carefully.' Whatever his thoughts on the matter are, his face remains impassive and a gleam enters his eye. It seems he approves of my plan. I watch him go, thinking that, as with Mael, I can't lose with this new instruction for him. I'll either win some new allies, or Denewulf will be dead. I nod, trying to find some contentment. But the knowledge that Athelstan has gathered his men and is marching towards my border fills me with fear and anger in equal measure. Abruptly, I signal for my priest. I need to pray.

## 50

## 934, DERE STREET, THE KINGDOM OF THE SCOTS

*Prince Edmund, ætheling of the English*

'Ware.' The cry ripples through the air, and I rein in my mount, eyes peering all around me. This landscape is unknown to me, but there are scouts ahead, and so far, this has been the first warning we've received from them.

I swallow heavily, my hand reaching for my seax, not that it gives the comfort I'd hoped. Ahead, my brother, the king, rides with his household warriors. I have my own men. Well, I have men given to me by the king. They're loyal to him and only secondly to me, but all the same, I find it comforting to have them close by. Unlike me, this isn't their first fight. Many of these men are from Mercia, and they've fought the Norse for years. Unlike me. I've never fought anything more than one of the king's warriors, with explicit instructions that he shouldn't wound me.

'Hold,' another voice calls, and I'm surprised how far the sound echoes, as though we're between hills, but we're not. I can see hills close by, but for the time being, we're on open ground.

'What is it?' I call forwards.

'I don't know, yet, my lord.' The voice that responds is that of Eahric, Ealdorman Athelstan's brother. He rides as a member of my war band and not that of his brother's. He's a giant of a man, and I'm grateful to know that he'll be at my side when this comes to a fight. But I'd hoped to advance further into the kingdom of the Scots than just here. I feel sure that if I turned my neck, I'd still be able to see the fortress at Bamburgh on its rocky outcropping.

And then the horses move forwards once more. I can't tell what caused us to stop, not until we round a corner, and I can see a collection of bloodied bodies on the side of the road. Some of my brother's household warriors pick over the bodies, stripping them of their valuables before tipping them into a tangled, briar-filled ditch.

'Who were they?' I call, wishing my voice hadn't wavered on the question.

'My lord, they were men from the kingdom of the Scots. A small force. No doubt sent to determine our location.'

'And they're all dead?'

'Yes, my lord. None of them survived to return to the king of the Scots.' A smirk touches the cheeks of the man who speaks to me. I can see where he bleeds from a cut to his neck, and one or two of the men limp, or sit, pale-faced, recovering from the skirmish. I recognise him as one of Athelstan's favoured fighting allies, Flodwin. I'm sure Sigelac will be close.

'Any casualties?' Eahric calls, and I realise that should have been my first question.

'No, my lord. None. The Scots don't seem to have been expecting us to be quite so far north.'

We move on past the brief mess of broken bodies, my heart pounding heavily in my chest.

'It's always the same, my lord.' Eahric speaks with compassion. 'The first body broken in battle is a terrible thing. But the first kill will be worse, I warn you. But it gets everyone like that, even your brother, the king. Stay close to my side, and I'll ensure nothing happens to you,' the tall man offers. He has his brother Ealdorman Athelstan's height, but a much larger girth. For all that, I've seen him fight, and he moves with a swiftness I don't possess and fear I never will.

'My thanks,' I retort, wishing my voice sounded louder than it does. There's a palpable sense of excitement amongst the warriors who ride close to me, and voices call one to another, joking about what they'll do to our enemy when we encounter them. Suddenly, I'm not so sure of myself. I've trained to fight, and I know I've been taught by the best, but this is entirely different. For the briefest of time, I consider reining in, returning to the south, and my mother, and begging her to make my young brother the ætheling. But I know I can't do that. My mother wouldn't allow it, and if I'm honest with myself, I don't want it either. I want to be the image of my older brother. I want to live up to the stories I've heard of my grandfather and father, and Eahric's words ring true. All must face their fears. And all must live to fight another day. I only hope I can do that. And the sooner it's done, the better.

## 51

### 934, THE KINGDOM OF THE SCOTS

*Hywel, king of the South Welsh*

I don't understand what King Constantin's intentions are. I know we're deep in the territory of the Scots, and yet, so far, aside from the small scouting party, we've encountered no one. There's been no resistance to Athelstan's intentions. I confess I'm disappointed. Not only does my cousin Idwal still live and breathe, but if I'm not mistaken, the English king might soon be king of the Scots as well.

We've long since left behind the extent of Dere Street. Now we ride on unfamiliar tracks relying on others knowing where they go. The English king assures me, and I've seen the constant messengers to know he speaks the truth, that the English fleet is keeping pace with us, for all they're not visible from where we ride. I would have expected King Athelstan to stay closer to the fleet, especially as we make our way through Constantin's lands. But Athelstan is confident. I'd say he was too confident, but that's not the case. King Constantin has sent no one to counter this attack. Had King Athelstan marched into my kingdom, I'd have been far less subservient. I'd have ridden out to attack him and sent him fleeing from my kingdom.

But not King Constantin.

I can only surmise that Constantin is leading Athelstan to a place where he can be assured of a victory. Perhaps, while we ride northwards, Constantin, his son, Idwal, and his heir, Mael Coluim, are busily assembling the war bands of the Scots people. Maybe news of our numbers has gone ahead, and the only chance that Constantin has is to amass everyone in a single place.

I'm aghast that Constantin has been so blindsided by all this. Surely, he should have had some idea of what was going to happen when he interfered in the kingdom of Bamburgh? Or is he perhaps too old and feeble to understand the meaning behind people's warnings? I wish I knew.

'Cousin.' I turn to face Idwal. He rides close to me, forging a path through my warriors. I raise my hand and dismiss their concerns. Idwal won't kill me. At least not here.

'Cousin,' I retort.

'Well, this is a fine outing, isn't it? Almost like when you went to Rome?' he queries, the smile on his lips assuring me that he's enjoying himself. I never thought to see that.

'It does seem particularly easy,' I confirm, almost not wishing to say the words, for fear the Scots might erupt from behind a distant hill. The land of the Scots king is lush and filled with vast valleys and soaring peaks. In the distance, I'm sure I can still see snow crowning some of them, for all it's the height of summer. We've passed settlements and prosperous-looking farms. King Athelstan has ordered that the people shouldn't be attacked, not unless they come at us with blades in hand.

Men and women who speak with a soft inflexion bow low, eyes shielded to see the English king's wyvern and double-headed eagle banners that fly to the front of the long line of men and horses. They don't run in fear, the majority even lowering their heads as the king passes. It's strange. It feels wrong, and yet if the Scots king hasn't called his people to war, then they have no choice but to allow passage through their lands.

I see King Athelstan's will at work here. He doesn't need to conquer these people. He didn't conquer them at York. He won them over with kindness and reassurance that he merely wanted to protect them. If he had the men to leave at every settlement along this route, would he leave them there and promise the same thing? For now, we journey northwards.

'Easy,' Idwal says. 'Are we sure King Constantin isn't dead? His warriors fled? Perhaps they've even determined to journey to the islands between here and Dublin rather than actually fight a battle? Do we know that Constantin has *ever* fought a battle?'

I would tell Idwal to hold his tongue. We all know that King Constantin was once a mighty warrior. If he isn't any longer, then we shouldn't dismiss the fact that he once was. 'I don't know what King Constantin intends,' I confirm instead. I wish I did know.

'I imagine he hopes that King Athelstan will drown on one of his ships. The damn fool doesn't realise that the king leads a land army as well as a ship army.'

I shake my head and run my hand over my forehead. It's pleasantly warm, not hot. I don't sweat. In fact, I don't even wear my helm, content to let the sun touch the top of my head and warm it.

'Where's his son? Where's his heir?' Idwal continues to muse. I can tell he's had this conversation on a number of occasions so far. These words are well rehearsed, and it seems I'm just the most recent to have to listen to them.

'Where do you think Constantin is?'

'Fled back to Dublin to demand that Olaf Gothfrithson aids him. You do know he lived there when he was a child, don't you?' I nod. I do know this. The path to the kingship of the Scots is far from an easy one.

I open my mouth to say more, but only then I don't. Up ahead, it seems, the Scots have finally decided to find some stones, and the roadway is blocked by a decent-sized force. Or so it seems to my eyes.

'Halt.' The cry comes from the front, and I reach for my helm and slide it over my head, wincing at the heat from the iron on my hand. It's warmer than it seems, after all.

'At last,' Idwal murmurs, his eyes wide with anticipation. 'Let's see if these Scots really fight as well as everyone says.' He chuckles, and then turns his mount towards where his warriors ride beside mine. I eye them. These men look the part, but if it comes to a fight, will they be able to protect their lord king? And not just from the Scots, but from any other who might think to use this as an excuse to kill an ally who could become an enemy? A movement catches my attention, and my eyes settle on Morgan ap Owain. Now, there's a man filled with ambition. If Idwal is comfortable around me, he could certainly do with being more careful around him.

'Be ready,' I call to my warriors, but I don't dismount. Now that I can see more, it's evident to me that this force is small and stands no chance against the might of King Athelstan and his war host. No, I admit, this won't be the battle it should be. In fact, it might not be a battle at all.

## 52

### 934, CAIT, THE FAR NORTH, THE KINGDOM OF THE SCOTS

*Athelstan, king of the English*

My men assure me that the haze I can see far out to sea is the Outer Isles, the Orkneys. I squint into the setting sun, trying to see the green of an island, but it's no good. The clouds hang too low, and I can't see any features.

Beneath me, my horse shifts under my weight. I pat it reassuringly on the neck. We've come a long way, from the borderlands right up to the farthest reach of the lands of the Scots, and my horse has been a steady presence throughout that time. We've not had to rush, or gallop, or really do much more than wake every day and resume our journey northwards. What began as an attempt to see just where the Scots king would meet my force in battle has resulted in me nearing the very tip of his kingdom.

I've journeyed through a landscape rich in brown hills, peaks still covered in snow, the thunder of rivers loud in my ears, the sight of so much landlocked water startling. And now, I'm here. My ship army is at dock below the escarpment upon which I stand while I peer at the islands over the grey and menacing sea. I might like to visit there, only that place is ruled by the Norse, and not the king of the Scots.

I turn my head inwards, keen to see this kingdom of the Scots for what it is. Constantin has played me for a total fool. His failure to meet the terms of our treaty, to forward the tithe to me as and when he should, has all been intentional. His land is vibrant, and his people wealthy in resources. My anger at Constantin has already peaked, and yet, if I could get my hands on him now, I'd still be furious enough to inflict personal injury. He needs to know that I'm not to be treated in such a way.

Edmund has Ealdorman Ælfstan at his side, and I have his brother, Athelstan, my cousin by marriage, beside me. Together, we stand, and we look, and we absorb. This landscape isn't alien to us, but it's much wilder than the heartlands of the English kingdom. Here everything is just so much larger in scope.

A commotion in front of me, and a man rushes forward, only stopping when Ealdorman Athelstan kicks his horse forward to prevent him from getting any closer. He's not someone I recognise, but he knows who I am.

I watch Ealdorman Athelstan speaking to the man, wondering what this could be about. Ealdorman Athelstan looks at me and then moves aside to let the man through. He must carry words that I need to hear.

'My lord king,' he says, sweeping to his knees. With a raised eyebrow at Ealdorman Athelstan and a reassuring nod from him, I tell the man to stand.

'And you are?' I inquire, and the man looks nervously around before replying.

'My name is not as important as my message,' he finally says, and again the ealdorman nods. Clearly, the man hasn't told him his name either.

'And what is that message?' I ask, more than curious about this strange man, who has a decided tilt to his nose. I think it was broken once, and healed poorly. He must be a warrior, then, I assume. But for whom, I have no idea.

'Constantin's son is coming with a war band. They've been following you for days now, ever since you took ship and sailed over the Tay. They wanted you here, trapped, with the Norse of the Orkneys at your back and the Scots in front. They've forged an alliance with the Norse. They'll come with their ships and counter your ship army while your land army fight the Scots.'

'And when will the attack come, and which son is it?' The news that there might finally be a fight, as opposed to a skirmish, thrills me. I wish to subdue King Constantin in battle. Having him all but refuse to face me is far from proving that I'm his overlord.

'Ildulb, my lord king, and tomorrow, before first light, I would imagine. And, my lord king, the first light here is very, very early at this time of the year. I would keep a guard all night and be ready for anything.'

'And who sent you?' I ask, and the man grins and bows once more.

'Someone who would be happy to see Constantin and his herd of bastard sons dead.' And so, his message delivered, the man turns away, and I watch him with interest. What strange trick could this be, or is it the truth, and why would he tell me? The man was one of Constantin's people for all that he spoke my language well.

I ponder the implications as Edmund, Ealdorman Ælfstan and Ealdorman Athelstan look to me for a reaction.

'A camp and a defensive formation?' Edmund enquires lightly, the thrum of his voice impossible to ignore. I nod in agreement, pleased that, as young as he is, Edmund is aware of the needs of my men. Whether the message is real or not, I can't ignore it.

'And send some scouts out as well, one to the south, one to the east and one to the west, and one back along the coasts in each direction. Ealdorman Ælfstan, you know how to command the men. Ensure it's done, and that they know to return as soon as possible. I would know the numbers we face. Ealdorman Athelstan, inform the fleet. Have them ready to defend themselves should the enemy come from the Orkneys.' I didn't believe they'd ally with the Scots, but perhaps, the vast greyness between their home and Cait isn't the impediment it might seem to be.

'Yes, my lord king.' Ealdorman Athelstan lowers his head, and turns his horse quickly, to direct the animal down the path up which some of the ship men already labour bringing supplies that were easier to transport by ship than land.

And so, it seems, I'll have my fight with King Constantin. I envisaged it taking place on the borderlands with the Scots kingdom, not here, almost at its extremities. But I'm not fearful. Whatever force the Norse of the Orkneys have, I know my ship men will counter them. A smile touches my lips. I was adamant when I became king that peace would be the way forward, but King Constantin of the Scots has determined that peace is not the solution. I'll show him tomorrow why it would have been better to have taken that option.

## 53

### 934, BATTLE AT CAIT

*Prince Edmund, ætheling of the English*

I slept like the dead, which has occasioned much amusement from the brother ealdormen. Ælfstan and Athelstan, more my brother's allies than mine, have still determined to incorporate me in their group of warriors preparing for battle.

I yawn wildly, peering into the gloom of the coming day.

'Are we not too early?' I question. I'm sure that the daylight must still be some time away.

'They warned us that daylight came early, and anyway, ships have been sighted, as have warriors on horseback coming from the south.'

This has me jumping to be more prepared. I shrug into my byrnie, fastening the belt tightly to prevent my weapons from falling to the ground. I detect a tremor in my hands and quickly move them as though to convince myself I'm not fearful.

'King Athelstan bids us hurry to attend his war counsel,' Ealdorman Athelstan informs me, running his eyes up and down my body as though to check he's content with the way I present myself. I try and find a smile for my face, but it's difficult. He nods all the same.

'First blood, young Edmund, first blood. It'll be terrifying, but once done, it need never be done again.' I think his words are meant to reassure, but they don't. Instead, I turn to follow him as he picks a path through the fires that have lit the campsite during the night. A stubborn breeze blows from the north. I glance that way, but I can't even see the king's ship army let alone the fleet from Orkney as the cloud seems to merge with the sea.

My brother is standing outside his canvas, resplendent in his battle gear, shimmering in the blaze from a large fire that must have kept him warm throughout the night. Servants dash through the massing men, offering warm pottage and warm wine. I take mine and swallow eagerly while Ealdorman Athelstan watches me with trepidation.

'Be careful, or you'll be wearing that when you take a kill. Most prefer to fight on an empty belly.' I pause then, spoon halfway to my mouth, and realise that few of the others are indeed eating. I slow and consider heeding the ealdorman's words, but then continue to eat. My mother would assure me that, as a growing boy, I need to eat. If I'm sick later, then I'm sick later. I have more clothes.

I eye those who've been invited to this meeting. The archbishops and bishops stand to the left. The ealdormen to the right. And in between the two sides, as though they need to be kept a firm eye on, are the kings of the Welsh, and the Danish jarls from Mercia, the kingdom of the East Angles, and Northumbria. There are many of us.

My brother catches my eye, and beckons me closer. I forge a path to him, and he reaches out and grips my shoulder firmly, lowering his head so that he can look me in the eye.

'Brother,' he begins. 'Today will be your first battle. Today, I imagine, you'll take your first kill. But you're to be careful. Eadric and Æthelwald will fight at your side, the brothers of ealdormen Ælfstan and Athelstan. They'll ensure nothing untoward happens to you, but you must still fight for yourself. They won't be able to defend you from our enemy.'

'I understand, my lord king. Thank you.' I swallow heavily against the leaden fear in my stomach. Perhaps I shouldn't have eaten all that pottage after all.

'I had men who ensured my safety, and they still allowed me to gather injuries. And I learned to fight for them, just as they fought for me,' the king continues. I wonder why he takes the time to speak to me here and now. Surely, he has better things to be getting on with rather than worrying about me? 'Stay alive, brother, or your mother will flay me alive.' Athelstan laughs as he speaks, but I can tell he means those words. I consider my mother, far away, in Wessex. What must she think of me, her oldest son, fighting against the kingdom of the Scots? I hope I can make her proud of me. Certainly, I don't wish to fall in battle against England's enemy. I've heard her speak often enough of the death of her father in battle against the Norse, a man she has no memory of. If she speaks about him with such ferocity, then how would she react if her son were to fall?

'I promise, brother, that I'll not allow my lady mother to flay you alive.'

And now Athelstan does smile and claps me on the shoulder as our fellow warriors do.

Before us, the combined force of Athelstan's army is readying itself for the coming battle. The enemy, the Scots, have been sighted and will soon be close enough for the attack to begin. As of yet, I've seen none of the Norse ships from the Orkneys, but that doesn't mean they won't come.

The Welsh kings and their warriors will be split amongst the English forces. The Mercians will fight with the warriors from the ealdordom of the East Angles. The Wessex warriors will stand with those from the Five Boroughs, and the warriors of York will be held in reserve. I know that not all are keen to engage with the king of the Scots. But, under the command of their archbishop, they'll do so, if they're needed.

Hastily, I join the brothers of Ealdorman Ælfstan and Athelstan. The two men are prepared for what will come next, and yet, they must also fight to protect me.

'Stay close, and listen for all commands,' Eahric informs me in his deep voice. 'It can be hard to make sense of everything on the battlefield.'

I nod, and then realise he doesn't see me as we stride to join the forward line of English warriors.

'I'll do as you suggest,' I confirm.

'You'll be fine,' Eahric reassures me as we come to a stop. Ahead stretches the lines of the English warriors. We're not in the front line or even the second, but I can see where there's an expanse before the first line. Into that, I assume, the Scots will come.

I sight the Wessex wyvern and the double-headed eagle of Mercia, on the combined banner that Athelstan has adopted. I also hear men talking one to another or praying or weeping. But many of the men merely stand and wait, talking to those who surround them. It's as though they wait for a summer fair to begin and not a battle.

'There are bets on how many of the Scots men there will be,' Æthelwald informs me conversationally. 'Some say less than a thousand, others over five thousand.'

'And what if,' I ask, swallowing down my fear at such an enormous force, 'there are some who think somewhere between those two numbers?' Æthelwald chuckles at my confusion while a man in front of me turns and grins as well.

'I don't care how many there are, as long as I get to kill a few of 'em,' he offers, and I meet his grin. Here, he doesn't call me 'my lord' or bow to me. I find I like that.

'They're coming.' The murmur begins and grows and swells. I swallow again, wishing now that I'd thought to piss, but I didn't, and now, it seems, it's too late.

'Remember,' Eahric cautions me. 'Stay close and stay alive. Or while your mother chastises King Athelstan, it'll be Æthelwald and I who face the wrath of the king.' I nod, feeling sick and wishing my hand was less slick in my glove, but it's all too late for that now, as the line of men begins to advance. I must fight for my king and my brother. And I must stay alive.

The sound of wood on wood assures me that the battle has begun. I can hear the grunt and heave of men as they begin to test the strength of those they face along the shield wall. I wasn't sure that the Scots would use shields, as the English do, but it seems they do. I watch as those in front of me surge forward, their weight behind the man in front of them, who in turn, thrust their weight against the man in front of them. Through the overlapping shields, it's impossible to see much of anything, but the smell is enough to tell me what's happening.

Men bellow and swear, curse and pray, and for a moment I don't know what to do. I've been taught how to fight, how to attack, and how to protect myself, but against so many, and amongst so many, how am I to do so?

'Keep up, Edmund,' Eahric's cheerful voice calls to me, and I stagger forward, the line moving, and both Eahric and Æthelwald going with it. From far away, I can hear voices issuing commands. Some I understand, many I don't.

'It won't be long,' Eahric's voice thrums with conviction, 'and we'll be in the thick of it. See, some of the men already waver and fall.' He points down, and I see trails of blood leading to gaping wounds that bleed on men grown still. How, I want to ask, have men already fallen to their deaths when I'm still to ensure the grip on my seax is firm?

I hear the crash of wood hitting metal, and see one of the warriors in front of me stagger as though hit by a great weight. He turns and then falls.

'Bugger,' Æthelwald complains, bending to retrieve the man from being trampled over. I see that he still breathes, but his eyes are closed as though deeply asleep. Someone takes his place quickly while I turn and see, behind me, one of the many servants dashing forward to remove the man so that he doesn't get tangled in the legs of his fellow warriors.

A glint of iron, and I see spears being thrust between the legs of those ahead. Eahric reacts quickly, jabbing down with his war axe and even stamping on some of the barbed points so that whoever holds them has no opportunity to retract their weapon. And the English force surges forward again.

'Be careful,' Æthelwald urges me, 'this is happening quickly. When the shield wall fractures, stay by our side. Don't just run off after the rest of the men. They'll lead you into trouble.'

I nod and watch, licking my lips, observing the way the shield wall buckles in some places and advances in others. I can see why Æthelwald urges me to caution.

'Watch out overhead.' Eahric speaks next, and instinctively I look upwards and then realise that's the surest way to die with a spear in my throat. I look only at the man in front of me.

'Good, Edmund, good.' I know Eahric doesn't speak to condescend.

Another surge, and this time the men at the front of the shield wall don't cease running, and I remember Æthelwald's words and just stop myself from darting after them. The shield wall has collapsed already, although, in some places, it does still hold. For a moment, I catch a glimpse of my brother, the king, cleaving his way through men at the front of the shield wall. His actions are precise and well timed, almost as though these men want to die on the edge of his blade. Flodwin and Sigelac don't move from my brother's side. I've hardly seen them on the journey north, but I should have realised they'd be fighting next to their king.

'Edmund.' Eahric calling my name returns me to the here and now. A group of enemy warriors, shields in the hands of some, surges towards me. For a moment, panic consumes me. I'm a child. What am I doing here? I can't beat these men. I can't kill these men. Only then, there's no choice.

Eahric launches his war axe at the man to the fore, while Æthelwald takes on another two to the left. That leaves me with one man, seax bright with shed blood, menacing me. I eye him. He doesn't seem as tall as some of the others. His head is covered in a fine helm of polished iron, his byrnie matches his helm, and his seax glints, not just with blood, but with the iridescence of a blade that's been pattern-welded. This man is no mere warrior. He's someone important.

He launches his seax at me, and I move aside, allowing the passage of it to shiver down my left arm. Immediately, I stab with my seax, hoping to catch him off guard. His blade meets mine. He's quick on his feet, light and alert. He jabs at me, perhaps hoping to catch beneath my beardless chin, but I step backwards, and his blade passes me by without harm. This time, I run at him, keen to draw first blood. My heart hammers, but I feel surprisingly calm.

My seax misses him, and I almost overbalance, trying to turn quickly and counter his next move, but I keep my feet and just manage to evade his blade. He growls, the sound low and guttural. His eyes are as quick as his arm, trying to decide on the next move. I'm aware of men calling one to another, but I don't understand their language. It must be that of the Scots people. I launch myself at my enemy once more, keen to finally land a blow against him, and this time, he's a little slower to dance out of the way. I think I might have him. Only then he turns it against me. And as my blade harmlessly glances off his byrnie, I feel a stab of pain on my lower leg as he bends to attack me where I wear the least protection.

The sight of my shed blood spurs me on, and now I can't allow him to determine what happens next. I jab and stab, using my fist as well as my seax, but in no discernible order. The pulsing pain of my leg injury adds a rhythm to my movements that none but me must detect.

I thrust an elbow into his face and then stab with my seax. His bunched hand veers up at me, but I grip it and hold it firm, and he can't get away from me, not while I hold him. Once more, I jab with my seax, aiming for the exposed skin on his arm, and a thin line of blood blooms along it, dripping eagerly onto the ground beneath us.

He winces with pain, showing me his teeth and gums as I thrust again with my seax, this time further up his arm, trying to find more flesh to pierce. His blade slices at me, taking advantage of my preoccupation. But I still grip his arm. I eye him. In a moment of clarity, I realise that he can be no older than me. Unlike the rest of the men, we're both slight of build, wearing equipment that's seen more grease than blood, and still, I reverse the hold on my seax and stab upwards, under his held arm, and up into the flesh beneath his armpit. I've been told it's a quick way for a man to die, and I imagine it'll be an even quicker way for a boy to meet his death.

At my action, a shriek fills the air, and I turn, letting go of my enemy, aware of him falling heavily to the ground and that Eahric and Æthelwald are both fighting only one man between them, who, eyes wild, tries to get beyond their guard. I feel I should know him, and yet I'm sure I've never met him. He wears the colours of our enemy, and as I've never met one of the Scots, apart from Constantin's son, Alpin, I can't know him.

My thoughts spiral and sound comes from far away, and the shrieks of the wild man die away, as all I can hear is the retching of my guts, as I bend double and lose all of my pottage into the churned ground of the soil.

I don't know whom I killed, but it seemed someone cared a great deal for them. I'm grateful that Eahric and Æthelwald are there to protect me, for my body shivers and shakes, and it's impossible to grip my seax. Without them there, I'd be dead. The thought makes my stomach roll all over again, but there's nothing left to leave my stomach, for all I retch, time after time.

## 54

### 934, CAIT, THE KINGDOM OF THE SCOTS

*Athelstan, the king of the English*

The battle is over before it began. The Scots, no number to match that of my combined might, have been defeated, and yet, even here, I can hear the keening of one man, one warrior amongst all the others. His shrieking and screaming are unsettling, the hairs on the back of my neck standing up. I run my hand down my sweat-soaked face, but can't shake the strange feeling from my body.

Eagerly, I seek out Edmund and smile to see him bent double, holding his stomach, emptying all that he ate this morning onto the ground and perhaps some of last night's meal as well.

Edmund has taken his first kill. The hardest part is to come, but he'll be a warrior king, just as I am, when he's called upon to do so. Yet, my gaze quickly turns away, my eyes narrowing. Why, I consider, do Eahric and Æthelwald hold back that man? I look at him, and then I look again. The man is dishevelled, his helm missing, and his mass of hair blows in the stiffening breeze, but something draws me to him. Somehow, I recognise him.

Quickly, I speed my pace and stand before Eahric and Æthelwald, Sigelac and Flodwin stepping between me, my brother and the raving man who thinks to fight both warriors. It's clear his intention is to reach my brother. And it's from him that the shrieking and screaming are emanating.

'Who are you?' I demand to know while Ealdorman Athelstan, alert to what's happening, joins our small grouping. He bends to look at the fallen figure, the man my brother killed. With more care than many might expect, my cousin lifts the broken man's body and removes his helm, and a soft sigh erupts from his lips.

'His son?' Ealdorman Athelstan murmurs to me, the shrieking so loud I think they might hear it from the border with England.

'Release him,' I urge my warriors, confident that I can fight this grieving father if need be. The restrained man doesn't rush to my brother, coughing and heaving on the ground, but instead to the man, or rather, the boy lying dead there. He scoops him into his arms, and keens, head thrown back, into the growing wind. I watch him carefully, sure that I know him, and then my cousin by marriage speaks.

'You're Ildulb, son of Constantin?' And suddenly I know why I recognise him. He looks like his brother, Alpin, an honoured guest at my court for many years. Some would say Alpin is a prisoner for his father's behaviour. I name him as a guest. I bow my head and know a moment of sorrow.

'And he's my son,' Ildulb growls, his gums red with the blood of the English he's slain. He looks more beast than man; his bloodied face streaked with dirt and tears. I pity him. I swallow. I was so relieved to see my brother yet lived, and yet, for Edmund to live, he's killed another man's child.

'Take him from here. Bury him as you would your dead.' I have to harden my heart to what I'm witnessing. There was no need for children to die. It was my intention that no father should mourn a child and no child should mourn a father, but King Constantin refused to accede to those requirements of the peace at Eamont. He even risked the life of his son, Alpin. Only I refused to punish my honoured guest for his father's transgressions. 'Allow his fellow Scots warriors to assist him.' Many of the Scots are dead or fled, but some remain, watching their lord with sadness and unease on their faces. They want to help. No doubt, they'd like to kill us all, but they stand no chance.

'He is dead,' Ildulb snarls, and suddenly, he's on his feet, weapon to hand, and almost at my brother's side.

Sigelac is the quickest to respond, but I'm not far behind him. Flodwin lifts my brother bodily, unheeding of his retching, and physically moves him aside, as though he weighs no more than a sack of flour, and isn't a fully armed and armoured warrior.

My seax hovers at Ildulb's neck, Sigelac's war axe ready to strike him should he try and duck down and avoid me. I can react just as quickly as my warriors should the need arise.

Ildulb breathes heavily, his chest heaving, and I caution the rest of my warriors with my eyes.

'Take your son,' I say softly. 'Return him to your father, and tell him that I only want peace, not war. Tell him to send King Ealdred's son to me in Wessex. And tell him he'll be expected, at my court, in two months' time. If he doesn't appear, then I'll have no choice but to send your brother home in pieces.' I have no intention of doing that. I hope the threat of such actions will suffice.

I think Ildulb will argue with me and refuse to accept my words, but the fight leaves his body between one breath and the next, and I remove my seax, allowing him to stand. Eahric and Æthelwald beckon forwards four of the Scots men, and between them, they take hold of the still-warm body of the dead boy.

'I'll tell my father,' Ildulb informs me, his words broken and cracked. 'And I'll bury my son.'

'Then you're free to go, as are all your men who are wounded and yet live,' I add. In the face of such triumph, it feels only right to be magnanimous. And yet I'm angry, so very bloody angry. I've been fighting and killing my fellow men since I was no older than Edmund. I've spent my life trying to protect the English people, trying to ensure that none should attack us, that if the Norse did come, they'd meet a united front, and yet King Constantin of the Scots would sooner allow boys to die, fighting in his name, than join with me.

I turn and face the far north, the islands which I know the Norse call their home. It should be them who lie here, dead and dying. It should only ever be the Norse.

# EPILOGUE
## SEPTEMBER 934, CIRENCESTER, ENGLAND

*Constantin, king of the Scots*

I can barely meet King Athelstan's eye as he welcomes me to his court. My anger and resentment are difficult to contain. I'm here, as he bloody commanded, but I'm about as happy as a man about to be executed, and I know that Athelstan would have no compunction in executing me. He's seen off his brother, Edwin. Dead by drowning. They say Edwin chose such a punishment. But I know that drowning is the ancient punishment for conspiring against a ruling king. It's no surprise it happened soon after he approached Owain of Strathclyde to be included in my conspiracy against Athelstan.

A full week it's taken me to reach this place deep within the heartlands of the English, as far from the coast as it's possible to be. And as far from my kingdom as I've ever travelled. And with a heart full of anger and grief, it's been a long week. If the pomp of Athelstan's palace is anything to go by, it'll be a long two days here and then an even longer journey home to a kingdom still reeling from his lightning-quick attack that spanned all of my kingdom and has led to my resubmission to

Athelstan's overlordship. And the death of my beloved grandson. The fact that Ealdwulf of Bamburgh still lives burns inside me. It was all his fault. All of it. Well, the parts that weren't Athelstan's that is. He should have died at Cait, but he didn't, and now I don't know where he bloody is.

My son Ildulb has accompanied me, and I wish he hadn't. The grief for his son, killed in battle by Athelstan's young brother, is a heavy burden for him to carry. He neither smiles nor cries, but he's sullen and uncooperative. He has been for the whole two months since his young son met his untimely death on the slaughter field at Cait, and he returned to me with his limp body on a farm cart.

I should have refused Ildulb permission to attend when he asked, but I didn't have the heart. In my place as a father, I've always felt out of my depths. As a grandfather, I was better. As a grieving grandfather and father to a grieving son, I know I'm next to useless. I'd give Ildulb anything he asks of me now. Anything.

I know that I can't pray his son back to life, but I'd happily exchange my life for his son's. I've found it difficult to maintain my Christian faith since the boy's death. My prayers go unanswered, and I can find no inner peace. My God appears to be a being who expects too much from a mere man, even if that man is an anointed king.

King Athelstan's palace is no bigger than mine, the wooden hall an adequate structure, well decorated with shields and tapestries and pleasing to the eye. But it's surrounded by a large selection of buildings and cattle barns. It's a strange cross between a farm and a royal palace. But it's not my home, and I could laugh at the small feminine touches his stepmother has littered the place with. I don't care for flowers or sweet-smelling herbs or Athelstan's extensive collection of holy relics. As is now expected of me, I only want to show my face before his people, have them know that their king has gained the upper hand over me, Constantin, the king of the Scots, and then be gone once more to try and rebuild all that's been taken from me. The smell of winter is in the air, and I don't want to be caught away from home should the snow come early.

And I don't want to be bloody here at all.

The only possible piece of good news about this summons is that I've come alone. None of the other kings of the island is here, and for that, I'm grateful.

I have no love for the Welsh kings, but I'd not be able to tolerate the smug expression on Owain of Strathclyde's face either. He warned me about Athelstan, and I ignored him. I thought my lands unapproachable; after all, what would an English king be doing in the lands of the far north? Athelstan seems to make decisions that I don't think him capable of, and even now, I know that he'll do it again in the future. No matter how many times I think I've understood his motivations and his desire, he'll show that I know him not at all.

'My lord King Constantin,' the king's brother speaks, stepping towards me in his beautiful clothing. Does he know he's the one man I hope never to see again? Ever.

'Lord Edmund,' I reply as civilly as I can, my hand reaching for a sword that's not on my belt as I'm in the presence of the English king and his family. I'm a guest, but really a prisoner.

'You had a good journey?' Edmund asks, making polite conversation even though I don't want to speak to him. 'I found the roads to be good when I journeyed upon them.'

'Yes, your lands are fertile and well-guarded. Your roads are straight and well maintained,' I offer a little grumpily. I've seen as much of Athelstan and Edmund's lands now as he's seen of mine. The fact that I come as a subordinate, whereas Athelstan strode through my kingdom as though he owned it, isn't lost on me.

'We've spent much time and effort in reinforcing our borders and making our people feel safe with good law and order. We have an excellent coinage that gives our people the ability to trade well and with others from far afield.'

I don't comment that I've done the same. All my hard work seems to have fallen apart since Athelstan attacked my borders, when I thought to interfere in the affairs of Bamburgh, and messengers have chased me to Cirencester, telling me stories of problems that now infect my land. For much of it, I blame Mael Coluim and his ability to turn these problems to his advantage. I've even heard the words 'abdication' on the lips of some of his supporters. If they can't rely on King Athelstan to kill me, then they're prepared to explore other ways for their man to gain power in our homeland, especially after such a crushing defeat. Our allies in the Orkneys abandoned us, and Owain of Strathclyde arrived only after the defeat. The kingdom of the Scots is entirely alone.

My head is so filled with ideas and images, half-formed thoughts and regrets that I don't know what to think of first.

'King Athelstan is pleased that you've come,' Edmund offers, as though it was an invitation I could have chosen to ignore if I'd so wanted. Perhaps Edmund's forgotten that Athelstan had one of the ealdormen escort me here, almost under armed guard. I can't say that I don't like Ealdorman Guthrum, he is, after all, a robust and brave warrior, apparently high in his king's regard, but I'd rather have been allowed to give the impression that I'd come willingly.

'And I'm pleased to be here,' I offer, hoping the young prince will change the subject soon. 'It will be good to see my son, Alpin, once more.' At my side, Ildulb huffs in outrage, and I turn to caution him with my eyes. Only in that instant Edmund has realised who stands beside him.

'Lord Ildulb,' he says, his voice suddenly thick with emotion, 'I wish to express my sympathies for your loss.'

And that's too much for my son to take. To hear those words from the man who's made his grief a reality. Without my leave or that of the English prince, Ildulb strides from the palace. I hope he won't go far, but there's the possibility that I might not see him again until I return to my kingdom. I told him not to come, and yet I didn't refuse his request to accompany me.

'My apologies, my lord king,' Edmund offers, his voice still thick, grief evident on his face. I don't know if my grandson was the first man that Edmund ever killed, but if it was, Edmund will long remember that moment, and in time, I hope it will haunt his kingship. Should he live long enough to become king of the English.

'War is a bloody business.' I offer the only words I can force past my throat that don't choke me with hypocrisy.

'Yes, it is,' Edmund replies. 'Let us hope that the English and the Scots never have to meet in battle and strife again.'

I don't share Edmund's hope or even his desire for a future where I can't unleash my revenge on the English bastards. The day is coming when the Scots will lay waste to their land, their hopes and fears. I can assure Edmund of that. If I weren't acting as the submissive in a hostile land with a handful of warriors at my back, I'd take his head here and now.

But, while King Athelstan has belittled the kingdom of the Scots, claimed Bamburgh for himself, and returned to England victorious, I know that my scop spreads his incitement to war, and one day, and it will be far sooner than Athelstan, or Edmund, could possibly imagine, there'll be an uprising against Athelstan's imperium. Soon, he'll not be king of the English. Or king of Britain. If I have my way, he might not even be king at all.

# AUTHOR NOTES
## 925–934

The meeting of Athelstan, Constantin, Hywel, Ealdred, and an 'Owain' at Eamont in 927 is an accepted event in most histories of the time, and yet one historian, B. Hudson, has cast doubt on it, saying there is no proof that Constantin of the Scots ever made an alliance with Athelstan at Eamont. Eamont sets the scene for later events, and so I've adopted it as 'fact' for the novel.

The treaty of Eamont is only written about in the D version of the Anglo-Saxon Chronicle (ASC), and under the events of 926, not 927. (The Anglo-Saxon Chronicle survives in a number of 'recensions', all of them a little different and of differing ages, and known by the letters A–H.) The D version of the ASC is not believed to be a contemporary record of the period. But then, none of the entries that we have for this short period of time survive in a contemporary manuscript, the D text dating from the late eleventh century to the early twelfth century (so up to 200 years after these events took place). As such, we should never forget the potential for events to have been manipulated. The capture of York and the invasion of the land of the Scots in 934 are mentioned in the ASC E and F texts as well as the D (although there is confusion between events in 926 and 927). Much work has been done and continues to be done on the ASC, and the way the manuscripts have survived, and the formats they survive in. These annals, in the format we have them now, were not contemporary – no one sat there and wrote down what they thought we should know about the year that had just passed – indeed, these events regarding Athelstan are very unusual, but more will be said about that at the end of book 2.

There's uncertainty as to whether the Owain mentioned is the known historical person of Owain of Strathclyde, or whether it was the king of the Welsh kingdom of Gwent who was given the incorrect name of Owain. Again, historians will argue this. For the purpose of my story, I've determined to follow the argument that this Owain was from Strathclyde.

There is also confusion regarding Ealdred of Bamburgh and his son Ealdwulf, who might have been his brother. I have chosen to make Ealdwulf Ealdred's son in this instance, but it is possible that Ealdwulf was Ealdred's brother and that he was the one who caused Athelstan to intervene in Bamburgh, according to Alex Woolf in *From Pictland to Alba 789–1070*. If the source material for England is complex at this time, then that for the kingdom of the Scots is even more so. Irish sources are often relied upon, and I'm no expert on them.

Constantin was not the king of Scotland. He was the king of the Scots, or the king of Alba. He ruled over the combined kingdoms of Dal Riata, Cait, Fortriu and Atholl. It is complicated, but I've made every effort to ensure kings are named as they might have been known. For instance, for Athelstan there are charters naming him as king of Mercia and then king of the English, when he took up that position. Getting the terminology right is important. If the distinction was made contemporary to events (or as near to contemporary as our sources are), we should note it. England, as we know it, only formed under Athelstan. Prior to that, his father was king of the Anglo-Saxons, while his grandfather was king of Wessex.

Where possible, the events and the dates have been taken from known 'facts', often the charter evidence for Athelstan's reign, which provides a record of who was witnessing charters and where these royal meetings took place. These charters also reveal which of Athelstan's subordinate kings (named as *regulus*, little king, or *sub-regulus*, under king) were attending his witan and where these meetings took place. (The attestation of 'other' kings is something that only really occurs during the reign of Athelstan, and then a number of years later, under Eadred. It's not a regular occurrence throughout the period. It is unusual enough to take note of and to give credence to this idea of his 'imperium' over the kingdoms in Britain at the time). That said, these sources are not huge in number. There are many occasions when we simply don't know where Athelstan and his court were, but it is important to remember that it was a peripatetic court. Kings moved around their kingdoms to eat off their land and to lessen the strain on any one location. Winchester, often regarded as the capital of Wessex, was, in fact, just one of many of these places and one where kings were often, but not always, buried.

Of course, the charters that have survived are small in number and have only survived because they benefited someone, somewhere, to keep a written record of the event being recorded. Our history is a series of chance finds and bias on the part of pseudo-historians and chroniclers. We're lucky we have as much as we have and can gain as much information from what we do have. And this is the work of a number of eminent historians working in the field of Saxon England: Simon Keynes, Sarah Foot, Dorothy Whitelock, Pauline Stafford, David Dumville and many, many more. There is a monograph on Athelstan, written by Sarah Foot, which tells much more of Athelstan's life story. It is fascinating. Athelstan did indeed collect relics. He was often sent gifts of saints' bones. Alex Woolf has written about Scotland during this period, and Clare Downham has written about the Vikings throughout the United Kingdom and Ireland. Kari Maund, my former university lecturer, has also written about Wales at this time.

And yes, Athelstan's father, Edward, did marry three times and left his son with a vast number of sisters for whom he would be required to arrange their marriage (the exact number of sisters is unknown due to confusion in later sources and also because some of these sisters are quickly 'lost' to contemporary chroniclers, a fact I find astounding). Four of these sisters made prestigious marriages into families on the continent. At least three of these sisters spent their lives in nunneries, and possibly four, if Athelstan's full sister also entered a nunnery after the end of her marriage to Sihtric. This may seem strange, but the options for women were limited, and not all women who entered nunneries went on to become vowesses, but such a topic would fill another book. A widowed woman had more rights than an unmarried woman.

It's unknown when Lady Ælfflæd, Edward's second wife, died. It's believed she may have joined her daughters in Wilton nunnery, having been set aside by her husband. The same may be true of Ecgwynn, Edward's first wife, but she is so shadowy; if not for Athelstan's survival, she could almost be mythical. The ASC (D), which opens this book, contains one of very few references to these royal sisters, and in it a marriage is recorded between Athelstan's sister and a member of the 'Old Saxons'. This entry is particularly interesting as in two different versions of the ASC two different sisters are written about: in one, it is the marriage of Athelstan's full sister to Sihtric; in the other, it is a reference to the marriage of Eadhild to Otto, son of the king of the East Franks, recorded four years too early. It's believed this occurred because the original entry in the D text breaks off at this point, and the information was added by a later chronicler. (This isn't the only time a gap exists in a text. When writing about the number of children Alfred and his wife had, his biographer, Asser, leaves blank the number of stillborn children the couple had, so that, to this day, we still don't know.)

The truth about whether Athelstan had his stepbrother, Edwin, executed or whether he drowned at sea is open to interpretation. One historian has pointed out that being drowned at sea was an ancient Irish punishment for killing your brother (or plotting to), and Edwin might well have been involved in a concerted attempt to get rid of his brother in 933. We're told by a near-contemporary source that Edwin was buried at the monastery of Saint Bertin by one of Athelstan's continental cousins. This cousin, Lord Adelolf, was also buried at the same monastery when he died later in the same year. In the surviving record, which is slim and not always deemed authentic, Edwin does not witness any of his father's or brother's charters. I have determined to follow the line that Edwin was executed for his crimes against the king, and this execution took the form of being abandoned at sea in a boat without oars. This makes sense of the continental source, and Athelstan's later donation to the monastery.

Lord Osferth may or may not have been Alfred's illegitimate son. I've chosen to present him as his illegitimate son. There are historians who think he may have been related to Ealhswith's family somehow (Alfred's wife).

Titles – Athelstan's aunt, the countess of Flanders, is only named as this once during her life. It is possible that she may not have been known as the countess of Flanders during her lifetime, but her sons do seem to have been titled count of Flanders and count of Bolougne, after the death of her husband. It's unknown who Æthelweard, Athelstan's uncle, married, but he certainly had two sons.

Lady Eadgifu, Edward the Elder's third wife, is believed to have been the daughter of Ealdorman Sigehelm who was killed at the Battle of the Holme in 902/3 when Edward's cousin, the ætheling Æthelwold, allied with the Danes to win the kingdom back from Edward. It's often suggested that Alfred had reached an agreement with his older brother, who was king before him, in regard to who would rule after Alfred. In the end, it seems Alfred was able to manipulate events so that Edward became king, but it was not a universally accepted decision, and Æthelwold did all in his power to claim the Wessex kingship for himself. His family would continue to cause problems in the future.

The idea for this story grew from a frustration that it's rare to be taught the 'whole' history of the United Kingdom. I was raised in England and taught English history. I went to an English university where I was taught about Saxon England, and sometimes the Welsh kingdoms. What was happening in what is now Scotland was not taught to me, and it frustrated and perplexed me. And I confess, I am still largely lost in the Ireland of this time period. But I wanted to highlight the interconnectedness of these kingdoms, then as now. A large majority of this book was written when Scotland was being asked to vote on whether it should become independent or not in 2014. I am sure it very much influenced my thinking in devising the characters for my kings. I would dearly love to have been there if the treaty at Eamont truly happened. All those bruised feelings and desire to be seen as 'better' than their neighbours. If we think of Henry VIII and Francis of France, with their meeting at the Field of the Cloth of Gold, we can perhaps imagine how much one-upmanship there was.

During the tenth century, there are an increasing number of women gaining prominence in the sources in England. Lady Eadgifu, third wife to King Edward, known as the Elder, when he had a grandson who shared his first name, was an incredibly important political character. It could be argued, as I have done elsewhere, that without her gift of a long life, the Wessex royal family could have been faced with destruction. She is a fascinating woman, although largely absent from all court documents surviving from Athelstan's royal court. All the same, as the mother of Athelstan's eventual heirs, she must have been important, even if she never ascribed to one of his charters.

It can't be confirmed that Lady Æthelflæd of Mercia's daughter married Athelstan, known as the Half-King, and one of King Athelstan's ealdormen. There are arguments that both support and refute the idea, made elsewhere. For the purpose of fiction, I've adopted the idea. It makes sense of much that happens later in the tenth century.

The poem quoted as being invented by Constantin and the scop did exist, and almost as much controversy surrounds it as the battle of Brunanburh itself. It has been used variously by many historians for different reasons. For the purpose of the Brunanburh series, I've taken the suggestion of Nick Higham that it was a poem devised in Wales from 930 onwards to show unhappiness at the links with the English. That Constantin had a hand to play in it, is my own invention, although, you just never know! I have substantially amended the translation I've used, which can be found here https://exploringcelticciv.web.unc.edu/prsp-record/text-armes-prydein/

I am indebted to a talk I attended, given by Max Adams, in which the significance of Athelstan's journey to Chester Le Street was discussed. It occasioned a little bit of a last minute rewrite.

There is much more that I would share with my readers about the historical people behind these characters, and about the scop song, but I will stop now. Please do get in touch if you have any questions.

# ACKNOWLEDGMENTS

I would like to thank my editor, Caroline, for encouraging me to largely rewrite much of this book. I believe the story is much enhanced and allows the reader to learn more about contemporary events in the United Kingdom at this time, which are really rather complicated. Having fresh eyes look at something highlights any number of assumptions I originally made. Luckily, the rewrite coincided with new research I was doing on this time period, and it has allowed me to correct some minor mistakes, for which I'm grateful.

I would also like to thank the entire Boldwood Books team for all the hard work they do. They are fabulous. Thanks also to the cover designer who had a bit of a task with this one. And thank you to Ross and Susan who had the rather unenviable task of making sure I hadn't given anyone the wrong name or title. Thank you for your sharp eyes.

A huge shout out to my support group of EP, and CS, and all those who enjoyed the book in its original version, including MC, who helped me promote it back in 2014. As well as Stacy Townend, Amy McElroy and my advance reader team, and also my author buddies, Kelly Evans, Elizabeth R. Andersen, Eilis Quinn, Brenda Vinall-Mogel, Peter Gibbons and Donovan Cook. And, of course, Flintlock Covers for once more managing to produce an excellent map from my random ramblings, and not objecting when I changed my mind about some elements of it.

And to my readers. Thank you for enjoying my books, and I genuinely hope you enjoyed meeting the wonderful cast of people from the tenth century. It really was a fascinating time to be alive.

# MORE FROM MJ PORTER

We hope you enjoyed reading *King of Kings*. If you did, please leave a review.

If you'd like to gift a copy, this book is also available as an ebook, large print, hardback, digital audio download and audiobook CD.

Sign up to MJ Porter's mailing list for news, competitions and updates on future books.

https://bit.ly/MJPorterNews

*Son of Mercia*, the first book in The Eagle of Mercia Chronicles, is available now.

# ABOUT THE AUTHOR

**MJ Porter** is the author of many historical novels set predominantly in Seventh to Eleventh-Century England, and in Viking Age Denmark. Raised in the shadow of a building that was believed to house the bones of long-dead Kings of Mercia, meant that the author's writing destiny was set.

Visit MJ's website: www.mjporterauthor.com

Follow MJ on social media:

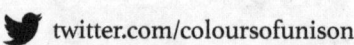 twitter.com/coloursofunison

 instagram.com/m_j_porter

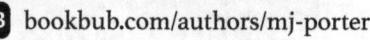 bookbub.com/authors/mj-porter

# Boldwood

Boldwood Books is an award-winning fiction publishing company seeking out the best stories from around the world.

Find out more at www.boldwoodbooks.com

Join our reader community for brilliant books, competitions and offers!

Follow us
@BoldwoodBooks
@BookandTonic

Sign up to our weekly deals newsletter

https://bit.ly/BoldwoodBNewsletter